Doctor Who

Short Trips: Zodiac

A Short-Story Collection
Edited by
Jacqueline Rayner

Big Finish

Published by Big Finish Productions Ltd
PO Box 1127
Maidenhead SL6 3LW

www.bigfinish.com

Range editors: Gary Russell & Ian Farrington
Managing Editor: Jason Haigh-Ellery

ISBN 1-84435-006-1

First published December 2002

Short Trips concept by Stephen Cole.
Thanks for everything, Steve.

Printed and bound in Great Britain by Biddles Ltd
www.biddles.co.uk

CONTENTS

Introduction and links by Jim Sangster

Introduction

as·trol·o·gy *n.* The study of the positions and aspects of celestial bodies in the belief that they have an influence on the course of natural occurrences and the affairs of individuals.

At this point in the fourth millennium, we can see how, throughout the history of the universe, almost all civilisations have at one time or another looked to the stars to find the answers to life, the universe and everything. In Earth history, we can see the influence of the Osirians whose pyramids first appeared in Egypt in about 10,500 BCE (Before Christian Era). These structures were decorated with astral charts that almost certainly first inspired the Egyptians to examine the night sky. Similar influences can be seen in Mayan, Aboriginal and Chinese development to the point where, on three separate continents across one planet, different cultures evolved away from mere sun-worship (such as the cult of Orb, which stretched right back to the development of early man) to the worship of *many* suns.

It was the ancient Greeks of Earth who first devised the zodiac system, in which a 'wheel of time' was divided into 12 equal but distinctly different houses, or 'signs' as they became known. The signs were divided alternately into either 'masculine' or 'feminine' depending on their perceived influences upon an individual. In the homeworld's solar system, these signs related to 'planets' in the firmament (which for the Ancients would also include the sun and the moon), with those planets lower in the night sky believed to be 'warmer' and therefore more feminine than the higher, cooler planets, which were masculine. Mercury was the exception, being neutral or hermaphrodite. And just as the movement of these bodies could affect the air and water of Earth, so too could that movement affect a child on the day it is born and thereby shape its personality and likely future.

In purely Earth-focused terms, we see the first real challenge to astrology in the rather grandly named 'Age of Reason' in the second millennium of the Christian Era. Here, the establishing sciences took the word 'astronomy' to distance themselves from the 'interminable mumbo jumbo' of the older science.

But it was the Great Breakout of the third and early fourth millennia that saw resurgence in the ancient faiths. As colonies broke ties with Earth Central, so their reliance on science began to dwindle and belief in astrology increased exponentially. Though many individuals played their part in the formation of what we now know as 'neo-astrology'. One man can be said to have shaped neo-astrology into the form we know today –

the astrologist Kasterborus. It was he who first studied the constellations from Earth's position and remapped them according to the layout of the stars in the neighbouring colony clusters (some saw this merely as a way of appeasing pressure groups such as the Sons of Earth). Planets such as Bellicantra, Stella Stora and Japetus quickly adopted Kasterborus's neo-astrology as the galactic standard; only a very few planets on the outer reaches refused to give credence to Kasterborus's system, preferring to create their own, principally Chloris, S14 and Levithia. The notoriously superstitious and cautious inhabitants of Gallifrey decided to name one of their constellations after Kasterborus in an all-too-rare display of a sense of humour.

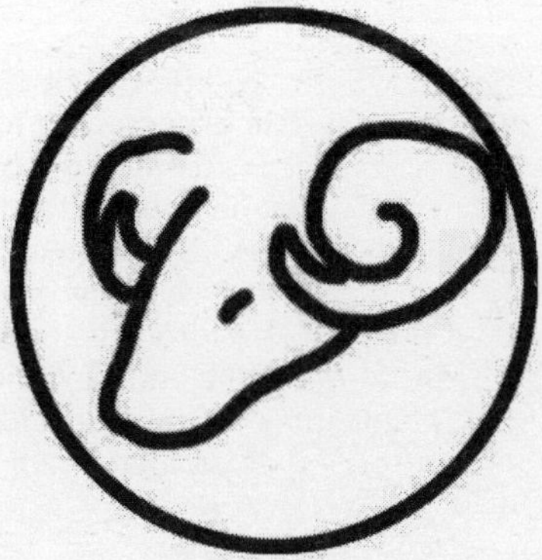

Though most of Kasterborus's calculations were destroyed in the horrific fire that devastated much of Cyrrhenis Minima's capitol, extensive restoration work on the remaining records show how respectful Kasterborus was towards the fundamental aspects of pure astrology, and how he used his skills not just to foretell the future, but to rewrite the past. The origins of the house of Aries, for example, were already confused before Kasterborus came to them. The Romans believed the ram to have been a manifestation of the Egyptian god Ammon, while for the Greeks it represented the golden ram that lent its fleece to legend. Curiously, in all origins, the ram was sacrificed in honour of the gods themselves; in Kasterborus's version, the ram simply ascended to the firmament without loss of blood.

Aries, the first sign of the zodiac, is the element of our personality that governs the 'self'. This is not to say that those born into this sign are 'selfish', so much as they are highly aware of their own self-interest. They can be wilful, argumentative, impatient and blunt - all traits governed by the fourth planet out from the nearest star (from the homeworld, this would be Mars, while from Estellios, it is Carval - both planets associated with war). Aries is an impulsive sign, symbolised by the ram...

Kasterborus, *Our Destiny is in the Stars*

Kasterborus says...

If today is your birthday: *A meeting of minds is well starred today. You may be invited to a party which will give you the chance to bring matters to a head...*

The True and Indisputable Facts in the Matter of the Ram's Skull

Mark Michalowski

This document is reproduced exactly as found.

October 2nd, 1849

My first encounter with the gentleman who - for his own purposes of anonymity - preferred to withhold his full name from the company, and went simply by the sobriquet of 'the Doctor', was scarcely five hours ago; when, at the behest of two other doctors of my acquaintance - Parsons and Wolffson - I had found myself entering the house of a certain Mr R——, a scholar and man of letters of whom I was cognizant but whom, before this very evening, I had not met.

On the journey to Mr R——'s house, I attempted to ascertain from the good doctors the purpose of our visit; but both were taciturn in the extreme, impressing upon me that, as a gentleman familiar with the unnatural and the bizarre, I was to be something of a learned witness to to-night's events. Before I could correct their impressions of me, we were at Mr R——'s residence and we alighted from the cab.

We were shown into a parlor by a servant who thenceforth made himself absent and I was introduced to our host, Mr R——, a rather unremarkable gentleman, possessed of a pale, insubstantial complexion with thin hair plastered back across his pate, who gave every impression of being of a nervous or hysterical nature - which did not predispose me well to the evening. Also in the room, on chairs and sofas or else standing by the curtained window were a number of other people. The two doctors and I were introduced to the gathered company which struck me as being of a very disparate composition: Miss Allardyce, a stern and somewhat matronly woman, and her young female companion, Abigail (a plump, sullen and charmless girl, possibly only just of marriageable age - fourteen years old at the very most); and Colonel Caine, a veritable model of the military classes with a florid complexion and a most pugnacious air about him who, barring his name, had said very little since our arrival, and who was sipping from a glass of cognac, grimacing.

But I was most interested in the trio who stood at the window - an elderly gentleman and two younger people, a man and a woman. Although the first seemed comfortable - if somewhat impatient - his companions looked sadly lost or perhaps just bored. I introduced myself to them – the younger was Mr Ian Chesterton, and his companion (perhaps his fiancée, or perhaps the elderly gentleman's daughter), Miss Barbara Wright. The other gentleman introduced himself simply as the Doctor – which elicited an expression of knowing disbelief from Miss Allardyce. As I asked him how they came to be there, he turned his gaze on me and gripped his lapels in the manner of a school teacher about to embark upon a peremptory lecture.

'We received a message from a friend of ours,' he said sharply, eyeing me with a curiosity that was somewhat disquieting. I asked him if we had previously met, but he smiled a most disarming smile and shook his head, saying that although he had not yet had the pleasure, he was fully acquainted with my works. I was on the point of questioning him and of attempting to ascertain further his provenance when Mr R—— gave a short cough and we all turned our attentions on him. He was standing in the doorway to the back room, his arms extended to hold out of the way the heavy brocade curtain that covered the door, with the clear implication that the evening was about to begin.

The Doctor seemed strangely reluctant to pass through.

'If I may ask,' he said, addressing Mr R——, 'are we to be informed of the nature of this evening's, ah, entertainment?'

At this, Colonel Caine bridled audibly, letting out a disgruntled snort.

'Entertainment sir? Entertainment?! I can assure you, this is no evening of "entertainment"!'

'My apologies,' replied the Doctor. 'The friend who secured our invitation for the evening was, shall we say, less than forthcoming about the purpose of this gathering. I am merely curious, that is all.'

'Miss G—— was less than forthcoming,' interjected Mr R——, 'because I have had to be very circumspect in my description of this evening, Doctor. I apologize for what must seem like excessive secrecy, but what I hope we will achieve here tonight is not something that I would wish to be disseminated to the public at large.'

At his words, I felt a cold hand grip my spine, and my eyes darted toward the still closed door to the back room. The Doctor nodded thoughtfully, and, in a silence somewhat thickened by Mr R——'s pronouncement, we all processed through, myself leading the way.

The windows had been draped with heavy velvet curtains and a fire that had been burning in the grate had been extinguished, leaving the air smoky and gray. A circular table, topped with a dark baize cloth, filled most of the room, and around it were ranged enough chairs for the gathered company. But what drew my – and, no doubt, the others' – eyes was the object that Mr R—— had placed in the center of the table, positioned carefully on a small round dais of dark wood. It was a skull – a goat's skull,

I first thought, although Mr R—— corrected Mrs Allardyce when she, too, commented on it presently, informing us all that it was the skull of a ram. The bone was a pale and sickly ivory color, bleached and unnaturally clean. The yellowish light from the three wall lamps stationed around the room glimmered softly on it, revealing a sheen that suggested that the skull had been polished - dare I say it, lovingly - over many years. Dark, ribbed horns curved and twisted out from it, their tips resting upon the cloth. Those awful, empty sockets, surrounded by raised ridges of sharp bone, gazed up at us, and even the residual warmth from the extinguished fire was insufficient to keep another sudden chill from clawing at my bones. Inscribed precisely between those sockets, in the flat of the forehead, was a clearly recognizable symbol - a five-pointed star, a pentagram, that most ancient of occult devices.

Being the first into the room, I had the opportunity to observe the reactions of the other participants in tonight's 'entertainment' - as the Doctor had put it. The Colonel gave the skull a most cursory glance, and I wondered briefly if perhaps he had seen it before. Indeed, it was possible that he had supplied it to Mr R——. I knew little of the Colonel, although I had heard of him by reputation. He was a stalwart of the Longridge Club where, rumor had it, he often held court at tedious length about his African hunting trips and expeditions to Egypt, so it was quite plausible that this skull had been one of his trophies.

His cognac glass still in his hand, the Colonel sat down heavily in one of the chairs as Mrs Allardyce and her ward entered. Whilst Mrs Allardyce seemed clearly disturbed by the animal remains (her hand flew to her mouth in a somewhat parodic gesture at which I had to stifle a laugh!), the child stared at it in what I can only describe as awe. There was certainly something ghoulish in the way she was drawn to it, her chubby fingers pawing at the thick cloth on the table.

Mr R—— was standing further into the room, watching, with a fascination equal to mine, the reaction of Abigail. Her mouth fell slightly open, her fat, pink lips glistening with saliva as her bright eyes darted around, drinking in every detail of the macabre exhibit. She was only cut short by Mrs Allardyce who whispered curtly that it was rude to stare, and pulled her around the table to their seats.

Next into the room were the Doctor and his entourage. I noted with interest that whilst Miss Wright and Mr Chesterton were drawn to the table and the skull, exchanging oddly disturbed glances, the Doctor himself seemed more concerned with the environs. He strode silently around, his thumbs tucked into the pockets of his vest, as he examined the dimmed chandelier that hung above the table. I watched him as he took a few steps backward and seemed to be attempting to peer under the table cloth. Then it occurred to me that this Doctor was anticipating some sort of charlatanism on the part of Mr R—— and was searching for signs of whatever artifices he imagined our host was anticipating employing. But when he did, finally, examine the skull and its enscribed symbol, a curious expression crossed his face, as if at the recollection of some dim and distant memory. He tapped his upper lip with his finger and then shook his head sharply before seating himself alongside his companions. Doctors Wolffson and Parsons followed them and exchanged an uncertain look: whether it was an acknowledgement of a shared secret or a shared suspicion, I could not be certain. They joined the other guests at the table, leaving only two chairs - for myself and for Mr R——, who took his place after he had passed around the room dimming the lights and placing a lit candle, ensconced within an elaborate brass candlestick entwined about with ivy leaves, upon the table. In silence, he completed the circle: proceeding clockwise around it - Abigail, Miss Allardyce, Colonel Caine, the Doctor, Miss Wright, myself, Mr Chesterton, Doctor Wolffson, Mr R—— and Doctor Parsons.

I caught a twinkle in the eyes of the Doctor: 'Very atmospheric lighting,' he commented wryly. 'I take it we are supposed to hold hands?'

'Not at all, Doctor,' said Mr R——. 'All that is required is that you keep your attention on the skull on the table.'

I smiled to myself at the thought that, at this moment, it seemed unlikely that anyone's attention was anywhere *other* than the skull. In the dim lamplight, its cavernous sockets seemed to gaze balefully at me, and I wished I had chosen my seat more carefully, so that I should not have fallen under its countenance.

'Focusing our psychic energies,' the Doctor murmured thoughtfully - although he spoke so quietly that it was possible that I had mis-heard him. 'Perhaps, Mr R——, this might be a good time to tell us what, exactly, is supposed to happen. Have we come all this way for nothing more than a séance?'

Mr R—— gave a gentle chuckle.

'This is considerably more than just a séance,' he replied. 'Mrs Allardyce's ward has what I believe is sometimes referred to as "the gift", second sight. With her help, we shall bridge the gulf between this plane of existence and the next.'

At this, there was an irritated sigh from Mr Chesterton, but Mr R—— continued as though he had not heard.

'My intention is that she will discover for us the ultimate secret, revealing to us knowledge that only those who have passed on can know. *The ultimate secret*, Doctor. *Immortality!*'

Mr R——'s eyes glimmered in the dim light and again I felt a cold hand press against my heart, as though attempting to still its beating. The Doctor's expression remained fixed, although I sensed a certain grimness, as if this were not the first time that he'd been in such a situation.

'Then it is a good thing that I am here,' he said with an air of finality.

The room fell silent again and the other guests turned their attentions back to the skull. As the seconds passed a palpable and altogether unpleasant change came over the room. The air around us, which previously had been still and warm, abruptly dropped in temperature, as if someone had silently thrown open a window. And yet, as far as I could perceive, there was no attendant draft of air, and the pale, oily light from the lamps stayed as hesitantly constant as it had been before. I felt a dryness in my throat as, illuminated from the side, a thick, milky cloud issued forth from Mr Chesterton's mouth. For one moment, I wondered if this was what I had heard referred to as ectoplasm. But, I realized with some relief, it was merely his breath, condensing in the increasing cold. I saw that Mr R—— was staring at me, and drew my attention back to the skull.

As the seconds ticked by in silence, I'm ashamed to say that I began to feel somewhat disappointed. True, the drop in temperature had been dramatic and unsettling, but since then, nothing had happened.

'Should we be thinking any particular thoughts?' came the whispered - and, dare I say it, mischievous - sound of the Doctor's voice suddenly, followed by an impatient 'tut' from one of the others - quite possibly the Colonel.

'Please Doctor,' said Mr R——. 'If you would be so kind as to keep looking at the -'

Mr R—— suddenly stopped.

Looking back on the moment when his words were cut dead, I can remember nothing other than a vague sense of irritation that he had not finished his utterance. It seems I was, regrettably, the only person to be unaware of the circumstances that had caused him to finish mid-sentence - perhaps due to the fact that, yet again, my attention had wandered from the skull to Mr R—— himself, whose eyes were gleaming wetly and maniacally. At his words I followed his gaze back to the skull on the table.

At first, I thought that the dim light, the atmosphere - and, perhaps, a degree of Mesmerism - were combining to induce some sort of hallucination; for something most peculiar was happening to the remnants of the unfortunate and long-dead creature before us. In the depths of the shadows that nestled in those dreadful hollows, something moved, a gentle and writhing sinuous motion, as worms rising from damp soil. Each socket seemed possessed of things alive and I heard a gasp from Miss Wright who, from her seat at my side, could clearly see the same things that I could. I broke off from the skull and let my eyes wander across the shadowed faces of the other guests. All but the Doctor - which hardly surprised me - and Abigail were staring fixedly at the skull. She was looking from one to another of the assembled group, her eyes wide and searching as if looking for some particular reaction, some specific response to the horror unfolding before our eyes. I had a sudden and inexplicable urge to pull away; to stand, bring up the lights and fling wide the curtains. But it was as if the very air had, at that moment, solidified and congealed, holding me in its frigid grasp as it insinuated writhing tendrils of darkness into my marrow. I found I was unable to breathe, my chest bound tightly as though by a huge, unnatural hand and a tingle, as from a galvanic battery, was playing upon my skin. Curiously, I realized that I could smell roses.

'Doctor…' came a hoarse whisper from Miss Wright. I tried to turn my head but I was held immobile by the force that had taken possession of us. All of us, with the notable and somewhat unnerving exception of Abigail, seemed transfixed. The girl's pale, round face was illuminated by something which appeared to emanate from within her: a paradoxically wan, lambent radiance; and I was brought to mind of a full moon. As I gazed at her, she opened her mouth and a voice that I can only describe as *unearthly* issued forth, bubbling as though being transmitted through the medium of some viscous, oily fluid.

'The door is open,' she said.

Her lips twisted into the most horrific parody of a smile that I have ever had the misfortune to see; and the foulness of her visage was compounded by the fact that she was no more than a child; although, at that moment, she had clearly left childish innocence far behind her.

'Proceed,' spoke up Mr R——.

'No.' This from the Doctor, who, against all the outward indicators of his frailty, had somehow managed to turn his head against the diabolical force which held us. He was staring at the girl, his jaw clenching and unclenching. 'This must stop,' he hissed through gritted teeth. 'What you're unleashing here is evil. Can't you feel that?' This last phrase was almost grunted, and if I had not previously been convinced of the malevolent provenance of this evening's events, his tone would have most certainly convinced me. Whatever the girl was doing, whatever doorway had been opened, I was in no doubt that what lay beyond it was, more than anything I ever witnessed before, totally and utterly inimical to us all.

But my train of thought was curtailed by further changes: a new metamorphosis was overcoming the skull before us. As if, in some bizarre way, we were witnessing the reversal of time, as though the world itself were winding backward, the skull began to clothe itself in flesh. Soft and pallid, the tissue formed on the polished bone, oozing out as a liquid from the surface of the skull. Within those horrible sockets, the wormlike forms continued to writhe, unaffected by the transubstantiation that overtook the rest of the head - for a head is what, by degrees, it was becoming.

No longer a naked skull, it now possessed a thick patina of pale flesh, quite unlike any flesh I have seen before. There was no intimation of blood vessels nor musculature, and I began to wonder whether this was merely some stage magic – perhaps a fluid or paste being pumped through the skull from beneath the table. Was that what the Doctor had been searching for? But the fluid did not drip or pool as one might have expected. It followed the contours of the skull, flowing around it and encasing it in a macabre parody of actual flesh. I became aware, for the first time, of a sweet, sickly odor, not unlike that of decomposition, which grew rapidly stronger, mingling with the scent of roses that I had previously noted, until I felt sure that I would be ill. My stomach churned in protest as the stench formed a miasma, thickening and curdling around us.

And then, of a sudden, the silence that filled the room was shattered by a gasp from Doctor Wolffson, and we all raised our eyes from the skull.

He was staring at Mrs Allardyce's girl, across the table from him. For a moment, I was unable to take in what my eyes beheld: my first thoughts were that my own eyesight was impaired or that the breathy clouds issuing forth from the company had obscured my view of the girl.

Amidst the grunts and moans of horror, shock and disgust from the other guests seated around the table, I realized that I was not mistaken. As though some sickening exchange were taking place, even as the flesh grew and crept upon the skull of the ram, Abigail's previous round and – uncharitable though it may be to say so – fat face was becoming thinner, visibly so, as we watched. Her jaw fell slackly open with a noise like the sound of tearing paper. Her eyes had rolled back in her skull so that only the whites were visible, and from within her dark and now cavernous mouth, a moan the like of which I would never have believed possible issued forth; and, to compound this ghastly sight, somewhere behind her tongue dark and sinuous shapes writhed.

I looked down at the ram's head. Now it was fully clothed in pale flesh. Curiously, there was none of the hair that I might have expected; and the eye sockets no longer held those wormlike forms. Instead, a single glossy black sphere filled each cavity, featureless and cold. They were staring at me.

My attention was suddenly drawn to the figure of the Doctor, who had placed his hands upon the surface of the table and who was in the process – labored and painful – of levering himself from his seat. The tendons stood out in his neck as he exerted what I imagine must have been an incredible force for a gentleman of his age, in order to extricate himself from the power that held the rest of us as flies trapped in amber. Inch by agonizing inch, as the rest of us looked on, he rose from his seat, shaking and unsteady. Beads of glistening sweat stood out on his pale forehead and I could plainly hear his stertorous breathing. I cast my eyes about the room:

the Colonel wore an expression of utter fear, and I suspected that his adventures had little prepared him for something like this. The doctors Parsons and Wolffson, too, looked on in terror, and I caught Parsons's eye for a moment before he returned his gaze to the skull, unable to turn his head to see Abigail, seated at his side.

The girl's face was, by now, little more than the head of a cadaver - almost fleshless, the surprisingly sharp cheekbones now protruding from the parchment skin that clung to them, taut and smooth. Her mouth was still open and those worms still crawled within it, flicking around her lips as if tasting the air. Her eye sockets were dark and empty now, and a foul fluid dribbled from the apertures, down over her cheeks like glistening tears of decay.

'Do not interfere, old man!' came the rumbling voice from within, and I sensed - as perhaps we all did - that whatever vile abomination had possessed her had realized that its hold was more precarious than it had first believed. If, indeed, this was some demon or spirit from the netherworld, attempting to gain a foothold in our realm, then the Doctor clearly intended to prevent it.

With jerky, spastic movements, the Doctor's hand moved across the table to where Colonel Caine had deposited his cognac glass - still, I noted with some grim amusement, half full. In one swift movement, he caught up the glass and threw its contents over the ram's head.

'You will not succeed,' the girl said gutturally. 'My reincarnation is almost complete.' In these last words there was a note of triumph which sent my spirits sinking, plummeting away; and, indeed, I wondered how soaking the ram's head in the Colonel's cognac could avail us of aught. To my knowledge, cognac was not one of those substances such as garlic and salt which are said to prove inimical to demonic forms.

'The candle, Barbara,' grunted the Doctor, his eyes darting between his companion and the elaborate candle stick, no more than a foot from her hand.

To my amazement - and to Miss Wright's great credit - she managed to speak through the tetanus which must surely have gripped her jaw.

'I - can't - move.'

My heart sank at the helplessness that had descended upon us; and then, to my great surprise, I found a strength within me which I had previously little suspected. As, like a light coming on in my brain, I realized the Doctor's plan, I found myself moving almost without thinking - which perhaps explains my ability to move at all - and threw - no! pushed! - my hand across the table. It contacted with the broad, ivy-wound base of the candlestick, knocking it over. A pale nimbus of blueish light sprang up where the flame made contact with the spilled cognac which, in an instant, raced across the intervening inches to the head and thence engulfed it, wrapping it in a flickering blue corona, curiously more intense than I would have imagined. It was as though, in a manner somehow more symbolic than literal, the flames were driving back whatever demon was attempting to invade this plane. The pressure which had pinned me in my seat lifted and I heard a chorus of sighs and imprecations from around me as the others, likewise, felt themselves released.

But amidst those imprecations came a low, animal moan which rapidly built to a shriek. Abigail rose in her seat as if elevated by invisible strings, and we all saw that her face - now little more than a skull beribboned with tattered shreds of purulent flesh - was likewise aflame. Yellow and blue it burned, spitting and sizzling like fat in a frying pan, as the poor, poor girl stood motionless, her mouth wide. The unearthly fire engulfed her head, the hair and lips and eyelids peeling back as they blackened and shriveled and added their substance to the conflagration. And yet - most chilling of all - she made no further movement and no effort to extinguish the flames. Like a wax dummy, she stood rigid as the flames spread rapidly down over her shoulders, igniting her dress; and thence across her chest and down her arms.

'In God's name!' cried Doctor Wolffson suddenly, shattering us all from our reveries. He attempted to rush around the table to the girl's aid, hopeless though it seemed. But he was stopped in his passage by the Doctor, who gripped his arm to hold him back. I caught something of a look transpire between them, and Wolffson shrank back, his face clearly betraying his shock at the Doctor's apparent callousness.

In a shameful, mutual silence, we watched the still-burning corpse of Mrs Allardyce's ward topple forward onto the table before it rolled aside and thumped, sickeningly, to the floor. On the table, the ram's head, charred and crisped, suddenly burst, spattering us all - and myself in particular - with the foul-smelling flesh that lay beneath the blackened skin.

Copious cognac - its connotations did not go unnoticed - was passed amongst the remaining guests as we sat or stood in the dining room. Mr R—— had lent me a change of clothing which, despite being somewhat less formal than my own had been, was gratefully received; although I still imagined I could detect the stench of that room and of the skull's vile flesh, clinging to me; and I felt almost disappointed that the heady rose scent that I had previously smelled was no longer in evidence. Miss Allardyce sat, sobbing, in a corner as the Colonel attempted - with little visible success - to comfort her. The Doctor, Miss Wright and Mr Chesterton had abstracted themselves to one corner and were muttering in low, conspiratorial voices. Not so low, however, that I could not hear them.

'So we came here to watch a young girl die, did we?' This Chesterton.

'We came here to prevent... something. Something evil, from gaining a foothold on this world.' The Doctor sounded stern, as though repeating a lecture he had given many times before.

'But she was just a girl, Doctor,' said Miss Wright, her voice choked with incipient tears.

The Doctor nodded sagely. 'A very gifted girl, Barbara. Or a very cursed one.' He gave a sour shake of his head, and for a moment, his eyes caught mine and I looked away. 'If Mr Poe hadn't summoned up such strength and courage' (I had no doubt this last was for my ears, and I felt strangely grateful and humbled) 'then I imagine that the poor girl's substance would have been used to rebuild the ram. Yes, I imagine that's not far from the truth. The ram - or, at any rate, whatever the ram was to become - would have reconstituted itself, acting as a vessel for whatever force was possessing the child.' He shook his head ruefully. 'And, thank goodness, we managed to sever its connection to this plane, to drive it back where it came from.'

Mr R—— had, it seemed, spoken to Mrs Allardyce and although I was not privy to their conversation, it appeared that some agreement had been reached between them regarding the story that they would tell to the police. No doubt some concoction regarding an accident with a candle. But what else, I asked myself, could be said that would not result in our immediate removal to a sanatorium? That we had been party to an attempt to gain the secrets of the dead? That, before our eyes, we had almost witnessed the materialization of some unimagined evil?

In numbed silence, we all bade our host goodnight, having made our own compact never to speak of this again. As I stepped out into the cool night air, refreshing after the grim atmosphere within, the Doctor and his companions passed me and bade me a good night.

'You have a great talent, Mr Poe,' the Doctor said with a smile. 'One day - I suspect - the world will rate you more highly than you may imagine.' He leaned forward as if to shelter his words from other ears. 'But a lighter touch with the prose wouldn't go amiss.' He smiled tightly - and, curiously, somewhat sadly - and turned away, leaving me wondering quite what he'd meant. I watched them go, feeling tired and leaden, and then re-entered the house to bid my farewells to the Colonel and Mr R—— - who expressed his desire that his name (and, oddly, that of Miss G——) be withheld from any account of this evening that I should choose to write up - before I returned to my rooms through the damp October air.

I have, it must be noted, often been described as having a 'fevered imagination', but I could not drive from my mind the image of that poor girl, standing before us like some ghastly human torch, whilst the skull burned and sizzled on the table in front of us. And had it been the candle's flickering light, or had the pentagram, inscribed upon the skull, glowed momentarily before it had been obscured by its unearthly flesh?

So it is done, and I have committed the events of the past few hours to paper. It is past midnight and my story is complete; and yet I continue writing as if, somehow, my continued existence depends upon the incompleteness of my tale. As I penned the final paragraphs of the account above, it seemed that the shadows were gathering around me, waiting for me to finish - perhaps to pass some critical judgment on my story.

I would like to believe that it is simply the horror that I have witnessed this evening that causes me to be so afraid of every dark cranny in my room, every movement that I see from the corners of my eyes. I had hoped that the transcribing of my tale would be - what an apposite phrase! - a form of exorcism for the demons that seem to have clung tenaciously to me since I left Mr R——'s house. But quite to the contrary, it is as if that oppressive, demonic presence is here with me now. And, although I know not for what reason, I am possessed of the unshakeable belief that the shadows around me are pleased - oh, horror! - that I have put down this account. Perhaps, as I have oft times suspected, there are other gateways, other means of egress into our world, of evil. And now that I have thought it, I am *sure* that I am right; that, simply through the medium of my words, I have somehow accomplished that which Mr R—— failed to do; whatever doorway to Hell that the Doctor sealed shut with the burning of the ram's skull has been opened again through the scrawls on the paper before me. About me, the shadows dance and writhe as if in triumph. The door - Lord save us all! - is, once again, open.

Edgar Allen Poe was found in the streets of Baltimore, disoriented and ill, on the afternoon of October 3rd, 1849, and taken to the Washington College Hospital where he died on October 7th. The cause of death still remains a mystery, although the Baltimore Clipper *described it as 'congestion of the brain'. Following Poe's burial, a mysterious stranger - still unidentified - visited his grave and left a bunch of roses and a bottle of cognac.*

This document appears to be the last thing Poe ever wrote.

The connection of this sign to bulls originally came from another Greek legend regarding Zeus's seduction of Europa, where he took the form of a beautiful white bull before kidnapping her and taking her to Crete where she bore him three sons. Kasterborus would appear to have confused this legend with another - that of the Minotaur - and tried to find its closest counterpart in galactic folklore to form his neo-taurean history.

Here we see Kasterborus trying too hard to adapt his studies to match contemporary circumstances. Many of his critics additionally felt that his rewriting of the sign of Taurus was crossing too far over into the realm of creative writing, particularly in the way he as good as accuses Taureans of being murderers and thieves to a man. (It's long been suspected that Kasterborus was simply having a dig at his publisher, a Taurean, for rejecting his discourse on how credit cards can be used instead of the traditional tarot deck.)

We'll skip that passage...

...the Great Journey of Life takes on added significance for those born under the sign of Taurus. Just as the plagues of Nimons devastated empires, so too the style and wit of those born under the sign of the bull can be devastating. And like the Nimons, Taureans can often be said to be acquisitive, wanting the luxuries of life and obsessing over them instead of the necessities or mundanities. Taureans have a natural sense for the finer things in life and actively seek them out for both themselves and their loved ones. For Taureans may be stubborn, but this is also their most positive attribute as they make the most loyal of friends, so long as their friends do not try to offer unsolicited advice - advice which will remain unheeded...

Kasterborus, Our Destiny is in the Stars

Kasterborus says...

If today is your birthday: *Things are never as bad as they seem. Today is not the day to push yourself too far. Take things easy and everything will work out fine.*

Growing Higher

Paul Leonard

In his dreams, he flew above the mountains. Pale blue in the earthlight, they seemed to heave below him, like the ghost of an ocean. He could feel sickness rising in his stomach, but there was no end to the waves: the crests piled up ahead of him, each layer higher than the last, until they were a vertical shield, blinding silver under the midday sun. The suit rushed him on towards the light; but he got no closer to it. Air alarms shrieked. Red lights blinked in the visor, and his brain became thick from lack of oxygen. But still he was getting no closer. In the surface below, white cracks opened, like an eggshell breaking from inside - and the fire was streaming in...

Sewa Singh awoke, shaking and sweating, and instantly remembered where he was and why he had dreamed that particular dream.

They would be here today, almost for certain.

He sat up, letting the sheet fall, and examined the black hairs that were turning to grey on his chest. Eighty-two years. His great-great-grandfather wouldn't have considered it a bad span of life, he thought bitterly. He swung out of the bed, slowly so as to avoid disturbing the young woman sleeping next to him. The air was warm and the carpet was soft on his feet. He padded through the half-darkness towards the shadow of an ebony cabinet, opened a small drawer and took out a golden control bracelet. Tiny keys glowed in the dark, made from emerald, lilac amethyst, ruby, sapphire, diamond. They no longer controlled anything; the bracelet had been off line for forty years. Primitive, he thought. Like me. But he put it on his right wrist anyway.

Pushing aside the silk curtains of the doorway, he stepped up into the mainroom. The sudden steely light sent stabs of pain through his eyes. He blinked, put out an arm to lean on the doorway, looked around. Black and silver stools were scattered like tall spiders across the moondust-coloured carpet. In their midst crouched a low table topped in white Imbrian stone. Beyond, the room curved gently away to the kitchen, a pattern of grey squares and green vines. The shape of the room was intended to imitate the torus in an orbit station. The style had been fashionable half a century ago when the unit had been built. Singh had always meant to do some alterations, bring it up to date a bit.

Well, it was too late to worry about that now.

'The possessions of the deceased, Sewa Singh, were sold at auction today...' he muttered, and wondered where he'd left the whisky bottle.

A floor-to-ceiling screen on the outer wall, several metres long, was set up as a false window. Presently it was showing the view above on the Surface, a flat landscape with a short horizon. The lunar rock glared like concrete in the noon sun. Metal rails ran across the ground, surrounded by dull orange coil guides. A couple of black slits near the horizon indicated the sites of landing ports.

Nothing moved.

Four months ago (a time of innocence, Singh thought), silver packages had rushed along those rails, red lights flickering as the cargoes accelerated towards orbital velocity. Trolleys loaded with grit had rolled up to the dumps. Shuttles had grumbled in and out of the ports every minute, sending a deep, soothing vibration through the floor of the apartments. Singh had liked that sound: in his more fanciful moments he had used to think of it as a heartbeat, a living beat, as if the Port, the Base, the entire mine System with all its machinery was part of a living animal. And he had watched the lines of redlit cargoes receding and seen arteries pulsing with red blood, moving the digested substance of the Moon to other parts of the body of the human race, where they would be built into new, living worlds...

It occurred to him that he ought to ask.

'System,' he commanded.

The house system indicated that it was ready, by means of a small chime.

'Any flights due in?'

A list appeared on the inner wallscreen: there were four entries. At the head of the list was the UN Administrative Support Ship *Diversity* – 'Special Run', due in at 0715.

Ten minutes.

'Passenger list, number one,' he rapped out.

There was a slight pause – a security check? – before the screen responded.

Akimboola, Joshu, Dr. UN Peace Corps, Senior Officer.
Cleomides, Aristo. UN Peace Corps, Sergeant.

Singh felt his stomach heave. They were really coming. He really would be taken to Earth, put on trial. Certainly he would be found guilty. Given 'socially useful work' to do. Planting trees. Helping the irreversibly senile to use the lavatory. Burying the dead.

And, whatever he did, in Earth's crushing gravity he would age. Muscles would lose their tone, cells would die, irreversible decay would occur in his own blood vessels and neural tissues.

It was something that he had come to think would never happen to him. He'd had a good job, and plenty of money. Antisenility drugs, replacement organs, low gravity - perhaps he would last until the day when people started to live for ever. But not now. Now Sewa Singh was going to die, like all the rest of them. He fingered the golden control bracelet, watched a date form in ruby letters on the gold.

'Four months...' he muttered.

Four months ago, he had been facing this same inner screen, confirming costs with a client in Osaka, when the news had come. There had been a world called Kuppam, newly built by the Yamoyata Company in high Earth orbit. It had been the largest, newest and best of its kind: the flagship of the makers. A steel and glass spheroid almost thirty kilometres across, filled with air and light, had rotated rapidly in order to generate a lunar-like 'gravity'. Inside there had been woodlands, hills, rivers, bridges, small towns with open-plan houses. Thousands of people had come to live there, to escape the heavy, dusty, corrupted Earth.

On the outside of Kuppam, in order to protect the delicate lifeshell from radiation and meteoroids, there had been a stationary casing of lunar rock. The junctions between the moving and the static shells had been supported by light-alloy bearings. Four months ago the supposedly impossible had happened: one of these bearings had sheared. That on its own would not have been serious, since the system was partially redundant, but within ninety seconds a second bearing had failed, and then a third. The inner shell had toppled wildly, slamming into the casing and breaching in several places. Air had rushed out, laden with fragments, widening the breaches. Within a few minutes the shell had disintegrated. Fifty thousand, five hundred and ninety-five people had died.

Sewa Singh had been the person responsible for the quality of the light-alloy used in the failed bearings.

'I see we'll have visitors soon.'

Singh jumped at the voice, looked up and saw that the girl had come into the room and was looking at the inner screen. She had washed and patterned: a wide stripe of purple decorated with silver stars ran across her black skin from shoulder to hip, and a light jasmine scent filled the air. Before he could speak she had crossed the room, pulled open a wallset, picked out a metal bowl and a wooden scoop.

'Perhaps I'd better make them some breakfast,' she commented.

Singh opened his mouth but it took a few seconds for him to make any words.

'They're coming to arrest me - take me away for ever - destroy my life - and you want to cook a meal for them?' He tried to laugh, but could only make a kind of choking sound.

She glanced at him. 'I'm quite serious.' From another wallset, she scooped out oats, soft lentils, dried apricots, and began to mix them in the bowl. 'If we all eat together, it will reduce the tension between us.'

Singh felt sick. She was nineteen. But even at that age, surely she knew?

'This isn't a quarrel at a children's party, Bernadette. Psycho-social techniques from Copernicus College aren't going to do any good in this situation. Perhaps you should go.'

She took the bowl to the sink, filled it with water, placed it on a hotspot on the grey-topped hob, fitted the lid into place. Then said, as she scrabbled in the wallset for cutlery, 'You'd better wash and dress.'

He watched her for a moment, as she walked past him with her arms full of wooden bowls and metal spoons, laid the table two-handed, fetched glasses and a jug of lemon juice. The movements of her swift young body were as implacable as steel.

'Go and wash,' she repeated levelly, when he just stood there.

He turned slowly, walked back towards the bedroom.

Bernadette Faraddin watched the man leave the room from the corner of her eye, then linked the electronic part of her brain to the house cameras to follow his progress. She saw him walk into the poolroom, toe the scented water, felt him key an instruction to the system. The Jacuzzi began to whirl. Meanwhile Singh crossed the green tiles to the lavatory and urinated.

Bernadette grinned. Obviously he didn't think she was watching him. He often forgot about the capabilities of her implants.

It was an old person's mental stiffness, she thought. At times it was hard to believe that Sewa Singh was eighty-two, with his childish jokes, his temper, his party nights, his wild-bull lovemaking. But then – at other times…

She'd once suggested that he have an implant fitted for himself. His reaction had amazed her: he'd almost exploded with anger, his eyes popping from their sockets. 'Bloody hell Bernadette! I'm not having a machine doing my brain's job for it! I want to stay alive – I, not some bloody computer!'

He had rarely mentioned the Kuppam disaster to her. He had attended Company hearings, she knew, and one infamous press conference. But all he would say in private was, 'There is nothing to be done. I am a lamb to their slaughter.'

Bernadette had made her own plans, nonetheless.

She switched off her link, turned to the hob, sniffed at the vapour that was rising from the hotpot. Vegetal, but a little bland: it needed spice, she decided. She walked past the machinery of the kitchen, following the curve of the room to an area thick with plants. Some of them had been here when she arrived – decorative things like damsel roses, silverbells, blood orchids, blue ferns – but she had brought others, mostly herbs in pots, from her student's digs at Copernicus. The plants wove in and around each other in the broad shafts of piped sunlight, growing higher than they ever would on Earth.

Bernadette set about gathering what she needed. Parsley, lemon verbena, stick bay, gingerleaf - she balanced the flavours in her mind, watched the predictive pH traces on her visual cortex display, imagined likely reactions and possible side products. Infographics and schematics of chain polymers filled her eyes. For a moment she was back at school, learning the basic uses of her implant's encyclopaedic access states. Even the many angled sunlight was the same, the smell of green, the humidity. Slowly, she relaxed.

When she returned to the mainroom she found Singh standing by the table, wearing a strong spicy scent and a neck-to-ankle pattern of primrose yellow decorated with grey crescents. She put her bundle of leaves down on the hob, smiled at him.

'I've picked these to flavour the breakfast.'

He stared at her as if she were a stranger, a thief broken into his apartment. She realised that there was a tumbler in his hand, and that part of the scent about him was whisky.

'I'm trying to help,' she said uncertainly.

He turned away, refilled his tumbler from a decanter on the table. Took several swallows.

His voice was slurred when he spoke. 'I've just seen their ship come in. It was beautiful, you know, just beautiful. Like a seed: a silver seed drifting down to Earth - to the Moon, I mean - to bury itself in the soil and reproduce.' He laughed, banged the palm of his free hand down on the table, turned and winked at her. 'Don't worry, Bernadette, I'm not drunk. I won't spoil the party. I'm just overcome with emotion at the prospects for my wonderful future.'

She walked up to him, making an effort to write a smile on her face, searching her memories, onboard and remote, in search of the best thing to say.

'SYSTEM!' bawled Singh. Bernadette jumped: stress readouts blinked in the corners of her eyes.

'SYSTEM!' He bawled it again, without giving the machine a chance to respond. There was a huge physical anger in his voice. He caught Bernadette's arm, gripped it so tightly that the bone hurt.

The system chimed.

'I want to see a tiger. Sabre. At Khadri.' Singh's breath came in rapid snorts. His grip on Bernadette's arm tightened further, so that columns of red damage-report readouts on her display added themselves to the whining nerves: she shut off both, so that she could concentrate.

In front of them, the wallscreen had become a window on Khadri, the orbital tiger reserve. Moist green leaves hung over dark soil. To the left, apparently behind the kitchen, was a still white pool. The scene was three-dimensional, the illusion so complete that the soil looked only a small step down from the carpet. After a few seconds there was a faint rustling, a whisper of breath, a sense of presence…

A tiger stepped out from the foliage. He walked past them without pausing, so close that Bernadette could feel the heat radiating from his body. When he reached the pool he stopped, sniffed the air, looked over his shoulder. His eyes were enormous, water-green, aware. Bernadette's stomach tightened.

'He knows we're watching, doesn't he?' she whispered.

But Singh still ignored her. He stared without a blink into the animal's eyes. After a while he said in a soft voice, 'Ah, that's my tiger.'

With a grunt, the tiger turned to drink from the pool, and Singh told the screen to revert. He released her arm, muttering, 'Sorry Bernadette.' He fiddled with a gold bracelet on his wrist. The device beeped faintly, like a tiny metal animal lost in a maze.

Singh turned and looked at her, his eyes solemn.

'I'm going to take a final look at the surface,' he said. 'If our visitors should arrive, give them some breakfast and tell them I will be back soon.' He carefully placed his half-empty tumbler in the centre of the table and strode out through the doorway leading to the airlock.

Bernadette stared at the grey curtain swinging behind him, listened to the clicks and hisses as he suited up. She was glad he was going out: if he stayed away until after the UN people had arrived, it would make it easier to do what she had in mind.

For a moment she did think he might be trying to escape, but then dismissed the notion as ridiculous. He couldn't make a move without their knowing it. If he tried to take a shuttle, or even a buggy, the base System would have instructions to refuse it clearance. A picture came into her head: Singh walking across the mountains in his old red Aztex suit, destination unknown, the true twentieth-century science-fiction hero. She grinned.

Singh had been gone less than five minutes when they arrived. Bernadette ran down the stone stairs leading from the mainroom to the street door, arriving just as it opened. Two figures stood there, wearing white earth suits with blue armbands and blue UN badges on the lapels. Behind them, the wide street was crowded: Moon people in patterns and dayskirts, Earth reporters in thick, dull-coloured clothing. Flycameras buzzed and clattered around the lemon trees, their long snouts pointing, lenses dark.

'Ms… Faraddin?'

She focused on the speaker: a young man. Light brown hair, a smile, eyes that fixed on hers with a mixture of firmness and compassion that she immediately found irritating.

'I am the –' He broke off, made an awkward grin. 'Dr John Smith, of the UN Peace Corps. This is my Sergeant, Fitz Kreiner. May we come in?'

She stepped aside. 'We thought you might be here soon.' She paused, smiled. 'I have some breakfast for you, in case you weren't able to eat on the ship.'

'That would be kind,' said Smith at once. 'Thank you.'

He didn't seem surprised, which Bernadette had somehow expected him to be.

In the mainroom, Bernadette gestured the two men to sit at the table. Smith sat down with his back to the kitchen, moving with the easy grace of one long used to many kinds of gravity. Kreiner, seemingly curious, walked over to the main wallscreen, and peered out at the motionless landscape. Looking at the Sergeant for the first time, Bernadette saw that he was pasty skinned and puffy faced, with a typical Earth person's heaviness of build. Unlike Smith, he moved awkwardly in the light gravity: when he sat down he grasped at the edge of the table while he pulled up his stool, as if he were still in freefall and expected to float away. Obviously he was new to space. Bernadette wondered if that fact might be useful.

She turned to the kitchen, signalled open a valve on the cooking pot. A jet of hot steam rushed out, smelling of bay and ginger. There was a robot hot-hand mounted on the oven; she linked to it, bent it down to remove the pressure lid, waited for the steam to clear, then released the link, took the wooden handles of the pot in her own hands and carried it to the table. The aromatic steam rose in front of her eyes as she walked: beads of condensation tickled on her nose and chin.

Smith spoke. 'Mr Singh is out, then?'

Bernadette nodded. 'He said he wouldn't be long. He wants to have a last look at the surface.'

'Of course,' said Smith. 'We quite understand.'

Kreiner gave his superior a swift glance, as if he were puzzled by this exchange. Bernadette wondered if there was some sort of disagreement between them on policy. If so, that might be useful too.

The proper etiquette was to serve the older man's portion first. She spooned the sticky green mash into Smith's bowl; he held it still for her whilst she did so. Looking down at his face, she noticed that he was wearing a discreet blue eyeshadow of the kind that had been fashionable for men about ten years ago. Obviously he liked the effect: Bernadette decided that she liked it too. And its very out-of-dateness made him seem less official, more human and accessible. She smiled at him.

Turning to Kreiner, she spooned out his portion. He didn't hold the bowl for her, continued staring out of the wallscreen.

Still, thought Bernadette, I'd better try to relate to him.

'You are from Europe, Mr Kreiner?'

'Er - yes. Umm - England, despite the name. My father's family were German.' He seemed embarrassed, as if he were trying to hide something. Bernadette wondered what his instructions were, in case of resistance.

She glanced at Smith, but there were no clues in his face, only that vague, compassionate, irritating smile. She watched as he took a mouthful of the food, chewed and swallowed, nodded approvingly.

'The herbs are fresh?'

'From the garden.' She indicated the tangled greenery, just visible around the curve of the kitchen.

He smiled. 'A very civilised way of living.'

Bernadette grinned to herself. She decided that now was as good a time as any to start the action.

'Will the trial be on Station?' she began, addressing the remark to Smith.

He flicked his eyes up to hers, and down again to the table.

'On Earth.'

'The gravity will be difficult for Sewa and me.'

She didn't stress the 'and me'. 'Let the other person feel their own surprise' - she could almost hear her Psycho-Soc tutor speaking.

But to her disappointment, Smith showed no sign of being surprised.

'We will provide a support suit for each of you, and time to acclimatise. And the necessary permits for you to travel with Mr Singh will be no difficulty in the circumstances.'

From the corner of her eye, she noticed a puzzled expression flicker across Kreiner's features, though his gaze never turned from the window. Good. She had surprised him, at least. She took a sip of lemon juice.

'Even with a support suit, the gravity could kill Sewa within a few months.' She kept her voice calm and level, made eye contact ('maximum influence that way'). 'Isn't it possible to have him tried here on the Moon - and punished, if he has to be, up here too? Wouldn't it be easier for everyone?'

She waited, but Smith only chewed stolidly.

'It can't be done,' said Kreiner, turning to face her for the first time. 'The Earth people want to see him tried on Earth. Lunar colonists have been getting away with too much. Going too fast.' He put a knuckle to his mouth for an instant, glanced up at Smith. 'That's just a personal opinion of course. Not even mine, really. Certainly not an official one.'

Bernadette looked from one to the other of them, Smith eating, Kreiner playing with his food, both of them avoiding her eyes. She wondered if they knew something about what was being planned.

Well, now was the time to find out.

'There are friends of mine at Copernicus -' she mentioned some names, senior Tutors, SystemOps, academics - 'who think that the Moon should be allowed her own jurisdiction in this case, rather than following the conventional UN process. They've formed a committee -'

Kreiner interrupted her.

'Which way did Singh go?'

She frowned at the Sergeant, irritated.

'I don't know. West, I should think.'

'Can you make this thing look west?' He gestured at the wallscreen.

She did so, using her link, without a word. The new view showed square stacks of cold furnaces, white gaping quarries surrounded by rubble-heaps, and, behind, the smooth domes of the eviscerated mountains. There was no movement.

Kreiner got up and stood by the screen, leaning forward and peering out of it as if it were a glass window, in the way Earth people always did. Bernadette noticed that he had hardly touched his food. Did he think that, despite everything, Singh might try to run away? If so, how would looking out of the window help?

Bernadette decided he couldn't be very bright. She turned back to Smith.

'Our committee feel that this is a show trial, that Earth just needs a scapegoat for a disaster that wasn't really anyone's fault. In this they represent a strong current of feeling amongst lunar citizens. If the UN insists on the policy that you have indicated, then it could have major consequences in political terms.' She hesitated. 'There's serious talk of independence.' Then, without giving them a chance to take that in: 'I personally will accompany Sewa throughout the trial, and any punishment that is allotted to him, and will maintain liaison for publicity purposes with -'

She broke off as her link sent an urgent signal buzzing through her nerves. She blinked, brought up the NewsScreen in her mind.

<u>UN Cops at Copernicus Port – "Singh must pay for Lunar Crime"</u> Joshu Akimboola and Aristo Cleomides have arrived at Copernicus port with permits for the arrest of Sewa Singh. *More*>>>

Bernadette didn't need "more". She glared at Smith.

'Okay, Mr Akimboola and Mr Cleomides. Why have you given false names?'

'Not false,' said Kreiner.

Smith looked down at his food, embarrassed. 'You see, we're not strictly the right people. Akimboola and Cleomides have just arrived.'

'So who are you? Why are there two sets of officers here? I can tell you now that deception by UN Officers will be taken very seriously by my friends. The Lunar Committee will not –'

She stopped. Smith and Kreiner had exchanged a glance across the table, and something in that glance had made her shiver.

Without conscious thought, she linked her eyes to the camera in the airlock. Singh's red Aztex suit was missing from the rack. She counted the foil-packed air bottles on the floor beneath, and looked in the dusty outer chamber to check that the emergency unit was still there. Yes. He'd only taken the suit. Half an hour's air.

He'd been gone thirty-five minutes.

She linked in to Base Traffic, checked for his suit tracer. It wasn't logged.

The electronic part of her mind seemed to act on its own. With frightening speed, she had accessed the Base System. An overview of the area around the base appeared. Beacons were green; radar blind spots were shadows. A broad blue shield, spreading like a flood over the landscape, indicated the places Singh could have reached in a light suit in the time available. There were three places where the blue and the radar shadow overlapped. She logged the coordinates, felt her way through the smooth interface of Emergency Shuttle Dispatch, at the same time connected to manual BaseCom to obtain the necessary authority...

'Wait.' Smith's voice, and a stop message appeared on her display, too, in pulsing blue with the tag 'UN/AUTH'.

'There is something that I need to tell you.' Smith went on, speaking slowly, carefully. 'Shortly after we arrived at the port, I had a conversation with Mr Singh. He stated that, rather than face the trial, and the slow death from senility that would probably follow, he would prefer to take his own life now, with dignity. I indicated that we would not stand in his way.'

Bernadette stared at Smith for a moment, then stood up. She was oddly conscious of the fact that she felt nothing of the things she should feel – fear, anger, desperation – only the necessities of the moment.

'You can't stop me from trying to save him,' she said. 'There's still time.' And she already had the line open to the duty officer at BaseCom.

Smith went on eating, placidly enough, but Bernadette found that her communications were cut.

'Mr Singh also specifically requested me –' he paused, blinked once; Bernadette had the curious impression that he was trying to stop himself from crying – 'to ensure that you did not interfere with his wishes.'

Bernadette shouted, 'He wanted you to let him die? You expect me to believe that? You think that *anyone* will believe it?'

Smith gave a shrug.

'I don't know. It's what happened. It's better than what Akimboola and Cleomides had planned – for him, and for all of you.' He looked up, met her eyes. 'I know how angry you are, and how much grief you're going to feel, and how justified some of your friends' complaints against Earth are. But remember, no human being has been killed in war for eighty-seven years. You can't let it start again now.'

The BaseCom display faded. Bernadette became aware of Singh's whisky glass, still standing on the table, incongruous in the middle of breakfast. She sat down, feeling heavy, as if she were in a shuttle at take-off.

'He wasn't a criminal.' Her jaw felt heavy, too, as she spoke. Stiff. A unit of machinery that needed greasing. 'He was just a romantic. A careless fool. He wanted to live - for ever. He wanted everyone to live for ever. Growing higher. Growing up to be gods.' She looked up at the older man. 'Is that where you think we're going, Dr Smith? Or aren't we going anywhere? I mean, what's the point in going anywhere if there isn't - if he isn't - if there's no spirit left in us -'

She wasn't crying. She wanted to, but she wasn't crying.

Smith reached out and laid a hand on her arm, just below the place where Singh had bruised it. His touch was gentle, sexless.

'You are young,' he said, 'And from what I hear about the new treatments that are available now, it seems likely that you will be young for a very long time.' He let go his hand. 'It remains to be seen what price you will pay for that.'

He stood and joined Kreiner at the screen.

Bernadette swallowed, got up, gathered the empty bowls. Her legs felt weak, as if Earth's huge gravity had reached out and was pulling her down. She carried the bowls and the glasses across to the kitchen, placed them in a steel basin on the worktop, lowered the grey ceramic lid. There was a hissing sound, and a thin trail of steam emerged from a vent. She watched it for a moment, then went and stood behind the others, staring over their shoulders at the empty horizon.

At last Kreiner spoke. 'How much air did he have in that suit?'

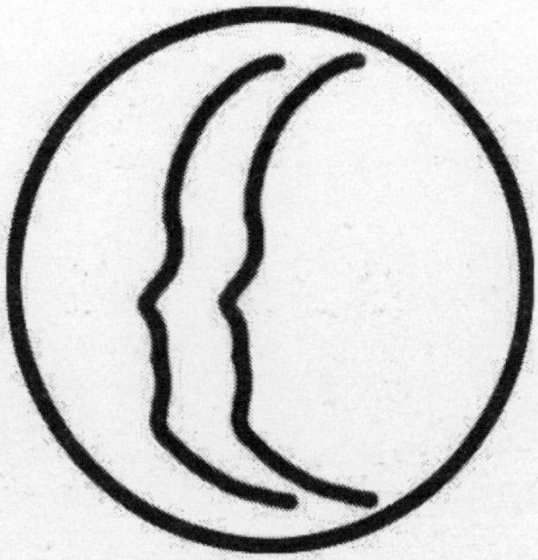

Sceptics of neo-astrology generally focused on one single aspect – that many noted astrologers continued to discuss prophecies in terms of the constellations visible from the old homeworld, Earth. Such patterns in the stars could not be said to have the same influence upon individuals if that individual was living many light years from the point where, say, Aquarius was once visible.

For Gemini, Kasterborus had the double challenge of taking into account twin constellations. In mythology, the twins themselves were Castor and Pollux, favoured mortals of Zeus who, as members of the Argonauts, had helped Jason rescue the Golden Fleece (see Aries). Killed in battle with their cousins, the Leucippidae, the twins were taken by Zeus and placed for eternity in the heavens as the twin stars that still bear their name.

The Gemini is in fact two signs in one: a reflective, introspective side that constantly questions the self; and the extrovert, the achiever, the persuader. Many Geminis use their extrovert side as a mask, hiding behind their louder personality to prevent others from seeing their true self. This aspect often makes them extremely competitive, always wanting to win, always needing to have the last word in every discussion.

Their ruling planet is Mercury, regardless of whichever solar system the individual is born into.

Kasterborus, *Our Destiny is in the Stars*

Kasterborus says...

If today is your birthday: *Check travel arrangements carefully before setting off on any long trips. And remember – you can have too much of a good thing.*

Twin Piques

Anthony Keetch

The Doctor beamed as he was carried along on the shoulders of the cheering crowd, ticker tape stranded in his mop of hair, confetti staining his collar like paper dandruff. Jamie, a pretty girl on each arm, was surfing the front of the joyous crowd on foot. He too had been held aloft initially, but a kilt/breeze situation had made this unwise, so there had been a mutual decision for the Scottish lad to walk. Whatever, his smile threatened to split his face in two.

King Gavin XXIII, flanked by his majestic retinue of impossibly butch guards, stood at the door of the TARDIS, an expression of dignified pleasure on his handsome face. He was a middle-aged man, tall, broad of shoulder, clean-shaven, with a jaw that implied a man who would brook no dissent, rather belied by the twinkle in his eye.

As his subjects marched the time travellers to the idyllic copse lined with aromatic lilac-leaved trees where the TARDIS had landed, the guards leaped to attention, and King Gavin strode forward to meet the excited crowd. The Doctor was gently lowered to the ground, and the two giggling girls tugged Jamie out of the throng.

'Father!' Japonica squealed and kissed the King.

'Order him to stay!' Corianda pleaded. 'Please!' Gavin smiled at his daughters, then took the hands of the Doctor and Jamie and held them high.

The King turned to face the crowd who fell immediately and respectfully silent.

'My people!' he boomed. 'Today has been the greatest day in our history. And we owe it all to our two friends here!' And the crowd bellowed its approval.

'Without their intervention and courage and sense of justice, my evil brother Conrad would be your king.' A hiss like a perforated zeppelin leaked from the crowd. His daughters clung to their father, as though their wicked uncle could snatch them away any minute.

'May the whiskers of his moustache curl up with shame and fall from his chin!' bellowed one old woman. The crowd concurred, quite noisily. They didn't like Conrad's moustache, it was yet another example of the pretender's narcissism.

King Gavin stroked his own baby-smooth upper lip, and with a raised hand and a barely concealed grin, quietened his subjects.

'And along with the calamity of my brother's crowning would have come slavery, poverty, and rank cruelty. But fear no longer. He is vanquished and locked away for ever in the Tower of Judgement.'

As one, the crowd's heads swivelled to glance fearfully at the distant sight of the black spire, a baleful scar on the horizon.

'I know,' yelled one man in the crowd. 'Let us build a giant statue of our beloved King, to block out the view of the Tower and its malevolent occupant.'

The crowd considered. Nice idea, they thought, but was it too toadying? Gavin was known to be rather disparaging of sycophancy. Everyone glanced at the King.

'Well,' he pronounced. 'I can't stop you...'

'It's nice to be appreciated, eh, Doctor?'

The Doctor danced around the TARDIS console, flicking at the switches with even more brio than usual. 'Oh yes, Jamie. Not that we do what we do for the kudos, mind you.'

''Course not,' Jamie snorted.

The Doctor's hair twitched. 'But I think a rare moment of smugness isn't too unreasonable.'

Jamie preened. 'Aye, it made a nice change to receive a hero's send-off as opposed the usual skulking away while no one was looking. And do you realise that is the only planet I have ever visited where I didn't get locked up or shot at or knocked unconscious?'

The Doctor looked up from his finger work. 'Yes,' he said thoughtfully, 'a remarkably civilised world. Lovely weather too. Only rained at night, just like Camelot. And with that rogue of a brother out of the way, they can get on with their lives.'

'That Gavin was a nice fellow. For a king.'

'Charming!' The Doctor glanced mischievously at Jamie. 'And as for the princesses...'

Jamie's cheeks burned cerise and he decided that his dirk needed urgent polishing.

Then with the sound of a million elephants clearing their throats, the TARDIS shuddered to a halt.

The Doctor peered out of the TARDIS – and his jaw dropped.

'Jamie!' he called. 'Come and take a look.'

Jamie's chin joined the Doctor's on the ground.

Blue skies, a warm sun with a deliciously cooling breeze, air like vintage wine.

'But we haven'ae gone anywhere.'

'Well,' the Doctor's bow tie drooped in puzzlement, 'I rather suspect we must have travelled in time somewhat. It would have taken longer than we have been in flight to disperse that crowd.'

'So we've gone into their future?'

'Or the past.' The Doctor shut and locked the TARDIS door. 'Let's find out, shall we?'

'So now we know we've moved forward in time.'

They stared at the colossal statue which had been implausibly elevated since their departure a few minutes ago.

'Quite a feat of artistic engineering,' the Doctor said admiringly. 'I'm not sure if I approve of such idolatry, but...

Jamie clutched the Doctor's sleeve. 'But look at the face!' he gasped.

The Doctor examined the head of the statue. It was a remarkable likeness, he had to admit, albeit a tad too sentimental for his taste. The jaw, the mane of hair, the moustache...

Four eyebrows whizzed heavenwards.

'But...' gasped Jamie.

'Something must have happened after we left. Conrad must have escaped from the tower, overpowered Gavin, and usurped the throne.'

'And the statue?' asked Jamie.

'I suspect that it was not the labour of love it was intended to be. Look!' The Doctor pointed to the horizon. 'And the Tower of Judgement.'

The once imposing structure had flopped to the ground, its crumbled base the only reminder of its previous dominance of the landscape.

'Doctor! Doctor!'

A chubby man ran towards them, his ragged breath at odds with the look of delight on his face.

'It's Ernst!' the Doctor exclaimed.

'He's got awfu' old,' Jamie pointed out.

'Jamie, one streak of grey does not imply decrepitude.'

Ernst gave the Doctor a kiss on both cheeks, then before the Scots lad could duck, did the same to Jamie.

'Shall I be mother?'

Ernst had bustled the frantic pair to his beautiful cottage, with its thatched roof and crooked chimney out of which spiralled a twist of smoke. A fussy little man, locked owlishly behind inch-thick spectacles, he had made them so welcome that they were quite exhausted by the attention.

Jamie and the Doctor sat on a blissfully comfy sofa, their dangling legs not quite reaching the floor. Ernst dished out mugs of steaming liquid and slabs of cake.

'It is lovely to see you again,' he said. 'You haven't changed a bit, either of you. Still showing off those lovely lallies, Jamie?' Jamie nodded, mouth chock-a-block, not really sure what he had just been asked. 'Geffre will be home from work soon. He's in the Treasury now. Privy-Secretary or something, I dunno. Better than cleaning the privvies, I always say. You remember my friend Geffre?'

'Of course,' spluttered the Doctor, cake spraying over the immediate vicinity. 'Without the pair of you, it would have been impossible to knock the resistance movement into any sort of shape. Your world owes you both a great deal.' Ernst blushed.

The Doctor leaned forward. 'But what happened?' he inquired gently.

Ernst looked confused. 'When?' He nibbled at his sliver of cake.

'Since we left,' said Jamie.

'Which was how long ago exactly?' asked the Doctor.

Ernst did the numbers on his fingers. 'Just over ten years.'

'And how did Conrad become king, exactly?'

Ernst boggled at the Doctor. 'Erm... you helped him. How can you have forgotten?'

'Let me get this clear.' The Doctor mopped up the last crumbs of cake, licked his fingers, and chose his words carefully. 'Ten years ago, Jamie and I came to this world, and helped King Conrad...'

'...Good King Conrad, bless him!' Ernst interrupted.

'...to wrest the crown from his brother Gavin...'

'Boo hiss!' chorused Ernst and Geffre, his endlessly tall, languorous, but equally-spectacled friend who had just walked in from a long day at the Palace.

'...who was then locked up in the Tower of Judgement.'

'Well, at first,' Geffre explained slowly. 'But when Good King Conrad decided that the Tower was a blot on the landscape and to demolish it and replace it with a Palladium of Art for the Community, he sent Gavin into exile. A long way from here.'

'We've seen the last of that rat-bag!' declared Ernst. 'He'll never dare show his scabby, disloyal, clean-shaven face back here.'

'And we owe it all to you and Jamie,' said Geffre.

'But, Doctor...' Jamie had long since left confusion behind and was now toying with bewilderment.

'Shh, Jamie, I'm thinking.' The Doctor's face was even more creased than usual. Something occurred to him. 'Now you're positive that you're not getting your kings mixed up?'

Ernst and Geffre stared at him blankly.

The Doctor clutched at his final straw. 'And you promise you're not just teasing us?'

Ernst and Geffre stared at each other blankly.

The Doctor sighed, his face crumpled like the hanky in his pocket. 'If it's not one thing, it's another.'

'Supper won't be ready for an hour at least,' declared Ernst. 'Why doesn't Geffre take you both for a drink at the tavern?'

Geffre strode purposely through the balmy twilight, his long legs leaving the Doctor and Jamie scuttling to keep up. A million insects gossiped noisily, but kept their distance.

'I don't understand, Doctor, what's going on?' Jamie whispered.

'I'm not sure, Jamie, but I expect there is some rational explanation.'

'But we helped Gavin,' protested Jamie. 'He was the good guy. He was the one the people wanted to be king. Conrad was a right... well, you know. Everyone said so. Now I could understand if they'd been hypnotised or something. That's usual.'

'Don't forget, Jamie, they are also convinced that we were on Conrad's side.'

'But we weren't!' Jamie stopped. 'Were we?'

The Doctor shook his head. 'I really don't know.'

The Doctor and Jamie sat on the grass outside, clutching their drinks. The noise inside had begun to weary them and they were both feeling rather light-headed, not entirely due to the potency of the local wine. Everyone had greeted them as returning heroes and had bombarded them with drinks and slaps on the back and updates on their lives. Luckily no one had asked the time travellers what they had been up to since their previous visit because it would have resulted in a very short conversation. Jamie muttered something to the Doctor about feeling a fraud, but the Doctor had responded that they weren't really, after all, they had fought to save the people from a tyrant - just not the one that everyone assumed.

It was almost time for them to return to Ernst's supper, so while Geffre 'paid a visit', the Doctor and Jamie waited for him outside the tavern. It was a gorgeous evening, the air was warm without being oppressive, only the sounds of nature could be heard, and the stars twinkled exactly the way they are supposed to.

'They seem very happy with Conrad as king, don't they, Doctor?' An interminable litany of praise for King Conrad had been forced on them for the past hour. It had become a bit boring eventually, like being bombarded with photos and anecdotes by a grandmother who is convinced her grandchild is a genius, a prodigy, or maybe even a messiah. Since his coronation, Conrad had instigated free medical help for all, ensured a more equitable distribution of wealth, built affordable housing, and made intolerance illegal and - more effectively - unfashionable. He had even ordered his Scientist Royal to invent calorie-free chocolate. The only complaint seemed to be that the telly wasn't as good any more, but as the Doctor pointed out, drama doesn't thrive in an atmosphere of nirvana.

'Yes, they do,' said the Doctor, 'and it's not right.'

'I don't see what the problem is.' Jamie shrugged, eyelids drooping, the wine having hit the spot. 'They've got a king they like and who doesn't chop their heads off for any silly wee excuse. Let's just leave it at that, eh?' He lay back and stared at the sky.

'Because there's something wrong, Jamie, I can feel it in my water. Gavin was a good man. I knew that as soon as I met him and we were right to fight for him.'

'Perhaps...' Jamie started, then paused.

'Perhaps what?'

Jamie shrugged nervously. 'Perhaps you... we were wrong.'

'Wrong?' The Doctor's face was unusually immobile. 'In what way?'

Jamie knew he was stuck in this hole so he had to make the most of it. 'Maybe, we were on the wrong side. Perhaps Gavin was the villain, after all.'

'Fiddlesticks!' The Doctor folded his arms. 'I know my dictators. No, the important questions are: Why have the people changed their allegiance? How come history has been rewritten? Why do they think we were fighting for the wrong side? And most peculiarly, what is behind Conrad's suspicious benevolence?'

Jamie gave no response. 'I realise those were rhetorical questions, Jamie, but I would appreciate...' He noticed that Jamie was laid prostrate on the ground, his knees bent, hands behind his head. 'Oh, Jamie do pay attention.' This enigma was making the Doctor cross.

Jamie sat up rather too quickly. His head spun and he clutched his forehead. 'I've just noticed something odd.'

'Yes, well, oddness does seem to be *a la mode* in these parts.'

'You know I spent last night with the princesses...'

The Doctor coughed. 'Now, Jamie, you're a grown lad and I can't stop you doing... Just be glad the King didn't find out...'

'No, Doctor, the lassies took me up the hill and showed me their constellations.'

The Doctor looked uncomfortable.

'The stars,' Jamie explained. 'They pointed them out to me and told me their names. I can't remember them all, although I know Princess Japonica was born under the Sign of the Wardrobe. It just looked like four stars quite near each other to me. I couldn'ae see a wardrobe.'

The Doctor gulped down the last of his drink and shut his eyes.

'Now, I'm no expert on the stars, although I've visited a few of them since I joined you.' Jamie shook his head. 'But I think those stars up there are all in a different place from last night.'

The Doctor's eyes snapped open.

'Yes, I am sure they're all higgledy-piggledy.'

The Doctor stared into the heavens and slapped the ground. A grin cracked his face and he leaped up and danced a little jig. Not for the first time, Jamie was secretly relieved that he had taken the precaution of chopping up the recorder, not that it ever prevented the Doctor producing a fresh one from somewhere.

Geffre left the tavern. 'Ready for sups, chaps?'

The next morning - naturally with an azure sky and perfectly choreographed butterflies - after a breakfast as delicious and table-breaking as the previous night's supper, the Doctor and Jamie set off to the TARDIS.

'But, Doctor, I can't believe it.'

'It's the only explanation.'

'But everything's exactly the same.'

'That's the whole point of doppelgänger worlds. They are rare, I admit, but they are a fascinating phenomenon. Two planets, absolutely identical down to the last leaf.'

'But what about Ernst and Geffre?'

'The same geology, flora, fauna, even individuals. It's a trillion billion to one chance, but', the Doctor sniffed, 'anything's possible.'

The Doctor stopped and surveyed the environment with great pleasure. 'Fascinating!'

'Bit of a coincidence, eh, Doctor, to land here straight away after the first planet?'

'Now, Jamie, don't knock coincidence. Very useful thing. Don't know where I'd have been without coincidence down the years.'

'So...' Jamie began.

'So?' the Doctor asked.

'What now, Doctor?

The Doctor rubbed his hands together. 'Ah!' he said. 'The people are happy, the planet is idyllic and the weather is glorious.'

'The telly isn't very good apparently though.'

'Yes, well, Jamie, there's nothing you and I could do about that.'

'So...'

'By rights, we should move on. Return to the TARDIS and move on. To the next adventure. There's nothing here for us to do.'

'Is that right?'

'Except...' the Doctor winked, 'to have a marvellous holiday!'

'I'll get the sun tan lotion.'

'And I'll get the bucket and spade.'

The pair of them scampered in the direction of the TARDIS.

'Do you think Ernst and Geffre will mind us staying with them?' Jamie asked.

'Mind? They are the perfect hosts. Although we'd better not impose for too long. Guests are like fish, they go off after three days.'

As the grove where the TARDIS rested came into view, Jamie paused and took a look back at the surrounding land. A cloud sidled in front of the sun, but soon realised it was not welcome and quickly dispersed. 'I wonder what's going on back at the other planet?' he asked.

The Doctor was fishing for the TARDIS key. 'In what way, Jamie?'

'If Conrad is the good guy, what does that make Gavin?'

The Doctor stared at Jamie.

'I mean,' he struggled to make sense of what he was thinking, 'did we help put the wrong man in power?'

'No,' the Doctor stated firmly. But for a second, a worried expression made a brief visit to his face. 'Obviously...' he began, an explanation almost but not quite within his reach. 'Um, obviously, on this planet, Conrad is the benevolent leader while back on the other planet, Gavin takes that role.'

'But you said the two planets were identical,' accused Jamie.

'They are,' protested the Doctor.

'Down to the tiniest leaf.'

'Um...'

'Suppose we've helped a tyrant gain power? What then?'

'We haven't. Look, didn't Gavin seem like a decent chap to you?'

'He did.'

'And what about his daughters? The princesses?'

'Japonica and Corianda?'

'Yes, you liked them, didn't you, Jamie?'

Jamie stuck his hands in his sporran and emitted a heartfelt 'Oh aye.'

'There you are then,' the Doctor stated firmly. 'Do you seriously think those girls would allow their father to turn into an autocrat?'

'A what?'

'A bully. A despot.' Jamie looked blank. 'A James the Seventh.'

Jamie's lip curled. 'No, probably not.'

'There's no probably about it. They were good girls, they'll keep their dad in check.'

'But...'

'Trust me.'

A mauve-feathered bird landed on the branch of a nearby tree and caw-caw-cawed as though laughing at a particularly dirty joke.

'I do,' Jamie stated, almost convincingly. 'But...'

The Doctor looked cross. 'But what?'

Jamie chewed on his lower lip. 'Suppose you're wrong?'

An outraged squawk escaped from the Doctor. 'I am never wrong!'

The pair of them looked at each other.

'I suppose we could always check,' said the Doctor, meekly.

'How can we do that?'

Silence. Then the Doctor snapped his fingers. 'The fast return switch!' He shrugged his shoulders. 'Well, it might work.'

Four very short legs ran as fast as they could to the TARDIS. Jamie arrived first. The Doctor flung him the key, and he opened the door and disappeared inside. The Doctor stopped at the door and patted the 'Emergency' notice. 'Don't let me down, old friend.'

'It all *seems* okay.'

'Appearances can be deceptive, Jamie. Haven't you learned that through all our travels?'

They stared up at the statue.

'Is it my imagination, Doctor, or is it taller than the one of Conrad?'

'There is a tape measure back in the TARDIS, Jamie. You can always measure it if you like.'

As expected the sun shone, birds twittered harmoniously, and the breeze lapped deliciously against their faces. They had yet to spot an ominous pall of smoke, or a corpse-laden gibbet, or even an officious noticeboard.

Instead, children played unsupervised in the street. Passing strangers nodded at each other with a smile. A man walking his dog scooped.

And not only had the Tower of Judgement disappeared, but the Palladium Of Art For The Community was almost complete - and, astonishingly, quite tastefully designed.

'Well, Doctor, what do you think?'

The Doctor surveyed the surroundings. As paradises go, it was bit suburban and unexciting for him, but then he wasn't expecting to live here. But neither did he get the itch to overthrow the local authority. Which made a nice change, and meant that someone was doing something right.

'I think,' he said, 'that I'd like a cup of tea.'

Ernst greeted them as though he hadn't seen them for years and hadn't cooked supper for them last night, which of course he hadn't. He dished out all the local gossip, most of which was pretty identical to what they had heard last night. Since Gavin had claimed the throne, life had progressed rather nicely, thank you very much; the streets were clean, the prisons were virtually empty, and a cure for gout had just been announced. Hurrah for Good King Gavin, he cheered. And yah boo to rotten old Conrad, justifiably exiled to the distant armpit of the world.

'Shame about the telly, though,' sympathised Jamie.

'Oh no,' protested Ernst, 'TV's getting better. Mostly repeats admittedly, but old stuff we haven't seen for donkey's years, when they knew how to tell a story well.'

Jamie and the Doctor finished their tea, accepted some of Ernst's home-made cake for their journey, and, imparting messages of love for Geffre, they departed.

'Now all we have to choose,' said Jamie, 'is which of the two planets we are going to spend our holiday on.'

'Hmm!' the Doctor muttered.

Jamie groaned. 'I know that "hmm".'

'Hmm?'

'No, not that one. That's a question "hmm". I mean the first "hmm", the itching-to-investigate-something-and get-us-into-a-terrible-mess "hmm".'

The Doctor smiled. 'You know me too well, Jamie.'

'What is there to investigate?' asked Jamie. 'Two planets, both very happy. End of story.'

'Two kings, both good men and wise rulers,' said the Doctor, 'albeit neither of them democratically elected. Why were they at war with each other?'

'Don't care,' said Jamie. 'Fancy an ice cream?'

'Yes,' said the Doctor. 'But after we've solved this dilemma.'

'There is no dilemma,' Jamie grumbled. 'Except what flavour.'

'But... but... but...' spluttered King Conrad. 'It's bigger on the inside than the out!'

'Oh aye,' said Jamie, 'so it is.'

He led Conrad into the TARDIS console room and held out a Chippendale chair for the royal posterior, but the king wandered about the console in a daze. 'With technology like this, it is little surprise that you were able to defeat my wicked brother.'

Jamie fidgeted awkwardly. He hadn't met Conrad before, although the king greeted him like an old friend. Conrad was uncannily like his brother, with the exception of the bushy moustache which engulfed the middle of his face. He even shared the same twinkle in the eye as Gavin, which sat oddly with the brutal reputation he initially held.

Eventually, his senses regained, Conrad ceased his aimless roaming and turned to face Jamie. 'Why have you brought me here, Jamie? I owe you and the Doctor my whole life, but I am a busy man, you understand.'

'Oh aye, we realise that,' Jamie said slowly. He chose his next words as carefully as he could. 'But we feel, the Doctor and I, that your world is missing just one thing which could help you be even more prosperous and, erm, happier than it is already.'

Conrad's eyes narrowed. 'And that is?' His hand automatically reached for where his sword usually hung.

'Oh, I'll leave the Doctor to explain it,' Jamie said, then quickly added, 'Besides, it's all his idea anyway.'

Conrad took his seat. 'Kindly inform the Doctor that I am ready to receive him whenever he is ready.'

'I'll do that.' Jamie raced down the corridor to the room which the Doctor had allocated for this - in Jamie's opinion - daft business. He knocked on the door, and the Doctor poked his head out.

'You-know-who is ready,' Jamie informed him. 'And very reluctantly unarmed.'

The Doctor nodded. 'Bring him here. But be prepared...'

Jamie, muscles taut, sweat dripping, a rictus smile etched on his face, led Conrad down the corridor. As they reached the door, Jamie wanted to say something, but couldn't decide what. He knocked on the door and then turned the handle. He gestured for the King to enter. As Conrad went in, Jamie poised himself to leap.

Two identical screams of anguish rent the air, as Conrad saw with whom he shared the room.

'How dare you break your exile!' Gavin and Conrad yelled at each other in unison. 'For that you will die!' Both reached for swords that weren't there. Remembering they were unarmed each leaped for the other's throat. Jamie hastily grabbed Conrad by the shoulders, while the Doctor, with astonishing ease, restrained Gavin.

'Now, majesties,' said the Doctor, 'we all need to have a little talk. Jamie, put the kettle on.'

Gavin and Conrad glowered at each other, matching lips curled in scorn.

Jamie stared at the surroundings. He had never been in here before. It was a long room, so long it had its own horizon. The walls and floor were covered with what looked like dimpled mattresses. Gavin sat on one side of the room, Conrad the other, the pair of them separated by a narrow river which flowed down the middle of the room into the distance. Occasionally, small life-forms could be seen near the surface of the water. Jamie didn't want to know what they were.

The two kings had hesitatingly agreed to listen to what the Doctor wished to say. But each had fixed his eyes on his hated brother, ready to rip the other's heart out if the opportunity made itself available.

The Doctor had spent the past ten minutes explaining the situation. But it became clear to Jamie that neither king was listening to a word the Doctor said.

Gavin glared at the Doctor. 'My people consider you a hero, Doctor. But they will cheerfully tear you in half for allowing that accursed monster to return to our land.'

'You think so?' Conrad spat. 'It is you they despise. Although, much as I am loathe to agree with such an asinine specimen of humanity, my people will find it hard to forgive this betrayal, Doctor.'

'Your people? Pah!'

'Yes, *my* people, usurper.'

The Doctor flopped down on to a chair and rested his cheeks in his palms. 'Oh dear.'

Jamie shook his head. 'I could have told you, Doctor.'

Gavin made to stand up. Jamie tensed. 'If this charade is finished, Doctor, I wish to leave. I have a sibling to kill.'

'Really?' Conrad sneered. 'You and whose army?'

Gavin considered. 'My own.'

'My army', said Conrad proudly, 'is bigger than yours.'

'Your army?' spat Gavin. 'A rag-tag of mercenaries and low-life scum.'

Conrad was shocked. 'A fine way to describe the Royal Retinue!'

'Actually,' Jamie pointed out, 'they're both the same.'

'As if the Royal Retinue would demean their courageous selves to serve a rascal such as you...'

'Gentlemen, please!' A loud thwack rent the air. The Doctor tucked his hand inside his armpit, trying to hide exactly how much hitting the table with his palm had hurt. 'Stop this childish behaviour!'

The two kings looked at him sulkily. Conrad muttered something under his breath.

'I heard that, Conrad,' the Doctor snapped. Gavin sniggered. 'You know, it's your own time you're wasting. I'm not going anywhere. I can stay here all night. And we are not leaving until this is sorted out.'

Gavin stared at the ceiling. Conrad examined his fingernails.

'I don't understand,' the Doctor said, sadly. 'You're both good kings. Among the best I have ever encountered. Admittedly, as Oscar said, a good king is the worst enemy of democracy.' He caught Jamie's eye. 'But now isn't the time, I expect. But,' he continued, 'if you are both wonderful rulers individually, just imagine how much better you'd be if you could work together.'

Simultaneous snorts erupted from the matching noses of Gavin and Conrad. Even Jamie looked incredulous. 'Oh aye, Doctor, you'll be suggesting the Daleks and the Cybermen share a highland fling next.'

'Share the throne with him?' Gavin boggled.

'I'd rather share my trousers with a leper,' said Conrad.

The Doctor restrained himself from tearing his hair out. 'But what is the problem?' he spluttered. 'I don't understand. Gavin, explain to me - what is so wrong with your brother?'

Gavin stared at Conrad with undisguised loathing. 'The list of his crimes is endless.'

'Pah!'

'Start at the very beginning,' suggested the Doctor. 'It's a very good place to start.'

Gavin smiled. This he would obviously enjoy. 'He eats with his mouth open.'

The Doctor stared at him. 'Oh?'

'And not just that,' Gavin continued outraged, 'he actually shovels food in while he's talking.'

'I do not!'

'Do!'

'Well, actually,' said Conrad, 'that's nothing. He breathes in a really annoying way.'

'How?' asked the Doctor, interested despite himself.

'It's a sort of... just... like this.' And Conrad demonstrated an over-emphasised hiss.

Gavin pulled a hurt face. 'I don't do that!'

'Well, you do actually,' said the Doctor apologetically. 'But I expect it's just adenoids. We can get that sorted out quite easily.'

'No one's getting anywhere near my nose with a scalpel just to keep that monkey-mannered oaf quiet.'

'He also', Conrad was clearly almost enjoying himself now, 'reads something funny and laughs out loud and everyone is supposed to ask him what's funny and if they don't then he's like a Moglan Beast with a sore head for the rest of the day.'

'Just because you've got no sense of humour,' accused Gavin.

'I have too.'

'Anyway,' shouted Gavin, 'at least I remember to put the seat down afterwards...'

The Doctor and Jamie slipped out of the room.

'I just don't understand!' the Doctor wailed again.

'It's very simple,' Jamie explained. 'They're family. It's quite normal.'

The Doctor stared at him. 'Is it?'

'Oh aye. If you had a brother, you'd be fighting with him all the time.'

The Doctor said nothing.

'It's just that they're both kings, so they've got armies and power and no one to tell them they're both being big girly dafties.'

'I suppose we had better separate them and get them back to their respective worlds.'

'Leave them for a while. They're having a whale of a time in there. Let them enjoy themselves. You never know, it might even get some of the silliness out of their systems.'

The Doctor nodded sadly.

* * *

Gavin and Conrad eventually exhausted themselves with their arguing and had now separated themselves. Gavin had removed his shoes and was paddling in the stream, seemingly oblivious to the small creatures nibbling at his toes, while Conrad was sprawled on his back in the corner, head on the floor, his legs up against the wall. Gavin pursed his lips and breathily whistled a popular tune while Conrad ground his teeth to powder.

Jamie led Conrad out of the TARDIS and back to his palace, while the Doctor returned Gavin to his own planet.

Neither brother said a word to each other.

That night, stuffed to the gills with another of Ernst's eat-till-you-explode suppers and consequently incapable of movement, Jamie and the Doctor sprawled in the garden, enjoying a meteor shower. Jamie had unwisely chosen a hammock, so when a sudden thought caused him to sit up, he regretted it.

'Doctor!' he exclaimed, clutching his stomach to stop the contents slopping about inside him.

'What is it, Jamie?' the Doctor yawned.

'When we arrived on this planet - or was it the other planet? - we asked Ernst how Conrad got into power, and he told us that we had helped him. But we didn't. Gavin yes, Conrad no.'

The Doctor thought about it. 'Not yet we haven't.'

'You mean we might in the future?'

'Either that or there is an another me hanging about the universe.'

Jamie's eyes widened to the size of the plates on which their vast dinner had been served. 'Another... Oh no, one of you is enough, I couldn't cope with two of you.'

'Neither could I,' said the Doctor.

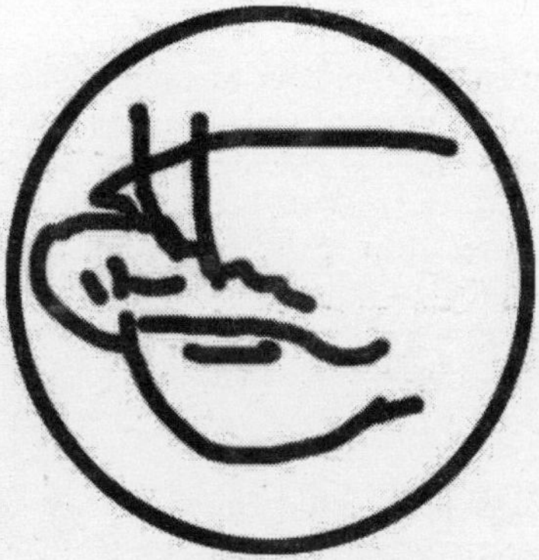

Cancer - the crab - was the first of the signs to be placed in the heavens by someone other than Zeus. The Carcinus was a huge malevolent crab sent by Zeus's queen, Hera, to distract Heracles during his battle with the Hydra. When Carcinus was slain by Heracles, Hera rewarded it by creating the constellation Cancer in its honour.

This origin was, regretfully, thrown out by Kasterborus in his attempt to make the legends resonate with a 'modern' audience. He didn't replace it with another myth, however - he just failed to mention its origins completely.

Colonists born into the house of Cancer are famous as the homemakers of the zodiac. Though very powerful and resilient, Cancerians are in fact terrified by their own strength and so tend to reserve it until certain lines are crossed, or they are pushed to their limit. They tend to be their own biggest fans and their own harshest critics as they never feel their best is good enough.

The comparison with crabs though is straightforward; just as with a crab, they can appear harsh or defensive on the outside because they are so soft and vulnerable on the inside. They are instinctive rather than analytical, fuelled by emotion more often than rational thought. And just like crabs, whose lives are governed by tides, it is the pull of the moon that is the greatest influence upon the Cancerian.

Kasterborus, *Our Destiny is in the Stars*

Kasterborus says...

If today is your birthday: *They say travel broadens the mind, but as all Cancerians know, there's no place like home.*

Still Lives

Ian Potter

Master Pangloss taught the metaphysico-theologo-cosmolonigology. He could prove to admiration that there is no effect without a cause; and, that in this best of all possible worlds, the Baron's castle was the most magnificent of all castles, and My Lady the best of all possible baronesses.

Voltaire, *Candide* (1759), trans. attributed to A T L Gift

Two identical snowflakes fell to the pavement as Helen walked by and melted before anyone could notice them.

This kind of thing happens a lot, no matter what people tell you, you just need to be looking the right way to see it.

Lightning strikes in the same place twice with such predictable regularity that conductors have been provided on some of its more popular routes. History repeats itself without becoming farcical so often it's tragic.

Patterns recur.

Helen took her old route to work again; down the stairs that smelled less of urine than the lift did; across the estate by the route where the lights worked, even though it was light enough to go the quick way, and past the paper shop to the tube. For old time's sake she went down on to the platform.

The train that was in was full as usual, and, as usual, she couldn't catch it, it wasn't going anywhere she wanted. Never again, she told herself again, never again, and began the walk to work.

June 22nd, and still snowing, and still no one to say, 'It's not natural, is it?' to. She was sick of this cold snap that had lasted months now, but even more sick of the mid-morning crowds impeding her route to HQ.

By her own reckoning she'd been living back here in Maida Vale for about five years now. Obviously, things had changed in that time. The country had slipped more towards the right, the ingredients in Coca Cola had been changed, and there'd even been a brief warm spell a year or so back, but so much was unchanging that her life seemed more and more futile with every breath she took.

Nothing of consequence altered much: the headlines in the paper, constant permutations on the same themes, slowly altered as the mood of the country shifted; the royals seemed to be falling further out of favour, fashions and faces in the street came and went, but all so slowly you barely detected it at all.

* * *

The pale mid-morning light, pouring unblinkingly through the squat's window, finally stirred Mark from sleep. As always, he groaned as he remembered where he was. Another day failing to change the world looming up in front of him and next to nothing in the fridge.

Scratching the same itch he'd been ignoring for months, he rolled his first smoke of the day and put an album he'd bought on vinyl, in his youth, into the cassette player.

He really hoped that itch wasn't crabs – he could easily have them. He'd gone through a particularly drunken self-pitying period a while back where he'd had sex with anyone who didn't move.

The album didn't sound quite like it used to; the tape was worn from replaying and it sounded like it'd been remastered too. The mixes were different on half the tracks and the running order had been swapped, but it was close enough to remind Mark of the good old days when you knew where you were, got up when it was light and went to bed when it went dark.

He kept the portable tape machine in his hand as he headed to the kitchen. It helped drown out the constant one-note rumble of the traffic. The tape trundled on as Mark made himself breakfast and sang along, until, after a few minutes, he and the tune went separate ways.

He had a horrible feeling they'd replaced one of his favourite guitar solos with an alternative take.

The traveller sits on the street, drinking cheap spirits with another rough sleeper, Kilburn Tony, enjoying the effect of the drink on his mind and wondering what the new day might bring.

He scratches his beard and pulls his blanket closer around him, as Tony retells his life again, in a still more streamlined fashion, whittling meaning and narrative from the random events that have shaped him.

The traveller watches a few lost snowflakes dance erratically on the eddies of his hot breath. He must be seeing double, he thinks, as he half convinces himself he has glimpsed two identical crystals in the air, one falling down and the other careering sideways crazily.

He passes the bottle back to Tony and the snowflakes crash together, obliterating themselves.

Journal of Dr Elizabeth Shaw
24th of July

D still going on about free will to himself, insufferable!

I'm no theologian, thank God. What philosophy I read at Cambridge stopped with Plato, long before all that pinhead dancing stuff, but it seems to me he's deluding himself.

Surely, what he says he saw – a universe next door where we all worked for the Nazis or whatever, suggests a deterministic cosmos, in which we react entirely to our surroundings, rather than the possibility we can map our own destinies.

I said as much to him myself, but he just quoted the bit from *Hamlet* at me, about there being more in Heaven and Earth than we dream of and went back to more dilettante fiddling with his gadgets.

Some scientist! As if making up half the terms he uses and spelling half the rest wrongly wasn't enough, he refuses to tackle *anything* rigorously.

If all the states of matter that can exist actually *do*, somewhere off in other dimensions to the sides of us, the fact we're only aware of taking one path between the possibilities doesn't mean we will those paths of our lives into being, merely that there *are* many paths.

One for young Kimpton at Queens I think, but I fear the variations in the worlds are just the results of quantum events reconciling one way or another. It all points to accumulated chance rather than any mysteriously acausal 'free will' shaping our lives. If I can see it why can't he? He's the supposed genius.

Mentioned all this to A L-S, saw him glaze over about three sentences in, but he eventually got the gist.

Forget that, for all he's a bit of a maths whizz on the quiet, his imagination remains steadfastly military.

A L-S says not facing the idea may be part of D feeling trapped here. He can't stomach the possibility of being trapped in a broader sense than he already is, of having no control of his destiny. He has to live believing he has free will, whether he has it or not. Apparently, that's why he always bangs on about being a free agent, not a UNIT employee.

Sounds like something he's pulled from one of Dr Sweetman's reports to be honest; all that stuff about how D's ego is compensating for his feelings of powerlessness.

I suppose there's some sense in what A L-S says though; if all our possible lives are true and we just happen to be conscious of one of them, then our lives have no meaning. No one wants to live believing that.

Mark got the day's paper from the usual place, and, as ever, nothing grabbed him as of interest on the news pages. Just the usual James Stevens *Good Science* bit and the same old mix of sex scandal, celebrity and home news elsewhere, so he leafed through to the TV pages after a brief laugh at Stevens's transparently Ministry-dictated good news stories.

It was pretty much the same old rubbish on the telly too, a few things he'd not seen before tucked away in there, but nothing major.

Chorley's People was transvestites again, the *Playpen* pals were making pretend boats out of cardboard boxes, *Occult Secrets of the Nazis* would be on BBC3 this evening, as they generally seemed to be, and ITV was still going to be doing that thing about cancer at 11, not that he'd see it.

He'd watched a lot of daytime telly a while ago, but its sameyness had become depressing. It sure as hell wasn't entertaining, and you couldn't really justify watching three hours of it in a sitting for what you learned as it droned away at you.

He clicked on the TV and flicked peremptorily through the channels.

Chloe was making a toilet tube mast, the advert for fish fingers was on, schools programmes were about to start on ITV. All totally predictable.

For once, the transvestite that Harold Chorley was leaning over wasn't wearing fishnets that really didn't go with the rest of his outfit. That made a pleasant change at least.

He headed out to get some more beer. The cans he'd got before crashing out for his kip a few hours ago seemed to have mysteriously gone walkabout.

For years afterwards he would thank all the powers he could imagine for making him head to the off licence that day.

Helen arrived at work after a few hours of walking, hoping, as usual, that today one of the doors might be ajar and she could slip in. As ever, a few figures stood tantalisingly near the entrances, frozen like statues, and every door remained shut.

She would stay here and hope, for as long as she could, just like last time, and the time before. She felt sure that one day she'd wake and her moment would have come.

The sign outside UNIT HQ now read European Axis Military Corps, as it had done for years to Helen's eyes, but it was just possible that the same people were still within those impenetrable walls. People who might just help Corporal Helen Martin get her life back.

Mark had been behind the rubbish tip near the project outbuildings when it happened. Everything had seemed to dim slightly, like in the power cuts the Eastchester project was supposed to stop, and he'd felt a little queasy.

For a second he thought he'd fainted and imagined the world dimming. Then he noticed the noise. The constant drill rumbling had changed pitch, dropped an octave or so and, perhaps odder, become a softer, more regular sound like a musical note.

There'd probably been some kind of brown-out, a dip in the electrics across the National Grid, and everything had slowed down. The Ministry of Energy had made statements about that. It was all part of teething problems at Nuton apparently.

He'd finished his illicit fag and gone back to work thinking nothing of it, until he remembered Eastchester had a mini reactor of its own, it didn't get power from Nuton. A second more thought and he wondered how a brown-out had made things go dark out of doors in the daytime.

Half an hour later Mark had discovered the true horror of what had happened to him.

Journal of Dr Elizabeth Shaw
25th of July

Lot of A L-S's goons running about flapping about our missing sentry, still.

They're convinced the Soviets have her, and she's gone over to the other side; think they'd be happier if she'd turned into a wereperson like those others.

I suppose, if she were a sleeper agent, the Stahlman project might be something her masters would want information on. There've been rumours they're planning something similar in Siberia.

I'm sure A L-S thinks women are more prone to defecting, old-fashioned that way. He hardly ever deploys the female troops in prominent roles, and has Bell pretty much deskbound.

I think Helen's probably just had enough of UNIT and gone AWOL. I can understand that after Eastchester.

Dear Lord: AWOL! This organisation's getting to me, I'm starting to think like the military: little, and in initials.

Helen had known it was some kind of time experiment she'd being guarding so her first assumption on finding herself trapped in this world of statues was that she'd been caught up in some kind of loop, her whole existence now somehow channelled into one moment.

She'd quickly ruled that out - she could move freely, retracing her steps, occupying the same space multiple times, which would surely be impossible if her matter had been repeatedly superimposed in the same instant of time.

She could see, if dimly at first, so photons were hitting her eyes, and she could hear, if only a low monotonous drone, and she could, with effort, move other objects.

Time was passing in *some* way.

When she'd felt the world lurch and had woken in the half light, she'd immediately run round into the building she knew was the cause of it all - the old hut where that dandy in the nightclub comedian's shirt was always messing about with his computer console and what have you.

The door had been open and the Brigadier and Miss Shaw stood framed in its opening. Helen had snapped to attention and waited for instructions, but none came.

Five minutes passed without movement from the top brass, during which time Helen had slipped from stone-faced military acceptance of the Brigadier's latest jape, to nervous hysteria when no punchline came.

Her laughter, unreprimanded, had slowly turned to fear.

Hours of panic followed. Helen shook her superiors and they did not stir, screamed out in the busy canteen where all spoons were suspended mid mouthful and not a muscle flinched, cried out to God in the little on-site chapel and neither He nor the site chaplain moved.

Worst of all, in all those hours of fear, it never went dark and no clock bar Helen's wristwatch moved an inch.

She had cried herself to exhausted sleep in the mid-morning sun and woken up in the same. It was still 11.15 am on the 22nd of July and it didn't look as though it was ever going to change.

Journal of Dr Elizabeth Shaw
26th of July

I spoke to D about Helen but he was too busy drawing squiggles on napkins, talking about dimensional elasticity and how he could get enough power. I think he's trying to work out how to get his magic table back in its box again.

I said he should do that translocation of object thing he does.

He gave me a bunch of conjuror's paper flowers, and asked for a coffee with a filthy number of sugars in it.

I'm not convinced his ego needs any more bolstering myself. If it gets any larger he'll probably trip over it and kill himself.

Experimentation over the next few days, as Helen's watch described the endless elevenses, had taught her a few more things.

Movement was much easier within an elliptical area reaching from the doorway of the hut to the rubbish dump a few hundred yards behind it, so presumably everything within that area had been affected, to some degree, by whatever it was that had happened.

She could interact with small objects close to her body - it was an effort, but possible. She could eat. Of course she should have realised that; she had, after all, found herself able to breathe. She could move things around, but if she left them for too long her influence on them tended to fade away. A pencil picked up before bed would have miraculously returned to where it had been found when she awoke.

People, it appeared, were too large to influence in this way, you might be able to rearrange their clothes or pop something into their pockets, but they remained impassive and unreacting.

Eventually she'd decided her best hope for salvation was to find out where old frilly shirt and his vintage car had gone.

Presumably he'd headed back to UNIT HQ in London, that long pink baroque cake of a building in Maida Vale.

She'd started walking. If she'd been able to make a car work for her life would have been easier, but it seemed her influence wasn't great enough. She was clearly working against the normal flow of events, creating a little pocket of world around her that grudgingly followed her rules as she waded through it, and couldn't make anything as complex or as large as a jeep behave for her.

Kilburn Tony asks the traveller if he knows what it's like to be a drifter, to live without purpose, just because you don't know what else to do.

The traveller nods, he knows. He points at the snow. He drifted himself for years, never settling, incapable of fitting in with ordinary life, living between the cracks of society.

Kilburn Tony nods and says he understands.

The traveller says he has no idea.

The weather had been good back then. It'd been a pleasant sunny June morning that first month, which made sleeping in ditches easier. When the first rain had come, Helen had thought she was cured. There was movement in the world about her at last, but no. The rain was moving certainly, hitting her skin, certainly, drenching her clothes, but not at full speed, and not necessarily falling *downwards*.

Close scrutiny of individual raindrops showed that while some fell, others rose up over time, or slipped sideways where there was no wind. Still others hung implausibly in mid air for seconds, unmoving like everything else in the world.

That was the first time Helen had realised that there was change in the world that wasn't caused by her.

She wasn't stuck in the 22nd of July - she was going through all the other possible versions of the 22nd of July now.

On a large scale, little was different, but by watching the rainfall intently she could discern some of the tiny differences in the world she was living through, tiny imperceptible fluctuations in the air which governed where a raindrop fell. She had found herself strangely moved and comforted as some of the drops that hit her face dribbled down her chin before coming to rest in mid air as they left her sphere of influence.

The weeks walking through rain that had followed seemed somehow easier for the realisation that this mad limbo she was living in had rules.

Once Helen had given up staying outside UNIT HQ permanently in the hope of a door spontaneously becoming unlocked, she decided to develop a sensible routine, and impose something like normality on her world. She had found somewhere to stay in Maida Vale that had an open door, and lived in it as best she could, ignoring the statue people she shared it with at first, and, in time, coming to love their ridiculous *tableaux vivants*.

She started sleeping in eight-hour stints in each twenty-four and going over to UNIT at set times, arbitrarily creating her own days in each of which she stood vigil outside HQ as if on an ordinary shift of duty. Over time, however one measured that in a world where it was always 11.15 in the morning, she had begun to notice some of the quirks of her new existence and, through close attention, larger changes occurring around her.

If you waited long enough, you'd notice things altering. on a human scale, slight movements in the crowds, flares on trousers shrinking almost imperceptibly over a series of days, the text of novels in the local shop suddenly being different - not massively so, a comma for a semicolon, a bracket for a dash, but different.

More depressingly, when she'd woken up one day to find her diary had become blank at her bedside, she'd discovered that if you didn't keep things close by, your influence on them faded fast.

She started reading books in the local library, trying to make sense of her half life. The science section wasn't big, and most of it was aimed at thirteen-year-old boys but Helen had time to persevere. As far as she could make sense of it, it appeared her anomalous relationship to causality was some kind of quantum effect. She was travelling sideways in time into parallel universes, moving into what else 'now' might be rather than forwards into the future. It also seemed she created some kind of thin bubble around herself so things close to her travelled sideways with her, her interactions with them remaining intact - a little pocket of universe that cause and effect didn't know what to do about.

She could open an unlocked door, or eat a can of beans, and they stayed open or eaten while they were in contact with her body, but the further away from her an object got, the less fixed it was, more prone to change, to drifting sideways in time away from her, to be replaced by something similar but not quite the same.

All hope of her most developed plan working, leaving a note for frilly shirt requesting help, faded with this realisation.

Any note she could leave would only exist for a single moment across a limited number of possible worlds, there was no chance it could be read; and even if it could be, little chance anyone who read it would be able to travel back and sideways in time to aid her in her present.

She kept going though, living as if one day the UNIT door might be open and there might be some hope of salvation, though she suspected there was none.

* * *

'She's literally disappeared off the face of the Earth, Doctor!' announced the Brigadier, hoping his dramatic manner might pique the man's interest.

'Literally?' the Doctor asked disinterestedly. He appeared to be attaching electrodes to a potato, and what was worse, Miss Shaw seemed to be willingly helping.

'Literally.' The Brigadier soldiered on. 'We're baffled.'

The Doctor looked up, his mouth full of fuse wire. 'Well, perhaps if you started thinking laterally rather than literally, you'd have a solution. It's nothing to do with me wherever she's gone to, and to be frank I doubt it's a matter of any consequence. Blessed girl probably can't find her way home without help.' He beckoned Miss Shaw over, to help him with some calculations that were clearly far more important than a missing corporal. Probably weight to baking times for King Edwards.

The Brigadier tried another tack.

'Miss Shaw here, wondered if she could have turned into one of those werepeople.'

The Doctor sighed. 'Brigadier, not only is the suggestion beneath contempt, but the Latin derivation is all wrong. The "were" in werewolf comes from "vir", meaning man. "Werepeople", if such things existed, would just be people people.'

'Indeed. "People people"; we could do with a few of those working here.'

Miss Shaw giggled musically, and the Brigadier felt himself twinkling despite himself.

The Doctor softened noticeably, and then, almost as noticeably, feigned ferocious indignation to cover the lapse.

'Stop doing that infernal moustache twitching thing of yours, old man, will you! And Liz – stop smirking, we're involved in scientific research of the utmost importance here!' He toyed with the downy hair on the nape of his neck distractedly and took a deep breath before continuing.

'I'll put my mind to it at some point, old chap, just as soon as I've sorted out the little matter of dimensionally re-sublimating the console here.' He rapped at one of its control panels, causing something, somewhere inside, to drop noisily from its place. 'I assume you've looked everywhere she could possibly be?'

'Of course,' the Brigadier sighed.

'So, it's just where she could impossibly be that's left?' said the Doctor triumphantly. He clicked his fingers and beckoned imperiously. 'Pass me that voltameter, Liz.'

The Brigadier pressed on regardless.

'Quite. We assumed she was with you at first, vanished about when you went on your little jaunt, but obviously not. Looks like she's gone off somewhere else. That's why we've started grasping at werestraws.'

The Doctor's face paled briefly, then, as if shaking an unpleasant idea from his head, he returned to work with a start.

'I'll give it some thought, but I'm not sure I'll be able to help you,' he mumbled, stroking his chin.

The Brigadier turned sharply and exited. He was sure the Doctor would set his mind to the matter now. Under that crusty exterior he was an old softy if you knew how to play him properly, he reflected.

'Some idiot's spelled megawatts wrongly on my equipment here again!' the old softy ranted as the Brigadier retreated. 'Can no one here even spell? I'll stencil the other G in myself when I have time. Really! Amateurs!'

Journal of Dr Elizabeth Shaw
27th of July

I think D realised. If the thought had occurred to me, I can't believe it didn't to him. He pretended it hadn't because he knew if Helen'd been caught up in some residual energy from his transit and sent through time after him, she was already dead somewhere in the past and another reality, and he didn't want to believe he was powerless to change that.

It wasn't just D and his console that went sideways in time, Bessie went too. If all the space around him was displaced into another dimension, space beyond the hut behind him could have gone too. Presumably we didn't notice because the space from that other time appeared here. If Helen was patrolling behind the hut when D disappeared she could have been scooped off into that doomed world too.

When presented with a base full of frozen personnel Mark's first thought had been that he'd been turned into some super soldier for the Republic, moving and thinking faster than his comrades in arms now, thanks to some drug, or radiation from that nuclear power unit.

He'd read of such things in Swifty G Singh's black market propaganda pulps from Australia, not that anyone would ever publicly admit to reading such inflammatory material. No matter how exciting the four-coloured tales of action heroes smashing rival powers were, they were anti-Republican texts and you could end up in the camps for reading them.

He'd waited a very long time for the effect to wear off, or for a superior to come and explain it to him, perhaps even telling him what his new role was to be and giving him his superhero costume.

When no one had come, and his life failed to live up to its comic strip promise, he'd gone off the rails for a while - it was impossible to say how long - before deciding to head for barracks.

Perhaps someone at RSF HQ in Maida Vale could help him.

Of course no one there had been any use either, he hadn't really thought they would be, but at least the journey back had given him something to do and something to hope for.

More to the point, back in the city, where there were posters and magazines and the telly, Mark had discovered his frozen world was changing. Sure, it was always July the 22nd on every paper, but little details of life weren't stopping still over time. When the rains, and then snows, had begun they had fallen by rules no one could understand.

It was as if all of time, bar him, had got stuck in a moment and, because it couldn't go forward, it had to keep remaking the one instant over and over again in slightly different ways. All the future had run out and anything that wanted to happen had to be squeezed into the present in any way it could.

By the time he'd got there, even the RSF's name had melted away on the HQ building.

Mark had eventually found himself an empty house in Maida Vale and made it his home.

Not knowing what else to do any more he had done everything he could think of, trying to find things he could still enjoy in this half frozen life. He was glad he'd got drunk a lot, because he wasn't always proud of what he'd done when he remembered it. In time, his meaningless, incomprehensible life had developed routines and he'd become almost content with it.

His amazement then, when one 22nd of July, he saw another moving human being in the street was total. Here was hope.

Helen had been outside the EAMC HQ for a full working day now, and all she'd seen move bar the constantly dancing snowflakes was a squaddie's jacket, flicking in the slo-mo wind.

She was cold and tired now, and beginning to hallucinate; she was sure she'd heard faint variations in the background noise. She turned to head for home and then froze.

In front of her was a figure emerging from an off licence, laden with beer cans; a young man, long haired and bearded, dressed in some kind of grimy military fatigues.

A young man who was moving.

He was faint, ghostlike, but there. She called out to him, hoping her voice carried through the treacle time around her.

He looked over in amazement.

Helen was perhaps the most perfect thing Mark had ever seen, a prim young woman in a corporal's uniform, blonde cropped hair, half grown out now, shivering in the snow, steam rising from her mouth, so frail and waiflike that, to his eyes, she seemed translucent.

After five years alone, he'd never thought he'd ever see a real-life, breathing girl again. Even his dreams had started to be colonised by the mannequin people who filled the day.

He dropped his beer cans and screamed in joy.

Mark and Helen ran towards each other through the freestyle falling snow. As they approached they saw each other begin to gain solidity. They were getting realer. The nightmare was ending. If they could just reach each other then together they could fight the madness, create a two person stronghold against the insanity around them. As they drew close, to within inches of touching, each saw the other begin to fade away.

Melting like snowflakes, they slipped through each other's fingers, disappearing like their tracks in the snow.

'Eastchester?' Helen cried out. 'Were you at Eastchester?' The man nodded.

'Five years!' shouted Helen to the fading wraith boy. 'We've been doing this for five years, there can only be another five years to go!'

They were halfway through, she realised, this would all end soon. This young man was slipping sideways from one world, she was slipping from another. They'd been caught up in the wake of matter moving from one universe to another, probably a pair of frilly shirts doing an exchange visit, and had been dragged along behind them, the slow way. Presumably though, when they reached the other's world it would all stop. They'd be in the wrong realities but life could go on in its proper day after day fashion. Just another five years.

Joyously, with renewed hope, she kissed the space the man had once filled.

'Have you ever loved someone and lost them?' asks Kilburn Tony, accepting the bottle back from his companion on the street. 'Ever let the one you just knew was your perfect other half pass you by, Mark?'

'Yes,' says the traveller. 'But you have to move on, live in the moment, not get trapped in your past.'

'Too many might-have-beens,' says Kilburn Tony, like someone out of a soap opera.

The sun starts to rise on another cold August morning and Mark starts to cry again. It's a recurring pattern, thinks Kilburn Tony.

An aspect of the zodiac that seems to have caused the most problems for would-be astrologers is trying to ascertain the precise start and end dates of each sign. This difficult time of the month, known as the cusp, traditionally falls around the 21st or 22nd of an Earth month. But of course, not every planet has an orbit cycle of 365 days. Pity the inhabitants of M'ii'e where entire generations were born completely within their planet's first cycle of Leo.

Like the Crab of Cancer, the Lion of Leo represents another of the beasts faced by Heracles, the near-invulnerable Nemean Lion whose pelt Heracles skinned and used as armour. Kasterborus writes:

Of course, it is the pride of the Leo as much as their seeming invulnerability that causes their sign to be that of the lion. More than just a pun, the lion's pride makes him the king of the animals, and so too the Leo is in many ways the monarch of the zodiac, being ruled by the sun. There is an important distinction to be made for all Leos however - they are ruled by the centre of their solar system; they themselves are not the centre.

World leaders, trend-setters and entertainers often emerge from this sign, as they have the confidence and raw magnetism necessary to lead by example. This confidence can also make them targets for resentment and jealousy and in turn makes many Leos arrogant and dogmatic…

Kasterborus, *Our Destiny is in the Stars*

Kasterborus says...

If today is your birthday: *Though you might think it's right for you to demand people's attention today, not everyone will agree with you. Perseverance is the key...*

Constant Companion

Simon A Forward

'Oh, Doctor, can't we keep it?'

'Well, I'm really not sure, Zoe. That rather depends on whether it wants to be kept or not.'

'And how do we know it's safe? It's no like any cat I've ever seen.'

'That would most likely be because it's not actually a cat, Jamie.'

'Oh, aye, so what sort of creature is it then?'

'I can't rightly say. Whatever precise species it is, it does look in need of a home, wouldn't you say?'

The it under discussion was not exactly a cat. There wasn't even a mat for it to sit on, but it had nonetheless planted itself, for better or for worse, right on the TARDIS threshold.

It had been waiting there for them when they'd opened the doors. It gazed up at them with such calm expectancy that it might have been there well before the TARDIS materialised. Certainly, Zoe was persuaded it had been there, ready and hopeful, when the Doctor had examined the external readings, pronounced a mystifying absence of anything and declared that the best way to find out about where they were was to venture outside and see.

Jamie had jaunted keenly after the Doctor's heels, while Zoe hung back for a moment and considered recommending some other more careful alternative; but since the scanner was apparently malfunctioning, she couldn't actually think of any. So she just shrugged and hurried to catch up with the two men in the doorway.

But there they'd stopped. In the open doorway.

At first Zoe couldn't see what the hold-up was, unless it was just the profound strangeness of the world outside. Admittedly it might give anyone, even the Doctor, pause for thought.

Across an implausibly flat landscape, a gravel driveway led straight to the TARDIS door, the grass on either side guttering and flickering like green flame fanned by the breeze. The horizon, if there was one, was screened by an assortment of trees that couldn't make up their minds whether they were deciduous or evergreen - a state of indecision probably not helped by the way in which spring, summer and autumn all blew through them like a wind, kindly sparing them anything resembling winter.

Oh yes, it was a strange place, thought Zoe. Not really a place at all.

But that wasn't what had stopped the Doctor and Jamie in their tracks. No, she had to glance down and peer past their legs to see that.

Between them and the outside world, a lost orphan sat. So lost, it seemed, it might as well have been a baby in a basket. But it wasn't.

No, it was much more like a cat, even though it clearly wasn't one.

It was variations on a feline theme. A very regal mane of marmalade fur, tumbling back from its dear little face to cover most of its body and puff it up into a cuddly ball. A tail like a furry snake, flicking this way and that with a life of its own. Banana-coloured eyes, set deep in the marmalade fur, pupils water-bright and deep as black holes; whiskers like quills sprouting from tufts either side of a pert little chocolate nose. And a tentatively hopeful feline smile.

Utterly adorable. And totally alone.

The Doctor crouched down to scoop up the abandoned bundle of life at his feet. 'Now, who in their right mind would leave a pet like this in the middle of nowhere?'

'How do ye know it's no some sort of wild animal?'

'Oh, Jamie, look at how well groomed it is,' chimed in Zoe. 'Still,' she added, her eyes reluctantly scanning the surrounding not-landscape again, 'there don't seem to be any homes around for miles.'

'Quite, and it has no collar or name tag. We'd be ages trying to find its owner.' The Doctor fell to stroking the not-cat's back, listening to the deepening purr as the creature nestled in and smiled at Jamie and Zoe from over the Doctor's shoulder. The horizon outside seemed to stretch further away, as the Doctor apparently arrived at a decision. 'Well,' he turned and favoured Jamie and Zoe with a flash of his mischievous eyes, 'I've taken in my fair share of waifs and strays before, haven't I?'

The Doctor bustled past the two of them into the ship, the marmalade creature nuzzling in comfortably against his shoulder. Zoe couldn't help smiling, and not just at the Doctor's little quip. She followed him back inside.

Behind her, it was Jamie's turn to do some catching up. 'Och, now wait a minute, Doctor...'

'What should we call it, d'ye suppose?'

'Jamie's right, Doctor. We really ought to give him a name.'

'Yes, he does look like a him, doesn't he? Unfortunately the scans don't tell me anything about his biology, let alone his gender.' The Doctor fiddled with the stethoscope around his neck and studied his feline patient, who sat on the medical-bay couch like it was his throne. He had endured his examination with princely patience and now beamed up at them as if awaiting the official pronouncement of his clean bill of health.

'He looks very intelligent,' commented Zoe.

Jamie looked wise to her game. 'Aye, and now you're going to say he looks smarter than me.'

'Not a bit of it. I was only going to suggest we call him Einstein. What do you think, Doctor?'

'Hm?' The Doctor had been elsewhere, but Zoe's question reeled him back on to terra firma. 'Oh, I was thinking we might call him Marmaduke,' he said with an expression disproportionately thoughtful to the matter in hand, but one that he leavened immediately with a softly whimsical smile. 'After his marmalade colour and he does look rather like royalty sitting there, wouldn't you say?'

'Yes,' nodded Zoe. 'He does look like a Marmaduke.'

'Welcome aboard the TARDIS, little fellow.' Jamie gently cuffed the newest member of the crew under his catlike chin. 'If you're half as mad as these two, ye'll fit right in soon enough.'

'Oh no! Now I really can't have this at all!'

Jamie wandered around the TARDIS control room so he could get a better view of what all the fuss was about - even though he already had a fair general idea. The Doctor was on all fours, his head lost somewhere inside the hexagonal base of the console. He was apparently in the process of crawling further inside, leaving only his coat-tails, checked trousers and battered old shoes protruding.

Jamie bent low, craning for a view past the Doctor's shoulders. He hadn't imagined there could be that much room under the console, what with all the ship's workings and so on.

The Doctor must have read his mind, because before he'd had a chance to voice the obvious question, a muffled and slightly flustered answer floated out from the innards of the console plinth.

'It's Marmaduke!' Jamie could have guessed that much. 'He's lodged himself in amongst the temporal relay circuits and he won't come out!'

Jamie thought he'd best stifle the laugh that badly wanted to come out right then. 'Uh, have ye no tried putting some milk out for him?'

There was a pause. 'No,' confessed the Doctor, his abashed tone dampened to some degree by the confines of the console interior. 'No, I haven't. That's a very good idea, Jamie. Perhaps you'd be so good as to ask Zoe to bring a saucer of milk from the TARDIS galley?'

'Aye, I can even fetch it myself.'

Jamie sauntered off, a grin making itself at home on his face. Every new companion, he supposed, went through a period of adjustment.

The Doctor eventually tempted Marmaduke out of his nesting place with the milk and plenty of gentle, if faintly strained, coaxing. The incident hadn't been the little fellow's first misdemeanour and by now everyone on board the TARDIS was familiar enough with his habits to know it wouldn't be his last.

There was the time when they'd been about to set out and explore the latest world the TARDIS had brought them to, only to discover Marmaduke had infiltrated the ship's extensive wardrobe and shredded much of the quality cold-weather clothing. They found the little chap himself swinging from a fancy eighteenth-century ball gown, his claws rendering it less and less fancy by the second.

There was the occasion he'd bedded himself down on Jamie's pipes, pummelling the bag incessantly and digging threads loose with his claws. After which, Jamie thought to store them in a high cupboard. Only to find that Marmaduke, apparently more than capable of rising to a challenge, had got at them again.

There were the repeated occasions he would fancy Zoe's computer keyboard as the perfect place to settle, but only when she was trying to work on one of her little projects. Jamie had found her mounting frustration increasingly amusing, of course, until the second bagpipe incident.

Then there was the time the Doctor found Marmaduke playing with his recorder. Nothing musical, just batting it lightly into a spin with his little paw, then pouncing over to arrest its spin and attack it from the other side. The Doctor, keen to retrieve the instrument as an aid to concentration right then, reached tentatively for it while appealing to Marmaduke's better nature in soothing tones. Marmaduke had not finished with the recorder, however, and in fact seemed pleased to find that the Doctor's hand had decided to join in the game. 'Ow!' The Doctor snatched his hand back and sucked at the tiny wound where the playful claws had raked his skin. Every time he encountered Marmaduke that day, the Doctor navigated a slow, wide path around him and met the little animal's feline contentment with a shadowed scowl.

Such wisdom shone out of those eyes, it wasn't difficult to imagine that his sweet, innocent expressions were entirely feigned.

Then too there were the countless times he was found sharpening his claws on the TARDIS walls, and the Doctor deduced that he must be a special little creature indeed, because he'd never seen anything mark those walls as deeply as that miniature lion's finely honed talons.

Of course all of this was fairly standard cat-type destruction, but Zoe and Jamie could tell that the scale of it was beginning to tell on the Doctor's nerves far more than their own. Very often they would hear the poor Doctor getting in a loud flap, and go running to his rescue, only to see him have one of his 'funny turns'. That was what the Doctor called them, and he would worry his companions by answering remarks or questions that had just occurred to them before they'd voiced them aloud.

It was very disconcerting for them, especially as the Doctor would usually follow this up with a dizzy spell and then collapse in an untidy heap.

All of which Marmaduke would study with a kind of baffled concern. Then he would scurry over, hop on top of the untidy heap and curl up.

When the heap regained consciousness, he could only marvel at the creature's devotion to him. It was very touching.

The final straw came when the Doctor, Jamie and Zoe returned from one of their more modest escapades to find the TARDIS control room looking like a bomb had hit it. A small furry marmalade-coloured bomb.

There was no evidence to indicate Marmaduke had exploded, but it did look like he'd been climbing the walls. There were deep grooves running down two of the panels at least, a number of the roundels were hanging open, chewed and tangled wires spilling out, and the floor was strewn with all manner of artefacts, no doubt mistaken for toys, disinterred from the various store cupboards around the control room.

'Oh now this really is too much!' The Doctor threw up his arms like he might take off, and Jamie and Zoe could only trade quiet rolls of the eyes as he flew here and there around the control room, thankfully still firmly on the ground, but only just. Zoe thought he bounced around rather like a smoke particle in a Brownian motion experiment.

'There's nothing Brownian about it! I'm not colliding with anything, now am I?' shouted the Doctor desperately. His thinking was clearly as straight as the frenetic path he was taking around the control room.

'Doctor, you're doing it again,' worried Zoe. 'I didn't speak.'

'Well, please be quiet, both of you!' The Doctor stopped his pacing long enough to fire an urgent plea at them from the other side of the room, then he was off again, springing at cupboards and throwing them wide open. 'I'm looking for the cat, Jamie, what do you think! It's all to do with the cat!'

'I didn'ae say anything!' protested Jamie, adding a shrug at Zoe. 'Besides, I thought you -'

'I know I said it wasn't a cat! It's not a cat! I'm just calling it a cat right now because we don't have any other name for what it is and we might as well call it something it resembles, which is a cat!'

The Doctor hurled himself into a cupboard and started burrowing around. 'Now will you please both help me find the cat!'

'Doctor, you really ought to -' Zoe's advice didn't make it all the way out before the Doctor poked his head back out of the cupboard, a frantic appeal etched deep in his blanched features.

'Calm down? How can I calm down when you two won't stop thinking!' He tapped his crown. 'It's getting very crowded in here! All I can hear are your thoughts bouncing around in my head and I can't shut them out! I can't hear myself think with you two chattering away in here!'

'But –' tried Jamie.

'I don't know how, Jamie! But it has something to do with that cat! It's been getting steadily worse since we took him in.'

'Doctor, are you sure it's not –'

'No, Zoe, it's not just the frustration and I'm not getting overwrought! There's some sort of telepathic amplification going on and we need to get rid of it!'

'You mean get –'

'Yes, I mean get rid of the cat!'

'Och,' Jamie complained to Zoe, 'will he no let us get a sentence out?'

Zoe put a finger to her lips and tipped her eyes in the Doctor's direction. Jamie followed the gesture to see the Doctor pounce at one of the roundels. After one swift skimming pulse of the sonic screwdriver, the Doctor yanked it open and there, curled up in a nest of wiring, Marmaduke was lifting his head and searching the Doctor's gaze through sleepy eyes.

'I'm not even going to ask how you got in there!'

'He'd be very unlikely to answer anyway, Doctor.'

'Yes, thank you, I'm well aware of that, Zoe. Especially as I've heard you think it already.' The Doctor stooped to reach in and haul Marmaduke out of his cradle. The furry bundle came freely enough and even purred in anticipation of a good cuddle. The Doctor, though, did not look at his most cuddly, and Jamie could have sworn whole new furrows had erupted across his brow.

Plonking Marmaduke down on the floor, the Doctor leaned back against the roundel to shut it in place, and stayed leaning there for a while to recover his composure. Marmaduke smiled up at everybody, still purring.

'Before either of you ask,' exhaled the Doctor wearily, 'yes, I am really going to get rid of him. I know it's very sad, but we can't have that sort of thing going on, now can we? Besides,' he added more gently, 'I'm only going to drop him back where we found him. He'll be perfectly all right.'

'How do you –'

'Zoe, please, I just know. He was perfectly healthy when we found him and quite probably he'll find his own way home or his owner will be out looking for him. Either way, I'm afraid we can't keep him in the TARDIS. It just won't do. Now, please don't make this any more difficult than it is already, either of you.' A familiar misty kindness crept into his eyes. 'Perhaps you two had best step out of the room while I set the controls and take him back, hm?'

'Come on, Doctor, we won't make any trouble, will we, Zoe?'

Zoe studied the Doctor's expression with some care. 'I think the Doctor means he just wants some peace and quiet in his head, Jamie. If we're a bit deeper in the TARDIS, he won't be able to hear our thoughts.'

The Doctor beamed at her, a school teacher's proud smile. 'I think that time you read my mind.'

Jamie and Zoe allowed themselves to be gently ushered out, and the Doctor headed straight for the console, head down and ready to fix in the coordinates. Gradually beginning to relax, he started humming a little ditty, occasionally breaking off to glance around at the devastation. Yes, he was definitely going to have to do some tidying up. Perhaps Jamie and Zoe would be kind enough to help, once their extra little passenger had been dropped off.

Thinking of which –

The Doctor glanced up.

He'd set the TARDIS in motion and Marmaduke was lounging on the central column, riding it up and down, his bright feline eyes anchored on the Doctor's gaze by some invisible chains.

The Doctor considered trying to out-stare him, but he somehow knew that was a lost cause.

'It's not there! The world isn't there any more!'

Jamie and Zoe had trod light-footed back into the control room, thinking to say their goodbyes to Marmaduke, but now it looked like there weren't going to be any. They opened their mouths to speak, but decided there was probably no need.

'I mean,' the Doctor answered them, driving the door control home, 'it's gone! Vanished! People come and go, but places can generally be expected to stay! They might change, that's fair, but a place should stay in the same place, don't you think?'

There was, of course, no need to respond. Besides, the Doctor was busying himself, scooting around the console and hastily laying in another course.

'Well, there's nothing else for it. We'll simply have to find him another home.'

The Doctor shook his head and took to watching the steady rise and fall of the cat as he set the TARDIS in motion again.

It was a lonely country house, wrapped in a coat of ivy, other climbing plants twined around the columns in front of the doorway. It looked like nobody had lived there for centuries, but the Doctor maintained he knew the owner well and was sure she would love another animal to add to her domestic menagerie.

The Doctor set the cat basket down on the porch and they all ducked back down the drive. The three of them walked quietly back along the country lane to the TARDIS, Jamie and Zoe speculating how much they would miss the little fellow.

They needn't have worried.

Marmaduke was scratching at the hatstand just inside the TARDIS doorway. He glanced up as they entered, but he didn't appear to have missed them much at all.

'All right, I've set the program. All you have to do, Zoe, is key in that sequence when I tell you. Do you understand?'

'Of course.' Zoe was hurt that he should even need to ask. She glanced down at the numbered sequence scrawled on the scrap of paper and put it down to the Doctor's distracted mental state.

The Doctor nodded happily, then favoured Marmaduke with a genial smile, producing a large ball of pink wool from the depths of his pocket. With a few deft movements, he unravelled a nice thick thread to leave it trailing on the floor. Coaxing and encouraging all the way, he teased Marmaduke out into and along the corridor, flicking the wool all along like a fat rat's tail.

The cat pranced and pounced after it, enjoying the game.

At the far end, the Doctor tugged open the door and tossed the ball of wool inside. Marmaduke sprang eagerly after it. The Doctor slammed the door closed, and sagged back. He shouted, 'Now, Zoe! Now!'

Moments later he walked back into the control room, mopping his brow with his oversized handkerchief. He managed a brave smile for Jamie and Zoe. 'There, I reconfigured that corridor as a Möbius strip. That should keep him occupied for a bit.'

He regarded Jamie patiently. 'Well,' he prodded, 'aren't you going to ask me what that is?'

'Oh,' Jamie came to life, 'I thought you'd have heard the question in your head.'

'No, no, no - I think it's a case of out of sight, out of mind,' breathed the Doctor in hushed, satisfied tones. 'It's a, a kind of infinite loop. He should be happy enough running around there until I can think of something better.'

He frowned at Zoe, his turn to be hurt. 'Now, Zoe, when have you ever known me to be over-confident?'

She looked worried. He realised her lips hadn't moved.

'Oh.' The Doctor's face sank slowly like a reluctant stone. Something warm and soft brushed against his legs. It purred.

The Doctor slid the cat box up on to the luggage rack and tried not to meet the forlorn expression on Marmaduke's face, peering out through the bars. An expression designed for breaking hearts; one of them at least.

Features involuntarily sombre, the Doctor beat a retreat up the carriage and hopped off the train. Jamie and Zoe waited for him on the platform.

He laid a hand on a shoulder each. 'I don't like it any more than you do, but trust me, it's for the best.'

'Aye, if you say so, Doctor.'

'Now, Jamie, this place is one of the Seven Hundred Wonders of the Universe.' Listening to the signals heralding the train's imminent departure, he drew the two of them along the platform to where there was a limited view of the giant structure arcing out across the vast ocean. 'The Equatorial Bridge circles this entire world. See those support towers? Each of them is a tower housing thousands of people. Below us is a pedestrian deck, full of shopping complexes, places of work, everything you'd expect from a vibrant worldwide community. Someone is sure to find him and take him in. And what's more they're unlikely to be telepathic, so there's very little risk of anyone experiencing those unfortunate side effects.'

'Aye, if you say so, Doctor,' was all Jamie could say again.

Zoe was silent though as the train pulled away.

The Doctor waved it off with his oversized handkerchief, then blew his nose noisily before leading his companions back to the TARDIS.

The cat came back.

They left him on a hyperspace cruise liner bound for the Carmalan Domains. The Doctor promised Jamie and Zoe the Carmalan people were a generous, hospitable race and that Marmaduke would be right at home.

He wasn't, of course. He was in the TARDIS.

They deposited him with a rescue centre on the cosmopolitan world of Moga. All manner of races teemed in the streets and the grav-ways, many of them had pets, and the rescue centre catered for the full spectrum of weird and wonderful abandoned creatures.

The staff were delighted with their new inmate and promised they would do their utmost to find him a good home. Marmaduke saved them the bother, and found his own.

He was back in the TARDIS in no time at all.

'Come on! They don't much care for my sort around here!'

The Doctor herded Jamie and Zoe back along the ledge, the rain beating them all into a huddle, while lightning flared up against the craggy, scarred cliff-faces. The Doctor had to shout to make his reassurances heard above the storm.

'The Sisterhood will take good care of him. They're all telepaths, but there's more than one of them, and you know what they say about a problem shared!'

Jamie and Zoe offered no answer, and the Doctor was just grateful when he finally shepherded them into the TARDIS. They all got themselves busy shaking off the worst of the rain.

The Doctor clapped his hands, then froze.

Marmaduke was looking up from his favourite wicker chair, content in the warm and dry.

The Doctor sat on the floor of the control room and peered out from behind a mask of fingers, afraid to take a better look. His head was spinning and reverberating with the echoes of Jamie's and Zoe's thoughts, even though he'd sent them off to their rooms for the sake of his own sanity.

He moved a hand warily aside, instantly mesmerised by Marmaduke's gleaming banana-coloured gaze, looking down at him from his perch on the console.

'What am I going to do with you?' He regarded the creature with rueful amusement. 'At least now we know why your previous owner let you go, hm?'

Marmaduke blinked.

The Doctor jumped up and seized the cat energetically by his little shoulders. 'That's it!' he cried.

He raced excitedly around the console, fingers dancing over the controls like those of a crazed pianist, nudging Marmaduke out of the way as necessary. Behind him, he heard Jamie and Zoe edging back into the room to see what all the excitement was about. 'Before you ask,' he told them, 'I think it's a simple matter of finding our little friend's original owner.'

'Aye, and how are you –'

'We have to go back to where we found him!'

Zoe's mouth was half-open as the Doctor whirled around to face her. 'Yes, I know I tried that before, Zoe! But I think it's just a case of when we go back!'

The Doctor stepped out on to the gravel driveway, cradling Marmaduke in his arms.

'So you found me.'

The Doctor glanced around. The trees had closed in, a tight circle of shifting wood and foliage around the TARDIS. The grass, still burning like flame, was all rippling outwards from the centre, the wind blowing out between the trunks, as if all the air was running off the flat land like water.

A translucent old woman in a wispy black gown sat in a tatty old armchair.

'Yes,' said the Doctor. 'It didn't take long once I had the right idea. We've, ah, brought your pet back.'

Marmaduke perked up and leaped from the Doctor's arm into the woman's lap. She welcomed the animal with firm strokes, her bony fingers massaging its mane.

'Ah, my precious little Id-Cat. He's much more than a pet, you know. If I'm the Sorceress, he's my apprentice. The dear little soul, I've missed him so much.'

'You have, have you? Well, that rather serves you right, doesn't it? Perhaps you shouldn't go foisting him off on the first unsuspecting travellers who came your way!'

'Ah, temper fugit, Doctor,' she warned. 'But I understand. That's just it, you see. You can't live with him, can't live without him. It's the nature of the beast.'

'Yes, I discovered as much myself, thank you.' The Doctor surveyed the shrunken not-landscape. 'When we first came here, I seem to recall everything was a little more spacious and you put the thought of picking him up into our heads, didn't you? Then when we came back you were powerful enough to mask this place altogether, weren't you? Now, look! Feeling a little diminished, are we?'

'Oh yes, like a part of me is missing.' A sad sigh escaped between the woman's thin lips. 'I've sought solitude so often, but the loneliness is always impossible to bear. It's why I made him up in the first place.'

Marmaduke walked around in circles in his owner's lap before settling down.

'So let me see.' The Doctor reasoned it all through. 'You're a telepath –'

'Amongst other things.' She nodded to the rhythm of Marmaduke's purring.

'You couldn't stand the congestion of all those thoughts of others invading your mind –'

'And the others couldn't stand my eavesdropping,' the woman pointed out, her eyes riding an unseen cloud. 'So, yes, I sealed myself off here by mutual agreement of sorts. And, yes, invented a companion for myself.' She smiled and tickled Marmaduke's chin. 'Something to have and to hold. And to love.'

'Only the cat gives back something in return for all that care and affection, doesn't he? Amplifying your powers.'

'Oh hugely. He has a very giving heart.' She patted the feline head. Marmaduke narrowed his eyes with pleasure. 'Unfortunately, sometimes it can get too much, of course. There have been times I was sure I could hear every thought in the universe.'

'Very unpleasant for you, I should imagine.'

'And very clever of you, Doctor, to bring him back to me a few centuries later – when I could no longer mask my presence.'

The Doctor was modestly abashed at the flattery. 'You're very welcome.'

He cleared his throat awkwardly. 'Well, if that's all, I think I should be on my way.'

'What?' The old woman arched a silver brow. 'No torrent of questions about who I am? What I am?' She chuckled softly, and Marmaduke seemed to enjoy the vibration of laughter through her torso. 'Oh well, you know what they say about curiosity.'

'Madam,' the Doctor bowed graciously in her direction, 'against that cat, curiosity would always come a poor second.'

Taking in a last picture of Marmaduke, perfectly at home there in her lap, the Doctor turned and slipped back into the TARDIS.

The Doctor blinked and the image was gone. He was sure he'd seen a marmalade smudge against the back of the wicker chair. And as he picked up his recorder, dimmed the lights and ambled out into the corridor, he fancied he felt a marmalade blur brush past his legs and scamper into the shadows. And there in his bedroom, he caught - out of the corner of his eye - a marmalade pillow looking perfectly at home at the foot of his bed.

The Doctor sighed a sigh of relief and reflection. He wouldn't sleep tonight. Just sit up and read, perhaps.

He couldn't quite make up his mind whether he had defeated another menace or lost another companion. Somewhere very much in-between, he suspected.

And in-between was something of a lonely place to be.

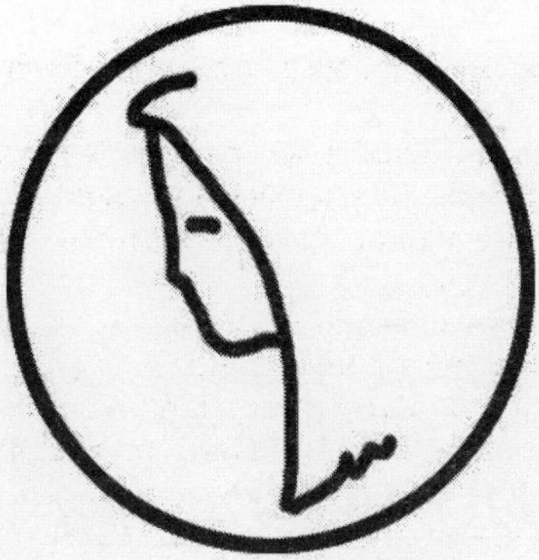

An interesting variation on conventional astrology can still be seen on some Fifth Galaxy planets where it is forbidden to depict graphically a member of their race for fear of corrupting their spiritual essence. For this reason, the signs that have always been illustrated with a human are shown with an inanimate object: in place of Gemini, we see two gems on opposite sides of a ring; Aquarius, the water-carrier, became a rather literal jug; and Virgo became a calculator, which in turn broke with tradition by making the sign only the second to have ever been represented by a machine.

Unusually, the original inspiration for this sign was a goddess. In Greek mythology, it was Astraea, the Goddess of Virtue, who was the last of the Titans to leave Earth for Olympia after the box of Pandora unleashed evil on to the Universe. In Roman mythology, it was Ceres, the Queen of the harvest, who represents the Virgoan trait of harvesting the best of everything. But the connection to Virgo, the virgin, has led to many misunderstandings about this sign. One in particular – that they are, as 'virgins', impotent and lacking in strength – Kasterborus was at pains to put right.

Virgo is the most hardworking, and therefore the most insightful and determined of the zodiac. For Virgoans, happiness is a fulfilling task or a challenge that gives them the opportunity to show their capabilities. They thrive on chaos because that gives them the greatest challenge, although much of the chaos in the lives of Virgoans is of their own making.

They are famously picky and pedantic, but that's mainly because few have standards as high as theirs; for them, tidiness and order are more a state of mind than of body. They can exist happily in a mess so long as they themselves know where everything is. In fact, were it not for their tendency towards obsessive introspection, they could easily become the single most powerful force in the zodiac.

Kasterborus, *Our Destiny is in the Stars*

Kasterborus says...

If today is your birthday: *Work matters are again to the fore, though a reunion with an old friend may not turn out as you expect...*

Virgin Lands

Sarah Groenewegen

She was in a car. A shiny new black Jeep Cherokee, obtained by the Doctor. Borrowed, mind, he'd said. Like the TARDIS? she'd asked, with a grin. He, grave as ever she had seen him, had shaken his head. No. Not like the TARDIS.

She sat in the driver's seat, a booted foot up on the dashboard wedged in between the steering wheel and the door. Her elbow was propped on the window sill, her fingers were tapping silently against the edge of the roof. She was listening to the radio, her lips a thin, pensive line. A woman was reading a bulletin in a five-minute news update with only one story: 'At least twenty-five people have died, according to Tasmanian Police. The gunman is still at large in the historic site of Port Arthur...'

She switched off the noise, and paused with her finger still resting on the radio button. Twenty-five today, fifteen kindy kids and their teachers a month or so before. She closed her eyes and saw again the carnage she'd witnessed on worlds and in time zones so far from here. Those memories made her wonder how and why someone could murder strangers, and prayed some other monster was behind it. There had to be something else there. Her people were not that evil. Surely. Even the Daleks, the Master... and her thoughts trailed off. She had to believe in monsters.

She had to believe in monsters to absolve her race of all its sins.

Ace had wanted to stay out front in the car, which suited Benny fine. She wanted to stretch her legs, check out the scenery. Oh, and see if the cliff face drop specified on the map really would deter unwanted visitors, or departures. An unwanted departure simply would not do.

The pathway was easy enough to find. It was past a large housefront down from the one Ace had parked outside and the Doctor had disappeared into. It was marked by the metre-wide space between two shrub-laden wooden fences. There was a single post sticking out from the ground like a forlorn sentry left behind by his squad aeons ago. White flakes of paint clung to its grey splinters making it look even more like a ghost. Benny brushed the tips of her fingers lightly over its top as though she was tousling the hair of that solitary ghost.

Innocence is a block of wood. Great. And she wondered at what it had seen, if it had eyes. 'Which it doesn't,' she said, firmly.

The path had probably been worn into the sandstone by years of people walking down to one of the small beaches below. At some stage someone had poured asphalt on it, to make it safer, she presumed, but the roots from plants and trees in the neighbouring backyards had made it all cracked and uneven again.

'You won't be able to get down to a public beach that way,' called a voice.

Benny stopped dead in her tracks and looked around at where the voice had come from. She couldn't see anyone.

'I keep telling Margaret there should be a sign, but she insists no one would even see it. The path, that is, not the sign.'

'Ah. I was actually only going for a walk. Take in the sea breeze and look at some of the lovely houses.' She craned her neck, trying to see the man who had spoken. Suddenly, his head appeared at the top of the fence. He looked like a caricature of an old sea captain with skin like tanned leather, and only the barest white wisps of hair around his pate. He needed a cravat, a peaked cap and a white corncob pipe hanging from his mouth.

'Where you from? I can't place your accent.'

She smiled sweetly at him. 'Here and there. Mostly there. I pick up accents like a dog does fleas. I take it you've lived here for some time and know a lot about the places around here?'

'You must've been in Sydney a while if you're already talking about property.' He laughed.

'Oh, I don't want to buy…'

'Good. None of these places are for sale. Not even LaMort's place up there.' His arthritis-gnarled hand pointed directly up at the house they were interested in on the top of the rise.

'Oh?' She said, all innocence. 'Why's that?'

'Well, now. This place here was my grandfather's house. I was born here, just before the War. Margaret's family hasn't been here that long, but long enough.'

'And LaMort?'

'See the jacaranda tree?'

She turned again to follow where his twisted hand pointed.

'When it's in bloom it is absolutely magnificent. On summer afternoons when the storms come in but the sun's still over the city… well, there's no other sight like it on God's earth.'

He trailed into silence, which made her look back at him. He was smiling, face crinkled up like a friendly old boot. She'd known enough old sea (okay, space) dogs to know there was no point in butting in on his reverie. He blinked, finally, and looked startled to see her still standing there.

'That's LaMort's. I've never been there and would never want to.' His tone had turned hard, and Benny saw the muscles in his jaw tighten. 'When I was a boy they used to say the place on the hill was haunted.'

* * *

Ace was still sitting in the jeep, gazing out along the sunbathed street but not really seeing it. Her mind was too busy matching up the memories of photos and plans and maps of the place she now sat opposite. They'd obtained the original architect's sketches, council schematics, and drawings from the sewerage workers who had come to change the pipes to deal with new drainage technology. There had been newspaper clippings dating from colonial times. Society columns, mostly, talking about the parties the place had hosted in the century and a half the house had existed.

The house was big and its location to die for. From the front at the top you could see the Harbour Bridge on clear days, and over the back the Pacific Ocean. Premier views, appropriate since the scandal sheets had hinted about Premiers of New South Wales knowing those views as well as they knew the owner of the building and land.

A small voice piped up from somewhere in her memories. It was her voice from long ago reminding her of daydreams she'd had as a child about rich old mansions and what it would be like to live in them. To fill the echoey old halls with life

or flames

It wasn't fair a scrawny society bitch like LaMort could own that place.

But, still, her fingers drummed their silent tattoo on the roof of the car as she waited.

The house was bright. White walls, huge windows looking out over the ocean that was blue and sparkling in the sun. Gulls were crying mournfully in the distance, and closer there was the chatter and noise of a party.

Her party.

She blinked water from her eyes as she surveyed the view inside. Pockets of people clustered together talking in hushed tones. Quiet. Talking about her. A guess borne out by the way they kept risking glances at her, and looking away again before they thought she'd had a chance to catch them.

One group she knew would be talking about her. Celebrity standover man Noddy Clarke in his cheap white suit and Brylcreemed hair combed over a huge bald patch, standing next to Alex Ball and Peter Petersen. Those two men dwarfed Clarke as they always did. Big detectives used to throwing their weight around so much they didn't need to any more. Both wearing sharp suits that looked shabby on them. Then they laughed, great belly-shaking laughs that made Clarke look even more nervous around them and she knew if she were closer she would be able to smell the fear in his sweat.

She turned away from the three crooks and caught sight of a boy standing at the top of the stairs, staring at her. She couldn't remember his name, but knew the pale-as-pastry face and dark mop of hair hanging limp over a surly expression. He was concentrating on her as a kid that age always does. She looked quickly away from him as Justice Yellowman arrived behind the boy, placing a hand on the child's shoulder.

She looked around again, taking in the small groups chattering amongst themselves. So many people she knew. Too many people, perhaps. Even the ridiculous people, like the little man in the crumpled linen suit standing near the punchbowl. The little man who refused to look away from her, contempt blazing from his intense blue eyes. She could see the filaments glowing from where she stood.

'Darling, such a lovely party.'

'Yes. Thank you.' She tore her eyes away from the little man, returning them reluctantly to where they should be looking.

'So many people to mourn.'

'Yes.'

She looked away again, the lure too strong. Fear stabbed in her chest. He was not there any more. She scanned the room and couldn't see him anywhere. And she had to see him, keep him in her sights.

She couldn't remember if he had been on the invitation list.

Ace still hadn't moved, and was becoming aware of the silence. She shifted her foot to the floor of the vehicle and took her aviator sunglasses off. She exhaled on to the reflective lenses, then wiped them off on her T-shirt. Putting them back on, she reflected they weren't exactly the most fashionable. Then, she'd never been exactly the most fashion conscious. Not that she cared. Fashion had never caught her attention and she sure as hell wasn't about to start following it now. Certainly not follow it as closely as she had followed the cars up the road to the house on the cliff where the party was swinging.

They were the gorgeous people of this city, and those rich enough not to have to worry about being gorgeous. Old men with silver hair and the women (most younger) they wore as their handbags, and younger men with hair so slicked it reflected like silver. No wonder they were called silvertails, she thought.

The passenger door opened. Ace looked over at the woman who climbed into the seat, reached into the glovebox and took a swig from the silver hipflask. She sighed. 'That's better.'

Ace kept looking at her.

'There's probably a way into the back, but the neighbour's nosy and chatty,' Benny reported, matter of fact.

'That why you needed the drink?'

'Tetchy,' she said, reaching out to turn the radio back on.

Ace reached out, grabbing Benny's hand before it reached the radio. 'No, don't.'
Benny looked at her.
'There's been another massacre. Tasmania.'
'That could explain why we're here. It's not that far from Sydney.'
'I don't know, Benny,' Ace whispered. 'There's something not quite right about it.' Her eyes flicked to the clock on the dashboard and she felt the familiar stab of pre-ops fear and quashed it. 'It's time,' she said, and she opened the door.

The doorbell rang. Like Eleanor Rigby she kept her face in a jar by the door for occasions such as these. A painted-on smile and a twinkle in her eye, meant for the possibility of an uninvited guest at this, her final party.
The smile became genuine when she saw the woman standing on the porch in front of her. She was slight in build, but that slightness was deceptive. She was betrayed by the way she held herself, poised catlike to strike at less than a moment's notice. Her angular jaw jutted out just that little bit to say she had every right to be there, when she didn't. She hadn't been invited, but that hadn't stopped her. 'Hi,' she said. 'I'm Ace.' Her accent betrayed her London origins, but she'd not come to Sydney via the usual route, of that LaMort was certain.
'Hello, Ace.' The name, as it travelled over her tongue, was at once right and wrong. 'Please. Come in.'
'Said the spider to the fly.' The woman dressed in black stepped over the threshold. 'Some party you've got going here.'
'It *is* a special occasion.'
'Your birthday?'
LaMort's smile froze. 'Not exactly.'
'Yeah, well I'll just mingle then, if that's all right.'
But, too bad if it wasn't.

This time, Benny crept around the back and she was rewarded by being left alone. This time, she made it to the fence line running along the back of the houses. This time, she was faced with two options: break into the neighbour's and then LaMort's, or traverse the cliff face and up where the jacaranda tree held its lonely vigil.
Which meant, of course, there was no choice.
It didn't mean getting into the neighbour's yard would be easy. The fence was old, but solid. Not impossible for someone fit and knowing a few tricks of derring-do.
Oh, all right. Fit enough and practised enough at breaking in.
The yard she landed in was guarded only by a rabbit in a hutch. Its reaction to Benny's sudden arrival in its domain was to freeze for a

second, then it resumed its nose-twitching existence. Benny ignored it, focusing attention instead on whether there was any other life in the space worth worrying about. All indications were that the rabbit was the only guard. No. There was a motion sensor near the door of the house, but Benny put that security feature in the same category as the rabbit: incidental to her mission.

She jogged over to the border fence and was up and over it as easily as the first fence

straight into a jungle hell.

She crashed into unexpected undergrowth and rolled into dark dankness. It smelt of rich humus, and she could also smell the activity of the bugs and worms and maggots working their way through the soil. And over the smell of the earthen humidity was a sickly sweet cloying smell.

Decay.

Death.

She fought to stop her own vomit adding to the stench.

Gagging for fresh air, Benny tried to run through the undergrowth towards where the house was meant to be. Where there'd be a break in the green canopy that stopped the sun from breaking through. But the plants were too dense and her imagination had them moving, conspiring to block her path.

Oh, for a machete.

Oh, for the house.

She was forced into a crawl. Forced to put her bare hands into the mulch of rotting leaves and animals. She couldn't see properly as she scrabbled forth, but she could feel the millions of little legs tickling her hands, her arms, and could even feel them creep into her trouser legs, and over her back beneath her shirt. Finally, she broke through to a set of rotted and ant-eaten wooden back veranda steps. As she stood, she brushed herself down, jiggling her legs to shake the bugs and millipedes from her trousers. Catching herself to stop her panic, she looked up at the ruin of a typical Australian colonial-style house.

'Now, *that* is not right,' she said.

The Doctor was in pain.

Not pain in the ordinary sense. There was no flower blossoming through his nervous system, playing with his mind. None of that excruciating, sheer pain scraping against his very existence. No feeling of something being inside wanting to break through him and be him.

It was more basic than that.

The type of raw pain he had once felt so long ago when Susan had left him. And again and again and again with all those others. Little deaths as they'd left him. Sometimes bigger deaths. Real deaths.

All the death in this house was beginning to affect him and it was time.

His nostrils flared as the sun broke through from a cloud, a living metaphor for what he knew.

She had left him, but he knew where she was likely to be.

Inside the impossibly large and exquisitely laid out house, Ace was bored. She had moved through what she thought must be every room, despite herself marvelling at the amazing view of the ocean below them, and the impeccable back garden.

Idly, she'd looked out for Benny, but hadn't seen her. No matter. She was either inside already, mingling just as she, or chatting to the neighbours again.

Like so many other parties she'd been to, the guests had clumped together. Children were playing downstairs in a room full of toys. Women dressed in twin sets and pearls and all looking like her mum at a wedding or a funeral congregated in the kitchen. She'd turned away as soon as she'd seen them, but she knew they'd be talking about children, nappies and recipes to placate hubby dear soon back from the pub.

She felt sick at the banality of the memories.

In other rooms the people hadn't been much better. All of them talking in closed circles, like those snobs at school who she hadn't thought about in such a long time.

Where the hell was the Doctor? And Benny? She should be in here by now.

Then she saw LaMort again. Tall and elegant in her simple black slip of a dress. Calves perfectly formed, helped in their shape by stiletto shoes that screamed hand-crafting by an Italian master. Diamonds glittered on a single strand at her throat and on several of her fingers. Ace had no doubt they were real and flawless.

The woman, her host, had turned to survey her domain. She evidently saw Ace and fluttered her fingers in her direction. Ace resisted waving back. It would be too crass, but she watched as LaMort kept climbing the stairs, then disappeared.

Quandary. Should she follow, or stay and wait for Benny? Then, no. She saw the Doctor, at last, walking with purpose through the crowd that parted as it always did. He was tracing LaMort's journey up the stairs. Intent, as always now, on his mission.

Whatever that was.

She took a step forward, then stopped when she heard a door open, and, 'Ace!'

She swivelled around. 'Benny? You look like you've just lost a round in a ring with a bloody jungle.'

'Astute observation, given that I have.'

Ace watched as Benny made to walk forward, seemingly oblivious to a crowd of silvertails meandering past. 'Benny!'

'What?'

'Watch out.'

'Oh,' and she did an odd little dance like she was trying to avoid stepping on something bad. 'Thanks. This place is a death trap. Where's the Doctor? Have you seen him?'

'Just then,' she said, shaking her head at Benny's antics, but dismissing them. There wasn't time. She pointed to where she'd just seen him. 'Up there. He was following LaMort.'

'Shall we?'

'Yeah.'

Anytime. Anywhere. She had all of time and space to choose from, and had chosen here - a house on the harbour edge of Sydney - and now - a few years shy of the end of the twentieth century - to end it all.

All of it.

She looked at the jar of pills spread out in her hand, and smiled at the idea of cheating all the gods.

'Why do it?'

She knew who it was from the sound of the Scottish burr. 'I know it's not original.'

'None of what you do is.'

'Come now, Doctor.' She looked up at his reflection in the bathroom mirror.

'No,' he snarled. 'You listen to me. *You* cannot die.'

'And who are you to say that?'

'*You* cannot die. *You* cannot leave your work. *I* will not let you.'

She laughed, but still refused to turn to face him. 'Oh, yes. You who have cheated me more than once. You're a fine one to talk. To try to tell me what to do.'

'Why are you doing this?'

With the change of his tack she closed her hand into a fist to protect the pills and their promise of oblivion and she turned to face him. He looked so deadly, earnest and scared. Scared of her? Of what he was doing? 'You are well to be wary of me,' she said.

'Wary? Oh, no. Not wary.'

She narrowed her eyes to focus on him, to try to read his intentions from his eyes. But his features remained as impenetrable as ever. His resolve was steadfast, shown by the way he was staring her down.

'You amuse me, Doctor,' she said, finally, moving nothing more than was necessary to talk. 'Just not enough to stop me from what I want to do.'

Under her gaze he seemed to change, shift visibly, his hardness almost melting as he said, ever so softly, 'Is that what you want? Something different? Something new?'

Benny watched as Ace bounded up the stairs, weaving her way upwards with a confidence Benny just did not share. The stairs were too dangerous. Wooden planks showing signs of age and wear. Too much weight in the wrong place and it would be more than a few white ants falling to their deaths.

Death.

That unmistakable smell she'd smelt in the garden outside was sending out its cloying tendrils all through the house. Wafting like wraiths in patches of cold air she passed through.

Ace looked back at Benny, saw her carefully climb the steps she'd bounded up. 'Come on!' she called, and saw Benny walk straight through one of the party guests. 'Weird,' she said, shaking her head at the impossibility, brain working to fill in the pieces.

She waited for Benny to catch up. 'Benny, what do you see here?'

'What?'

'Tell me what you see.'

'Do we have time for this?' Ace's face evidently reflected her impatient yes. 'A house that's seen better days, and those days were a very long time ago.'

'What about the people?'

'Well, there's a young woman with a ponytail wearing black, a short Scottish bloke in Panama holiday gear and probably another woman, appearance unknown.'

'No one else?'

'No.'

Realisation dawned. 'How many people do *you* see?'

Ace grinned. 'Stacks. Too many. Like this place is a TARDIS but for twenty-four hour party people. You just walked through a fat geezer who looks like he'd be happier on a hog.'

Hog? Harley Davidson motorbike, some part of her memory supplied. She shuddered.

'They're ghosts,' Benny said. 'They must be. I can feel them and they feel like ghosts.'

'Yeah?' said Ace. 'You know, things are starting to drop into place. The Professor just can't help dragging me into old houses full of ghosts. Come on,' and she grabbed Benny's arm and they kept going to the top.

There was more to it, Ace knew, than her flippant remark to Benny. There always was. Probably always would be.

Whatever.

She did stop saying excuse me to the dead men walking, but she couldn't bring herself to walk right through them. She still winced when she saw Benny doing that.

Then they were up on the final landing and there were no more people.

'The smell's worse up here,' said Benny.

'You what?'

'Can't you smell it? It's like something or someone's died up here and been left to rot.'

Ace sniffed, but there was nothing more than an old sea salt smell. She couldn't even smell the food from downstairs, or the people. 'It's LaMort. You can smell LaMort. It must be.'

Benny melodramatically slapped her hand to her forehead. 'Hell. Of course! LaMort. The Dead.'

Death again.

Ace shivered.

The Doctor had danced with death before, but this was different. Now there was no movement save the barely discernable in-out-in-out of their breathing. *His* breathing, he amended. *She* did not breathe.

He regarded her carefully. At surface glance she could have been young and beautiful. Like the diamonds she wore, her skin was flawless. Smooth. Stare at her as he had done and continued to do and you would see the sharp starkness of her white bones held together by taut skin that shifted in its colours.

A trick, he knew. Perception. Only the colours couldn't settle to one skin tone for him because for him it didn't matter. He wanted to grin, but didn't dare. It wasn't time and timing is everything.

Finally, he heard the noises he wanted to hear from the landing outside.

'She's here,' said Benny. 'In that room. It's where the smell's coming from.'

'Okay.'

'Ace, are you *sure* you can't smell it?'

Ace just nodded, face grim. Benny watched her as she reached out for a doorhandle on a door with moisture-warped paint. She twisted it, then pushed the door open. Both of them entered the room. Benny saw an old large bathroom, with an old-fashioned bathtub, walls flaking where the tiles had given up staying put. She could only guess what Ace could see, but supposed she could see the Doctor as well as she could for she walked to stand next to him. Now both of them were looking at the broken mirror of the vanity hanging over the sink.

And she realised the overpowering stench was coming from the sink.

No, closer. The middle distance; the same place the Doctor and Ace were looking at, she realised, and she wondered why the stink was less overwhelming at the source.

In case it was important, Benny took her place next to the Doctor and looked at the nothing where her friends were looking.

It did not surprise her that Ace belonged to the Doctor. It explained so much. Perhaps even the grin his face had broken into when Ace had entered.

But, even Ace and her mysteries were not enough.

She sighed, looked away from the Doctor's icy stare and down at her closed fist. She squeezed her fingers ever so slightly just to feel the reassuring shapes of the little pills.

'Bernice,' said the Doctor, quietly. But it was enough for her to look back up again.

'Yes, Doctor.'

The voice did not come from Ace, and there was no one else in the room. A trick?

'Tell me,' his voice continued. 'What have you seen in this house?'

The voice spoke of decay and rot. Of death.

It was matter-of-fact, this disembodied voice, and she had enough of it. 'Doctor!' she said, sharply, breaking into the litany. 'What is this?'

'I would like you to meet another friend of mine. Bernice Summerfield.'

'What trickery is this?'

'Actually, I wouldn't mind an explanation, too, Doctor,' said the voice.

Ace was waiting, too, but it was more to see if she was right.

'Bernice,' he began, which both surprised Ace and didn't. It wasn't the Doctor to exposit in a straight line. 'Tell us about yourself. Who are you? Where and when are you from?'

'Okay. CV of faux-Professor Bernice Summerfield coming right up.' Benny's tone betrayed as much surprise at the Doctor's request as Ace felt. Judging from LaMort's expression, his questions intrigued her, and Ace wondered at what LaMort could or could not see. She assumed Benny was not in her picture, though maybe she was after the word picture supplied. Ace found herself admiring Benny's succinct turns of phrase. She sure could tell a good story, and she wondered at how much was true.

'Thank you,' said the Doctor, concentrating everything on LaMort.

'So? I know you travel through time in ways different to most of us. I sensed it with Ace, and I have met you before, Doctor.'

Huh? Thought Ace. What had LaMort sensed? But she didn't get a chance to question out loud because the Doctor was asking Benny another question: 'Bernice, what do you think of death?'

Benny cleared her throat. Ace looked over at the noise and saw her friend had paled, sweat beading on her forehead. Not exactly the reaction she'd expected, and the Doctor just kept looking at LaMort.

'Ah, death. Yes. Interesting topic. Much more interesting to talk about than tax...'

'Benny.' His voice was low, warning.

Had those two planned something?

'Sorry. It's just a little bit difficult focusing on a talking sink as though the life of every human being from this point in time on depends on it.' She cleared her throat again. 'Okay. According to where and when I come from, death gets interesting, if you could call it that.'

'You mean there's a lot more of it,' Ace interjected.

Ace saw Benny look at the Doctor, then at her. She smiled back at Benny; the Doctor remained looking grim. They *had* planned this.

'I do not have to be busy to be satisfied, Doctor. It's not enough.'

'Barely two hundred years ago you visited Australia, then decided to stay and settle in Sydney. Why was that?' The Doctor's voice was startling in its gentleness.

'It was new,' LaMort said, simply.

'What about the indigenous population?' asked Benny, indignant. Ace fought the temptation to shush her.

'Oh, I knew them. Just differently. I know every soul on this planet.' Ace shivered as she realised what LaMort meant.

'That feeling of *new*,' the Doctor said. 'Think about the impending expansion from this world to many, many worlds. All new and clean, virginal, waiting for new souls. Waiting for *you* to see, to feel, to do what you *do*.'

'As new and clean as a virgin?' LaMort smiled again, then opened her hand and Ace saw a handful of pills drop through the bony outstretched fingers and heard them clatter and scatter on the floor. Ace saw every one of them as a question that would never be answered by the Doctor; and they changed before her eyes to images of souls she'd never met, melting into the cracks appearing in the floor. So, there was a place where they went. They didn't just disappear.

Twenty-five today; fifteen a month before; how many every second of her life?

She could never accept death, but Ace knew LaMort was not the monster she could use to absolve her race of its sins.

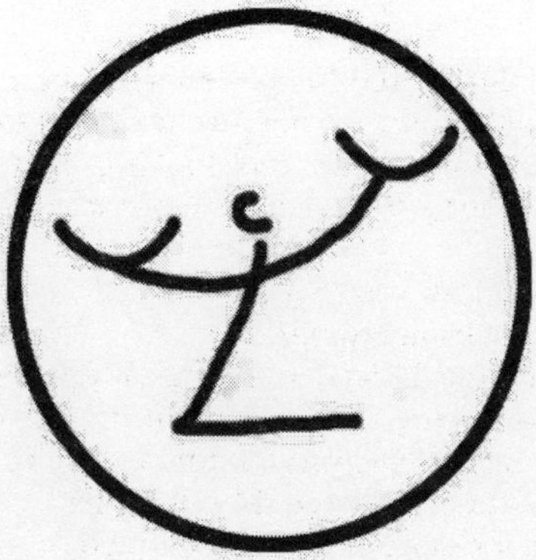

The Libran icon of scales would appear to date back to the Osirians whose hearts would be removed and then 'weighed' by Anubis, the god of the dead, to determine their worth in life. Only the beings whose hearts had fulfilled their destiny would be allowed to pass across to the great pyramid of Osiris. The histories of the Osirians of course passed down into human mythology through their involvement with the ancient Egyptians of Earth and through them to the Greeks and Romans in the form of the constellation of Libra, which convention draws as a set of scales.

Historically, those born under the sign of Libra have been depicted as obsessed with equality in all the houses of their chart. Yet Librans are more than capable of accepting imbalance so long as it is to their own benefit. They rarely shy away from conflict and often relish the chance to play 'Devil's Advocate'. However, the reason they can afford to be so deliberately perverse is that they are imbued with the ability to view both sides in a debate and assess which side is the most just to them. That they are depicted in the zodiac as a machine, a set of scales, is misleading as it is in fact a very emotional sign, one that cares a great deal and longs to share its own good fortune. The greatest injustice of all is when the Libran's generosity is rejected by its intended recipient. Only then do we see the fiery elements of the sign come to the fore. And as Libra is an air sign, combining air with fire can make for a dangerous mix...

Kasterborus, *Our Destiny is in the Stars*

Kasterborus says...

If today is your birthday: *You might be feeling trapped in your life right now, but a solution is in sight. Just remember that patience is a virtue...*

The Switching

Simon Guerrier

After a moment of dizzying blackness, the Doctor opened his eyes. He lay on his back, looking up at the ceiling. It needed retouching. Curls of dry paint peeled away from the surface.

'Well,' he said. With his ears still ringing his voice echoed oddly. He must have hit his head quite hard. In fact his whole body ached. 'Next time we'll try a smaller amount of solution!'

Thankfully no one was about to pass comment. But UNIT's finest would be racing this way to investigate the explosion. He would never live it down if they found him on the floor. Blowing himself up indeed! He really ought to be more careful.

Gingerly, he raised his head. He didn't recognise his surroundings. Where had his spacious laboratory gone? The little room he found himself in was an uninspiring grey, the brick walls painted sloppily. Beside where the Doctor lay, a bed was built into the wall.

He got to his feet as quickly as his sore limbs would allow, stopping to examine his clothes. Last thing he remembered, he'd been sporting a particularly fine smoking jacket with scarlet braid. Now he found himself in coarse, two-piece pyjamas with pastel blue stripes. There were cheap plimsolls on his feet. Not his style at all!

The Doctor looked around the room again.

'A prison cell!' he said.

Immediately he tried the door. It was heavy, metal and - as expected - locked. He stooped to try the small fisheye lens, set into the door at shoulder height. It was made for looking into the cell and not seeing out. Even squinting, he could see only indistinct grey forms outside.

He sighed. Best to remain calm. What did he remember, before the blackness? The lab. His experiment. That strange metal UNIT had found. If he had lost his memory, there was no telling what he might have done in the meantime. Maybe the metal had taken him over? Perhaps that was why they had locked him up. How much time had he lost?

The cell was like any other he had encountered - basic furnishings and little natural light. A bed, a table, a sink and a bucket. But on the bed there were various bits of junk. Stiffly, the Doctor sat down to examine them. A spiralled coil of steel looked like it had once been a coat hanger. It was attached to some wisps of copper wire, a bit of stone and something wrapped in tin foil. It would take skill to bend the coat hanger into such a precise shape - just the sort of thing he might throw together himself.

With his fingers still tingling and strange, the Doctor turned the items over. He couldn't fathom what the apparatus was meant to achieve. He tried inserting one end of the coil into the lock of the door, but it clearly wasn't any kind of key. He put all the bits back down on the bed, as he had found them.

Next he tried the table in the corner of the cell. There were two library books on it, both in English. He picked up one, a battered hardback called 'A History of the Plantagenets'. It had been stamped on the inside cover 'Prison Libraries Service', but did not say which particular prison library it belonged to. Turning over the first page, the Doctor found an oblong piece of paper pasted inside. Again headed 'Prison Libraries Service', it listed due dates for the book's return. The Doctor smiled at the current due date, the only one not crossed through in biro.

'Now we're getting somewhere!' he said.

The book was due back less than a week after the last day the Doctor remembered. So, unless the book was late, he could have lost no more than four or five days.

He gazed up at the window. There were bars across the small, square hollow and it let in only a miserable amount of light. On tiptoes, all he could see outside was some kind of watchtower. Judging by the architecture, this was one of the Victorian gaolhouses built on the panoptic model, where the warders on the tower could see into every room at once, and the prisoners each feel that the scrutiny is on them alone.

The shelf above the sink was crammed with all sorts of toiletries, all kinds of lotions and hair ointments he did not recognise. They were not his, and he noticed there was no razor.

'Perhaps they don't trust me with a blade,' he mused.

He checked the room carefully for other clues - even stripping the sheets off the bed. Nothing. Having looked under the sink and in the bucket, he had exhausted all options. And it was frustrating having no one to talk to.

'Perhaps I came up with a brilliant plan of escape,' he said to himself. His ears were not any better, and his voice still sounded strange. 'But whatever it was hasn't worked, and now I've lost my memory.'

He stood where he was, looking round the room again.

'Come on man, *think*.'

One hand on his hip, with the other he stroked his chin. And froze.

He snatched up one of the books, angling the cover in front of him so that the shiny dust jacket caught the light.

In the reflection, the distinguished, bearded face of the Master stared back at him. Horrified.

Some way away, in the Doctor's laboratory - and indeed in the Doctor's body - the Master was already busy.

He had picked himself off the floor, the muscle ache and vertigo being just as he'd anticipated. He flexed his fingers, trying to rid himself of the pins and needles prickling through them.

The Doctor's laboratory was a large, airy room with lots of natural light. The large windows looked out on to lush greenery. The Master strutted around, getting the feeling back in his legs, and spied the mirror above the lab's wash basin. He had a moment's grace for a little vanity.

He waggled his finger at the reflection, pulling a face. 'You've gone too far this time, Master!' he said, mimicking the Doctor's imperious tone. He tried a horrified face, and one of surprise. Then he crossed his eyes and stuck his tongue out. This face of the Doctor's really was very versatile, though the nose was far too prominent. It was odd, too, sporting a bare chin after all these years.

The Master used up a precious minute battling with the Doctor's infuriating, sticky-uppy hair, then hurried over to the TARDIS. The door didn't yield.

'Very untrusting to keep it locked up, Doctor,' he said, searching through his pockets for the key. The pockets were full of junk, including a small metal box with various controls on it. The Master recognised it immediately. It was the remote control for the Doctor's ridiculous car. Quite ingenious!

The Master dropped it on to the floor and stamped on it with his heel. The casing cracked. He kicked the box and it skittered across the floor and was lost under one of the workbenches.

He tried the pockets again, but could find no trace of a key. He bit his lip. He didn't have time for this!

A gas flame was alight on the tabletop. The Master dashed over, glancing through the Doctor's untidy notes. The man was testing samples of a metal alloy for unusual properties. Riveting! 'Do you really find it satisfying,' he mused, reading over the Doctor's experiments, 'when every one of your adventures can be solved with a schoolboy's knowledge of science?'

The Master turned off the Bunsen burner, then checked the desk drawers, rifling through the junk. No key, but he found a scalpel and slipped it into his pocket. Just in case. He began rummaging through the rest of the contents.

'Stop right there!'

The Master froze. Jo Grant, the Doctor's young assistant, stood in the doorway, her arms folded. Her scarlet sunglasses were huge and round, so she looked like she had borrowed her head from an insect. She wore a bikini covered in tassels, and her bare skin was pink.

'My dear Miss Grant,' said the Master. 'I do hope you've not been out under the sun in that scant attire. Not without protective lotion.'

'You're not going to get round me like that,' she said.

The Master gently put his hand into his pocket and found the scalpel there.

'I know exactly what you're up to,' she said.

The Master raised an eyebrow. 'You do?'

'You're trying to avoid the subject, and you're hoping I'll just go away, aren't you?'

Baffled, he nodded. 'A perfect deduction.'

'I suppose you're going to tell me you haven't got time now, that whatever the Brigadier's found is part of a spaceship and now we'll be invaded any second!'

'I wouldn't dare,' he said.

Had he misjudged that? What would the Doctor have said? Something much more patient, no doubt.

Jo folded her arms.

'You know Mike Yates has made every effort to make a good impression with you,' she said, her voice taking on a haughtiness the Master would not have expected. 'And every time, you're too busy or you're working or you just say something that makes him feel about two inches high. And then this morning... He was only checking the facts for his report, you know.' She shook her head. 'You just weren't very nice at all, were you?'

She was waiting for him to say something. 'My behaviour was completely uncalled for,' he said, as dolefully as he could manage. Yates was the officer who had arrested him, surely? Professional and personable enough. What had the Doctor said?

'Well, yes...' said Jo, thrown by this sudden contrition. She had presumably thought she was up for a fight. Perhaps he could end this quickly.

'I obviously overstepped the mark,' he said, 'and caused distress to you and to Captain Yates for which I can only offer my apologies.' Jo continued to stare at him, wide eyed. 'You're clearly very fond of him. And I've been rude. I'm sorry.'

She skipped over and kissed him on the cheek. 'Thank you!' she whispered, earnestly, in his ear. Then she turned and tottered away.

'Miss Grant!' the Master called after her. 'Would you happen to know where I might have put the TARDIS key?'

She grinned. 'Try round your neck,' she said, and ducked out through the door.

Sure enough, the key was on a chain, tucked into the ruffs of his shirt. The Master let himself into the Doctor's TARDIS.

'Guard!' called the Doctor, at the top of the Master's voice. 'Guard, can't you hear me?' He had been calling for a couple of minutes.

A voice eventually responded from the far side of the door. 'What is it this time?'

'I've had a bit of an accident, old boy,' called the Doctor cheerily. 'Can't you hear the running water?'

He had cut his hands pulling the sink out of the wall, but it had had the desired effect. Water was foaming from the broken pipe, and his cell was now ankle deep. His prison-issue plimsolls were not waterproof.

There was some hesitation from the other side of the door - using the spy hole, no doubt - and he could hear more footsteps. People talked in urgent whispers, and then the key was in the lock.

The door opened inwards. Four burly warders stood outside. They carried long black batons. Water rushed out, seeping over their boots. It poured away over the balcony behind them, and spattered down on to the ground below. Four floors up, the Doctor estimated: too high to jump.

'What *'ave* you bin up to?' snarled the first of the warders.

'Good afternoon,' said the Doctor pleasantly. 'Thank you for coming.'

'Face up against the wall!' ordered the warder. The Doctor did as he was told. The warder then stepped cautiously into the cell. He looked over the mess.

'Quite an "accident",' he surmised.

'I can be quite clumsy when I've a mind to it,' said the Doctor.

'Oi,' said one of the other warders, still standing in the doorway. 'Less of the mouth.'

'I do beg your pardon.'

The first warder scratched his chin, tapping the pieces of broken basin with his stick.

'Okay,' he said. 'We'll put him in another cell while we get this lot sorted.'

Two warders came forward into the cell. They flanked the Doctor.

'Right,' said one. 'No sudden movements.'

The Doctor nodded. And lashed out.

'Good grief!'

The Master couldn't believe what he had walked in on. The inside of the Doctor's TARDIS had always been a mess, but this was a disaster! The central console was a tangle of upended panelling, with bare wires showing. The casing of the time rotor had been removed, and some of the inner mechanisms had been dissected. Illegible scribbling in felt tip covered the panelling where the Doctor had dashed off notes and ideas. 'This button closes the doors!' read one label.

The Master looked it over as dispassionately as he could. It seemed the knowledge the Time Lords had taken from the Doctor included the most rudimentary skills. What had the man been up to? The transuranic spectrum gauge was hooked up to the relative chronometer! The housing of the spatial dampeners had been entirely taken apart!

He quickly, deftly, put the wires he could back where they should be, and closed down the panelling. The time rotor casing he found under the console - upside down and being used as a waste bin. He shook out the bits of paper and sandwich crusts, and hefted it back into place. Then his fingers dashed across the controls. A basic configuration menu popped up. On a whim, he changed a couple of settings.

He stopped, suddenly, and cast an eye over his work. It would have to do. He flicked the switches for take off.

Nothing happened.

He tried again, returning all the controls to zero, checking the dials and then working the controls forward gradually.

The console didn't even beep. He stared at it. And then at his hands, still clutching the instruments.

'Isomorphic controls...' muttered the Master. 'If this infernal machine is out of action for him, it's not going to work for me while I'm in his body!' He should have thought of that. Now what was he going to do?

'You're not going anywhere, are you?' asked Jo Grant, poking her head into the console room. Now she was barefoot, carrying her flip flops and sunglasses in one hand, and a scarlet plastic handbag in the other. 'Not without me coming too?'

'No...' he sighed. 'It seems not. The confounded thing refuses to move.'

'What *have* you done?' Jo was staring at the walls. The TARDIS's normal roundels had been replaced with shallow dishes.

The Master beamed. 'I've reconfigured a few things so that the internal architecture is much more... stylised,' he said.

'It's really glam and funky!' she said.

'Indeed. And with my limited grasp of this TARDIS's workings at present, it's going to take me for ever to puzzle out how to change it back. Even then it's set as the default setting.' He smiled. 'It's going to drive me mad!'

'But you still can't make the TARDIS go?'

'It appears not.'

'Have you tried thumping the controls?' she asked.

'My dear... *Jo*. Whatever would that achieve?'

'But you always do it!' she insisted. She was looking at him oddly.

'Very well,' he said. He leaned forward, and firmly rapped his knuckles on the flat section next to the time rotor. Rat-a-tat-tat!

Nothing happened.

He looked up at Jo.

'Oh well,' she said, dipping her head to one side. 'It probably makes you feel better. About the Time Lords.' And, since they evidently weren't going anywhere, she bobbed back out through the door and was gone.

The Master looked at his watch. He needed another plan, and quickly.

Brigadier Lethbridge-Stewart had been trying all day to catch up with paperwork, but his secretary had not grasped the meaning of 'no interruptions'. She kept supplying him with tea and biscuits - faster than he could put them away. The phone would not stop ringing. People kept coming to find him with chits to sign or leave to agree. A cheeky pair of lads had even come by to ask if they could join Miss Grant sunbathing! UNIT used to be such a sensible, serious place. What was it coming to?

There was a knock on his door.

'What now?!?' he thundered. The Doctor poked his head in.

'Not now, Doctor,' the Brigadier said. 'Whatever it is.'

'I'm sorry to intrude, sir,' said the Doctor. 'But I do only require a minute of your time.'

The Brigadier sat back in his seat, looking the Doctor up and down.

'You just addressed me as "Sir"...' he said, quietly.

The Doctor pulled a face. 'You *are* my employer...' he said. 'Isn't that the protocol?'

'Yes,' said the Brigadier. 'I suppose so.' He held his hand out, indicating the seat in front of him. 'Seeing how you ask so charmingly, what can I do for you? You're going to tell me that alien metal we got you is nothing of the sort?'

'Actually, no. I still have some tests to do.'

The Doctor took the chair.

'It's about the Master...' he said, seriously.

'Oh, you've heard already, have you?' asked the Brigadier. 'Suppose they fill you in before they even tell me, damn them!'

'I do beg your pardon,' said the Doctor, leaning forward. 'Heard what, exactly?'

The Brigadier helped himself to a biscuit. 'You mean I know something you don't?' he scoffed. 'Well, I've just this second got off the phone. Seems our old friend's been up to some new tricks. Caused quite a rumpus. You fancy some tea?'

The Doctor accepted the china cup and saucer, and the Brigadier poured from a delicate pot. He waited for the Doctor to take milk and sugar - but the Doctor just sipped the black tea as it was. Odd, even for him.

'You were saying?' said the Doctor. He hadn't commented on the tea either - usually he would want to name the blend, or mention how, five hundred years ago, he had been in Ceylon...

'Are you all right, old man?' asked the Brigadier.

'I assure you I am fine. Please, the Master...'

'Well. Appears to have tried some of that kung-fu stuff you get up to.

Took three of the staff to bring him down – with sticks! Now they've got him in full restraints.'The Brigadier chuckled.'I hear he didn't take to that too well!'

The Doctor smiled, demurely.

'So, what was it about him I can help you with?'

'Well...' said the Doctor. He thought for a moment.'I'd like to have him moved.'

The Brigadier put down his cup.'What did you say?'

'I would really appreciate the Master being moved to some other facility. Somewhere with a view.'

'Now really, Doctor, you must realise –' the Brigadier began.The Doctor was looking at him levelly.'You mean to say that this is what it's all been about? His adventures today?'

The Doctor shook his head.'Not entirely. But he's trapped.And... I know what that feels like. Especially to my people. But somewhere with something to look at, something to occupy his mind... that would make a significant difference to his behaviour, I can assure you. I appreciate it's very difficult, but you would have my express gratitude.And his, too.'

The Brigadier munched on another biscuit.

'Would it help if I drove you up there?' he said when he had finished. 'So you can see how he is? It's only an hour or so away.We could be back here before dusk.'

The Doctor shook his head again. 'I've taken up far too much of your valuable time,' he said.'Thank you for hearing me out.And for the tea.' He nodded, curtly, and left.

'That fellow gets odder by the day...' said the Brigadier, and returned to his work.

As the Master headed back to the Doctor's lab, a young, fresh-faced soldier stepped out into the corridor in front of him.The Master gave him a quick smile.The soldier stopped.

'Can I see some identification, sir?' said the soldier.

The Master made a show of going through his pockets.When he had searched them before, he had not seen a pass of any kind. He took hold of the scalpel.

'I'm sorry,' he said, warily.'I seem not to have brought anything with me.'

The solider winked, and stepped back out of the way.'Only having you on, Doctor,' he said.'We'll overlook it this once.Again.'

The Master smiled.

'There a problem?' said Sergeant Benton, sidling up behind him.

'Not at all, sir,' said the soldier, stiffly.'Just ensuring the Doctor had his card on him, sir.'

'Very good, Jack,' said Benton.The soldier saluted, first the Master and then Benton, and headed off down the corridor.

'Well,' said the Master, eager to be off. But now Benton was looking at him oddly. He guessed he ought not to have saluted back. How long had the Doctor been living with these people, and yet he refused to manage the most basic of courtesies?

'Is there something I can help you with, Mr Benton?'

'Not at all, Doc,' said Benton. 'I suppose you've heard about the Master?'

'It's... gratifying the security in the place is so stringent.'

Benton nodded. 'Still,' he said. 'I suppose we'd all be like caged animals in that place - even you, Doc.'

The Master could not help but laugh. 'Brigadier Stewart might not see it that way, you know.'

Benton stood up straight, and the Master saw the way he moved his hand to the pistol at his hip.

'"Stewart"?' said Benton. 'Now Doctor, you've never called the Brigadier that before. What's going on?'

Good old Benton, thought the Master. 'Tell me, Benton. Do I appear different to you today? Is there something unusual or out of character?'

Benton took a long look, and then he stared wide eyed.

'Oh, you don't fool me, sir,' he said.

The Master still had his hand in his pocket. He readied the scalpel blade.

'You've done something to your hair,' said Benton.

The Master smiled. 'You really are a remarkable species,' he said.

'Well, Doctor,' smiled Benton, chuffed, 'I must be getting along. Duties, you know. And I reckon you'll need to finish up on those bits we found.'

He saluted, and again looked quizzical when the Master saluted back. But he said nothing.

After Benton had gone, the Master walked down the corridor, and out through tall windows on to a veranda. It gave an exquisite view of the estate. He breathed in the cool, afternoon air and let the sun at his face. Bliss.

His ingenious escape plan had failed. It would have been glorious to leave the Doctor explaining to his human friends just why he had turned up at the prison unannounced and let the Master free. But not this time. Soon he would be back in a cell and despite his best efforts all he had achieved was getting himself chained to a wall, or something similarly crude. Whatever the humans felt best served justice and public order. And he had nixed any other ploys for a while - the Doctor would ensure he was kept under heightened surveillance after today's little outing.

He, feasibly, had time to leave a trap in the Doctor's laboratory, but the Doctor would be expecting that. It would be far more amusing *not* to, and leave the Doctor scouring for wires and explosives in vain.

But still. All things considered, it had been worthwhile just to stretch his legs. And he had rather enjoyed himself.

And then the Master had an idea. Something completely unlike him, but completely unlike the Doctor, too.

Two powerfully built warders had been stationed on permanent watch, on the far side of the room from the prisoner. One of the men bore a nasty bruise on the side of his face, where the Master had struck him earlier.

The other warder, Barry, could not quite believe what his colleagues had told him about this afternoon's incident. This had been the prisoner's most shocking, most violent attempt yet. Last time, he had effortlessly slipped off a set of handcuffs and convinced a warder to march him down to the main gate. But as soon as he had been confronted by another guard, he had given himself up. Barry had been one of the pair who put him back in his cell, and the prisoner had even apologised to them for all the fuss he'd caused.

But this vicious streak today - it just showed he really was the security risk the UNIT people claimed. A brilliant but unbalanced mind, the report had read. It had been in Barry's briefing today. And they had mentioned the prisoner's air of indignance this afternoon, that furious glare in his eyes as they chained him up. So they had taken precautions. Now the prisoner was chained to a seat, facing away from them so they could see that his ankles and wrists were bound.

As it happened, they saw nothing but immaculate manners from the prisoner. There was a moment's concern when, for a couple of seconds, the prisoner shook in his seat and rattled his chains like he was having a fit. But by the time Barry had walked over to have a look at him, he was calm again, head bowed humbly and with that look in his eye like he was just resigned to it all.

They untied the prisoner the following day, and he seemed to take the Prison Governor's lecture to heart. So they let him get some new library books out. Another one about the Magna Carta, Barry noticed. They didn't hear a peep from him in the next four days, and then UNIT had him moved to some other, private facility down on the coast. He had left behind him a letter of thanks to the warders, and a formal apology to each of the men he had injured.

Barry and his colleagues never heard what became of him.

His evening's duties over, Captain Mike Yates came to find Jo. She was hiding in her quarters. Right at the top of the UNIT building - and well away from the soldiers' mess - it was a tiny room with a sloping ceiling.

Jo sat on her bed, filling in some glossy magazine questionnaire. She still had her bikini on, and between her toes, there were bits of spongy substance. Her toenails were newly painted yellow.

'Mike!' she said. 'You better not be here unescorted!'

'I did actually want a discreet word,' he said, but he could feel his cheeks colouring. She had a habit of making him feel like this.

He perched on the edge of her writing desk, sliding the multitude of lipsticks and eyeliners out of the way first. He politely feigned not to notice the knickers on the floor. Jo put her magazine down.

'So,' she said. 'Is it the Doctor?'

'He's been acting oddly all day, Jo.'

'You noticed too?'

'I think we all have,' said Mike. 'The Brigadier came to talk to me only an hour ago, and apparently the Doctor had shouted at him. And you know why? Because the Brigadier's gone and done what the Doctor only asked him to do this very afternoon.'

'He wouldn't let me in the lab,' she muttered. 'And when I asked why not, he just roared at me.'

'That's terrible,' said Mike.

'It's funny,' she said. 'Because he seemed in such a good mood earlier.'

'And he didn't say what had got his goat?'

'He told me I was blind,' she said, pouting just at the thought of it. 'But I hadn't done anything. Not when he said it, anyway.'

'Benton said they'd discussed the Doctor's hair...'

Jo rubbed her eyes. 'But it's just not like him to be so unpleasant!'

'That's actually what I wanted to talk to you about, Jo,' said Mike. 'The Doctor *wasn't* unpleasant when he came and spoke to me. He was actually very good about it.'

'What do you mean?' she asked.

'Well,' he replied. 'I was in the mess this afternoon, and he came and sought me out. Wanted to say he was sorry for any impoliteness or lack of attention he might have shown me in the past. He said he respected me as a colleague and as a friend, and that he thought that... well, that *you* were eating yourself up over things he may have said and done. And then, before I could even say a word, he just ran off back to his lab. What do you make of that?'

Jo sighed. 'I don't know,' she said.

Yates stood up, and, as casually as he could, came and sat down beside her on the bed. 'I think I got his approval,' he told her.

Jo took his hands. 'Oh Mike!' she said. 'You never needed his approval!'

'Oh. Oh, well...' he said. 'Miss Grant,' he went on. 'Would it be forward of me...'

She was brandishing a great big grin. 'I'd love to go to dinner with you,' she said. 'I really would.'

He took her in his arms and kissed her.

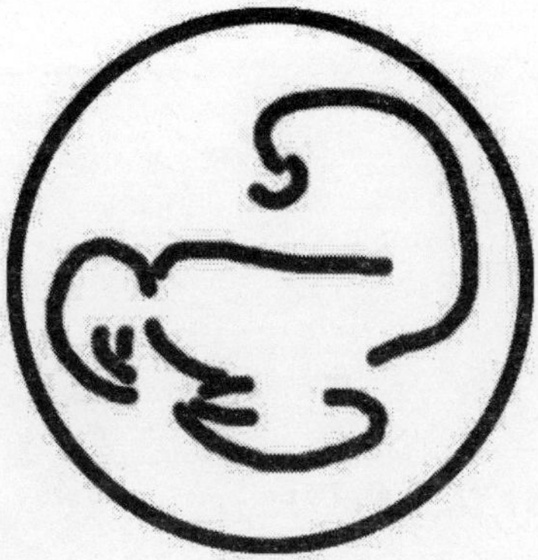

The story of Scorpio is quite an odd one. The goddess Artemis was believed to have had some issue with Orion, the giant. Some say he tried to rape one of Artemis's handmaidens, or perhaps it was just his boasting that he was a better archer than she that angered her. Whatever, Artemis decided to kill Orion and despatched a giant scorpion to do the deed. Orion's sword was no match for the beast's sting and he duly died. Artemis placed her loyal scorpion in the heavens as a reward. Had she hoped to silence Orion for ever, she was sadly mistaken; as Orion was the son of Poseidon, he too was placed in the heavens. Ironically for Artemis, the three-star chain of Orion's belt now makes Orion the most famous and easily recognised of all the constellations.

Miraculously, it was this origin that Kasterborus stuck to in his assembly of the neo-Scorpio chart.

Perhaps because of the origin of the sign as a vengeful beast, the poor Scorpion has had to endure more ill-informed assumptions about its sign than any other in the zodiac. Scorpios are not the rude, crude sex-obsessed people that many will have us believe. They are simply honest and devoid of some of the defensive pretensions of other houses. Neither are they vengeful like their mythological counterpart. They are willing to forgive most misdemeanours – they just refuse to forget any of them. Their greatest skill is a pertinent sense of humour that is the channel for much of their communication. Should, by some rare provocation, they feel the need to retaliate for a wrong-doing, their vengeance is usually as swift as the scorpion of legend: it is direct, to the point and almost always over as quickly as it began…

Kasterborus, *Our Destiny is in the Stars*

Kasterborus says...

If today is your birthday: Sometimes it pays to look at your exact opposites to see who you really are. Stay true to yourself and the right paths with be revealed to you.

Jealous, Possessive

Paul Magrs

The Capitol
November 1st

My dear Mark II,

Happy birthday! Many, many happy returns.

Do forgive me if the above nomenclature seems a little demeaning to your good self, and as if I were attempting to perform some awful act of one-upmanship. It's just one of those funny situations, isn't it? What do you call someone with the same name as yourself? It does give one an odd frisson of... well, one could say, existential angst. But given where you are currently trapped, that would hardly be tactful either, would it?

Anyway, I hope this little missive of mine reaches you and finds both you and your mistress flourishing in that curious and mysterious stellar enclave known only as E-Space. How my heart goes out to you both, wandering around for ever beyond all known space and time. Well, never mind. It doesn't do to dwell on these things, does it?

Here on Gallifrey the round of socialising is in full swing and it seems that hardly a day goes by without my attending some or other glittering function. It's rather gratifying, though embarrassing to a modest soul such as I, but it seems that I have become something of a celebrity here. Your mistress would probably know all about this, but off-worlders are rarely welcome on Gallifrey, and so the mistress Leela and I are fair game for all the curious stares and the polite but pointed enquiries about 'what life's really like Out There in the Big Bad Universe'. These Time Lords live a very sheltered life, it seems. And for once in my life I find myself the centre of attention. They delight in the tales of my many adventures. Really, I feel like the star of the show. For once.

Mistress Leela, it must be said, seems to attract a little less attention than do I. She is having just a smidgen of difficulty acclimatising to life under the awesome dome of the Capitol. She wears those frightful buckskins everywhere and whips her knife out at the slightest thing. Caused quite a stir at Chancellor Flavia's inauguration last month. And, of course, her own tales and anecdotes draw far less interest than my own.

She has no flair for tale-telling. 'Big scorpion creature inside Doctor's head. Doctor makes two of himself. Shrinks down very small. Injects himself in own ear. Goes to brain. Kills evil scorpion creature.' It's not exactly Tolstoy, is it?

Anyway, I thought that thing in the Doctor's brain looked rather more like a gigantic frozen prawn. Not that it matters. And you weren't born then, were you, my dear?

Well, my dear, I really must sign off now. There's a reception for the unveiling of a statue in honour of my good self in the glorious setting of the Panopticon. It's all to do with the good work I did in getting shut of those dreadful potato-headed Sontarans when they invaded and I decided to settle down in this congenial milieu for good. Honestly, I'm swept off my little feet, much of the time.

I don't think Mistress Leela is attending this reception with me. 'Who wants to see robot dog made out of rock? These Time Lords are stupid.'

Things have, I admit, become a little frosty between us of late.

Anyway, here's hoping that you are having an equally lovely time in your benighted universe,

Kind regards,

Mark I

E-Space
November 3rd

Dear Mark I,

Swept off your feet? Your heart goes out to me?

You haven't got any of those things! You're a robot! You're a robot dog! You've got a boxy square body and a square head and horrid antennae things like ears that keep breaking off. And you run about on rubber castors. Just the same as me! Exactly the same as me!

Since I received your letter, here in the 'benighted enclave' I've thought long and hard and resisted the temptation to write you a very stiff letter back. I've calmed down but I still have to say, I think you're GETTING ABOVE YOURSELF. It's all very well swanning about on Gallifrey and having tasteless monuments erected but really, I feel that you're STEALING MY THUNDER somewhat. And then addressing me in the most impertinent terms.

As it happens, E-Space is turning out to be something of a pleasant surprise. The Mistress and I spent a little time with those ghastly werewolf creatures and, for a dreadful while, it seemed that we were going to be doing some kind of charity work involving liberating slaves or some such.

But the Mistress and I had a good long talk about it and decided that we'd be far better off pleasing ourselves and putting our feet up. We've had a few long years working horribly hard (reconstituting the Key to Time was no doddle, as it happens) and we both agree that we could do with something of a rest. The rate of exchange being what it is, we find that we're both rather rich, here in E-Space, and so we are living it up, for once.

I am writing this from the lobby of a very swish hotel. The Mistress Romana is having her roots done in the Salon. This afternoon we're taking in some of the sights which are, we are assured, spectacular. Then, possibly, we shall go shopping, before returning to our hotel for dinner. This is our life now! And to think, just a matter of weeks ago, we were racketing about the place in that awful old police box.

Sometimes we do miss the Doctor-Master. We raise a glass to him at the end of every dinner and wonder how he's getting along. (I don't suppose you've heard anything?) But he was most remiss in simply dumping us in what seemed at the time to be a completely empty universe. He was always very cavalier.

So, my dear, I must go now, and prepare myself to face the world. I do enjoy receiving your occasional letters. But I prefer not to think that living in that draughty and dull place, surrounded by all those pompous dilettantes has TURNED YOUR HEAD at all. Please, stay as sweet as you are. And don't feel that you have to PUT ON AIRS for my sake. We share the SAME PEDIGREE, as you well know.

Kindest,

Mark II

The Capitol
November 6th

My dear,

I gather from the tone of your last that I might have offended you. Nothing could hurt me more than to think of your poor, lost, exiled self, running around in circles of frustrated pique. Let me mollify your overheated circuitry and point out that any honour bestowed in my direction is simply down to me and my own efforts and that I am not, as you suggest, getting ideas above my station. I am an extremely brave and resourceful robot dog and Gallifrey would no longer exist if it weren't for me, having been invaded by those brutes with potato-shaped heads. So there's simply no pretension on my part.

Perhaps you feel slighted that your own, worthy accomplishments have not been similarly rewarded? It is, actually, with sadness and regret that I have to inform you that no one here was actually aware that there was another K9 in existence. It seems your sojourn in (the really quite pleasant-sounding) E-Space has effectively rendered both you and the Mistress Romana utterly obscure. I ran a quick search in the Matrix and there was no record of this 'Key to Time' you mentioned in your letter. The repository of all Time Lord knowledge seemed to think that it might be some kind of computer game and that perhaps you are getting mixed up?

As to our being of the same pedigree... well, I really must be forward and query that assertion. As you know, I am the original K9, left with the Mistress Leela here on Gallifrey. And, missing me horribly, the Doctor-Master set to work immediately to attempt to replace me. Using the blueprints left to him by my inventor (I actually forget his name. Isn't that awful of me?) the bereft Doctor-Master knocked up a facsimile (IE: YOU) using some bits and pieces he had in an old cardboard box. The result was effective but, as I'm sure even you yourself can appreciate, hardly equal. I am sure that you did your level best to maintain the standards set by myself, but your limitations would be patently obvious to all but an imbecile. We all know what a botcher the Doctor-Master was.

Speaking of whom, I have received a number of very chatty postcards and letters just lately, from various terrifying locations in the Space-Time continuum. It seems that, for our erstwhile master, life continues apace, in the same old hair-raising fashion. He tells me that he has a new companion – a boy this time, which is a turn-up for the books. And that the Master (who is someone absolutely frightful from the Doctor-Master's past) is back on the scene. The Doctor-Master sounds somewhat frazzled and weary to me, reading between the lines. I do hope he's looking after himself. I am gratified, though, that he feels he can open up to me in this way. Our bond is very, very deep.

Odd that neither you nor your Mistress Romana have heard a peep out of him. And yet you say communications between E-Space and the real world are quite efficient?

Oh! I almost forgot. The thrilling news here is that Mistress Leela is expecting. It came as a shock to all of us, not least Master Andred. He is absolutely terrified of her at the best of times and is going around disconsolately, muttering and shaking his head. Between you and me, he doesn't look happy at all. And yet he used to be so satisfied by his work as a security guard.

Apparently it will be the first infant born on Gallifrey for many millennia.

Born the natural way, that is. Whatever that is. (We can assume it doesn't mean out of a cardboard box and a pile of spare parts! Ha ha ha!)

The happy news is causing quite a kerfuffle in the Capitol. I feel myself somewhat eclipsed.

Signing off now, with great affection –

The Original

E-Space
November 9th

Dear Prototype,

Just back from a TERRIFYING ADVENTURE with the Mistress Romana. I could go into details of the HORRIFYING EVENTS that transpired in the DEADLY SALON just after I completed my last letter to you, but I fear that you probably don't have the stomach for SUCH THINGS these days, having become such a SOCIALITE AND GOSSIP as your missives lead me to believe.

This is in haste, since we are leaving on a BRAND NEW QUEST this afternoon and the Mistress Romana requires my help in packing. She still takes a great many outfits on our adventures. 'Well, K9,' she says to me. 'Deadly danger is one thing, but looking a fright is quite another.' Luckily, I was never saddled with an ill-bred mistress who ran about well-nigh naked, brandishing steak knives about the place. The Mistress Romana's adventures tend to be rather glamorous. The quest we are embarking on this afternoon has something to do with the VERY FABRIC OF ALL TIME AND SPACE and, it seems, is sure to be a palaver. So forgive me if I keep this brisk.

Do pass on my regards to Leela and Andred. And our congratulations. Are they hoping for something human? I imagine your nose will be PUSHED OUT once the baby is born. The Mistress Romana agreed that such an advent will be very big news on her homeworld. What electronic dog could manage to maintain his public profile in such circumstances? I'm sure I don't know. Between us two, the mistress Romana did also say that she thought it a bit common: an asylum-seeking off-worlder moving in, marrying one of the guards and proceeding to GIVE BIRTH ALL OVER THE PLACE. But there we have it, as we both know, my mistress was VERY WELL BROUGHT UP.

No time just now to go into the business of the Matrix denying all knowledge of the Key to Time. Of course it all happened and of course it was all down to the superb efforts of the Doctor-Master, Mistress Romana and my humble self that the balance of order and chaos in the cosmos was kept in balance and check. It was quite a bother, all in all. And of course the Matrix held no records. This was something very hush hush and involved the Guardians, which are beings the hoi-polloi don't get to hear about, much less MEET AND HOBNOB with. Our adventures tend to be quite exclusive. IE NO GIANT PRAWNS OR POTATO-HEADS FOR US!

With fondness,

Mark II

The Capitol
November 12th

My dear,

Something dreadful has happened. I'm sure you won't have heard yet, but the most alarming reports have been coming in to the Capitol all day. I was the first to know, of course. The Mistress Leela has gone into shock and we're all very agitated.

There is no easy way to tell you this - but the Doctor-Master has had a fall!

There's no time to go into all of the details, but I thought I'd dash this off quickly. Apparently it's quite serious and he's not expected to recover. That is, we're expecting a regeneration at any moment. This is dreadful news. The Doctor we knew will be no more!

Let us bury the hatchet and put aside our differences in this difficult hour.

Apparently he was trying to save the universe. He should never have been up that gantry in the first place. Tripped on his own scarf or something.

In haste,

Mark I

One consideration that humans have had to face in their resurrection of ancient sciences is how they apply to other races. In around 200 BCE, the noted Greek philosopher Carneades once scoffed that to believe in astrology was to afford the same beliefs to every living thing; surely to suggest that the movement of the planets affects us would also mean that it influences dogs, spiders, fish and other animals? Though Carneades used this argument to discredit noted astrologers at the time, he unwittingly provided the route for Kasterborus and his followers that enabled them to adapt their findings to encompass all races, all species. And while this opened itself up to those who sought to exploit people by providing horoscopes for their parrots or hamsters, it also meant that Kasterborus became a man of influence over Phreni, Sirians, Delphons and many other non-humanoid races whose cultures responded to superstition.

When the kind and handsome centaur Chiron was accidentally shot by Heracles with a poisoned arrow, he was immobilised, but, as an immortal, unable to die. He endured the agony courageously until the Gods took pity on him and made him mortal so he could die and ascend to the heavens.

The most idealistic of the zodiac, Sagittarius is also the most extremist - their enthusiasm is all or nothing. They attract good luck - or, to be accurate, serendipity - as they rarely have to strive towards their goals. In fact it is when Sagittarians try too hard that they are often their own worst enemies. The human half of its iconography depicts the Sagittarians' stamina and keen insight. Their arrows are sharp and rarely misguided. The other half, the beast, represents their desire for action; a life of tranquillity is not for the individual born into this house, as they need to be constantly challenged and stimulated. Though their dynamic personality might lead to them being a little low on tact, they make up for it in enthusiasm and natural energy.

Kasterborus, *Our Destiny is in the Stars*

Kasterborus says...

If today is your birthday: *One word – serendipity. Let good luck bring to you that which is yours.*

Five Card Draw

Todd Green

The cool damp air of the dark hallway hit the Doctor's face in contrast to the monitored and recycled atmosphere of the TARDIS. He inhaled deeply, tasting it in his lungs. 'Medieval Earth,' he said. 'England, of course.' He looked up and down the hall, noting that many of its stones had crumbled away, leaving dark gaps which might hide cobwebs or rats. The floor was dirt, with hearty weeds poking through. The feeble light of sunset peered through the occasional small window. 'Bit of a fixer-upper, isn't it? And much older than the twelfth century, if those coordinates were right.' He looked out of a window and saw a wide moat filled with dark water, surrounding the... castle, then.

He looked back at the TARDIS standing in the passage, its outer police box shape more incongruous than usual against the stone. He hoped Peri would stay in the TARDIS library as he'd requested. He'd promised to show her the sights of the universe but somehow he didn't think this was the best place to start. For one, he didn't even know why he was here...

'Help me!' Back in the TARDIS, the voice had suddenly arrived in the Doctor's mind. *'You must help me.'* It was familiar, almost like his own.

The cry had hung in his mind as he'd stood by the console, the walls seeming to close around him, the console room feeling smaller. His feet had grown heavy, his calves sore as if after a long run. His heartsbeat echoed in his ears, and he felt the hot breath of pursuit on his neck. But the room had been empty. He closed his eyes, shutting out sensation but for the warm air still reaching the back of his neck. He was vaguely aware of his hand pressing coordinates into the system.

And the TARDIS had arrived here. Yet nobody he'd expect to find in twelfth-century Earth could reach into the TARDIS and draw him here. Whomever - or whatever - it was, they'd better have a reasonable explanation. Or not require much of him and shortly send him on his way. Such power commanded at least polite interest, if not respect.

The Doctor looked up and down the hall, looking for any indication of which way to go. But both directions seemed identically nondescript and deserted. Straining to hear any sounds of life, the Doctor turned completely around, then headed past the TARDIS along the passage. The hall led to a wooden door, flimsy with decay and hanging by one hinge. Beyond it the Doctor heard low voices and the scrape of chairs. He steeled himself to face whomever had called him. Pushing the door tentatively open, he pressed himself back against the wall, out of sight.

The voices stopped instantly. For a few seconds, nothing. Then... 'Well?

Are you coming in or shall we be waiting here all day?' The voice sounded ancient, as though travelling on centuries of air through the doorway to him. And somehow familiar...

The Doctor peered around the door and saw a wide room, faded banners skewed or lying crumpled on the dirt floor, a coat of arms broken into pieces in a cold, empty fireplace. Candles flickered half-heartedly about the room. Three men sat round a table in one corner, one of them standing as he entered.

'Ah, there you are, young man.' The man was old, with a mane of white hair swept behind his head. His eyes shone with wisdom and mischief and his face was lined with kindness... and worry. 'Come, sit down.'

'You,' the Doctor said to his earlier self. 'You're here as well? How?'

'I am sure all will be explained,' the old man said, rubbing one shoulder as he talked.

'And hopefully with good reason.' The figure in the middle turned and laid a finger to the side of his aristocratic nose. He smoothed the sleeves of his velvet smoking jacket as he looked from the Doctor to the old man.

The Doctor looked from one earlier self to the other, to... yet another. On the right sat a shorter man with a mop of black hair falling into his kind and sparkling eyes. His coat hung loosely around him, his shirt collar poking raggedly over the coat. He looked a bit of a vagabond, a hobo.

'All of us, together again.' The hobo smiled. 'Might as well make the most of it.'

The Doctor frowned. 'I'd rather get to the bottom of it,' he said. 'Who has brought us here?'

The old man reached into his coat. 'For the moment I suggest we find a way to pass the time.' He pulled a pack of playing cards from his pocket, separated them into two equal stacks, then shuffled them together once, twice.

'Pass the time? What are you doing?' the Doctor asked. 'Shouldn't we find out why we're here?'

A tall man burst breathlessly through a door across the room. He had blond curls and wore an outrageous coat stitched together from a dozen clashing fabrics. The Doctor glanced his future self up and down, thinking he looked more like a king's jester than a Time Lord, dressed to distract and amuse.

The jester paused, taking in their four familiar faces for only a second before reaching the table in two long strides. 'Did you see? Outside?' he said.

'Yes, of course we did,' said the aristocrat.

'The moat?' said the Doctor. It hadn't seemed exciting enough to warrant such an entrance.

'Sit down, if you will,' said the old man, motioning the Doctor and the jester to the empty seats. The jester sat, watching the old man dealing the cards and wincing as he extended his arm across the table. The Doctor leaned on the table.

'We're wasting time,' he said. 'I've left Peri back in the TARDIS and I don't want her wandering out. We should search this castle, the grounds outside, try to find out who -'

'I've been all through that,' said the old man. 'There's nothing in this abandoned castle to explain our presence.'

'And I wouldn't go outside at the moment,' said the jester.

'I'm sure whoever brought us here will show himself, in time,' said the hobo. 'A game might help pass the time.'

The Doctor stared at his other selves. 'You all seem rather calm about this.'

The aristocrat shrugged. 'I'm as curious as you, but for the moment I can wait. Anyone with the power to contact us inside the TARDIS might just as easily have done us harm.'

'They must want us here for a reason,' said the jester. 'We'll find out soon enough. What shall we play?

The old man set the remains of the pack on the table. 'Poker. I'll be dealer. I'm too tired to play.'

The Doctor considered. He could leave now, and let his other four selves face whatever had called them. Though it might contact him again, and there wasn't any immediate danger. At least not in this room... 'Just one hand,' he said. 'After that, if they aren't here, we search.'

'Very well, one hand.' The old man reached behind his chair and lifted a long, narrow leather case on to the table. 'You'll play for this.' He opened the case to display a gold bow, its limbs set with diamonds and rubies, its grip wrapped in brushed suede. A dozen arrows sat beside it, their tips polished gold and silver. It was a beautiful weapon, though the Doctor was surprised he didn't recall ever having possessed it.

'Is that solid gold?' said the hobo, touching the bow tentatively, as though proving its existence. 'It's lovely.'

'What is it?' said the jester, flicking the string in amusement, 'the bow of Rassilon?'

'There's no such thing, as you well know,' said the aristocrat. 'Where ever did you get it?'

'From the third emperor of the Cresap dynasty, of Gallutia,' said the old man, 'as thanks for persuading their enemies to lay down their arms at the battle of Andromeda.'

'The battle of Andromeda?' asked the Doctor. 'I don't remember that at all.'

'Nor do I,' said the aristocrat. The jester shook his head as well.

'I seem to recall some dispute at Gallutia,' said the hobo, 'but it's terribly vague.'

'I'm not surprised you don't recall,' said the old man. 'It was many years ago, after all. The emperor mentioned the bow had great and terrible powers and I should wield it with caution. Of course I'd never use it on a person, but it did improve my target shooting by an order of magnitude. In fact, there's an archery contest happening in the local village square tomorrow afternoon. Ben and Polly were visiting an old friend, so I landed the TARDIS in the surrounding forest for a bit of practice.'

The Doctor looked up. 'You decided to come here on your own?' Hadn't he been forced here like the others?

'So I thought,' said the old man. He glanced around the table. 'How many cards will each of you exchange?'

The Doctor looked at his hand. He had a pair of twos, in clubs and spades, and the four, seven and eight of diamonds. Nothing here likely to win the hand and take the prize, though he hadn't a clue what he'd do with a gold bow anyway. Might come in handy against Cybermen, but otherwise...

He watched the others sorting their hands. Should he keep the twos and count on someone else having an even worse hand, or throw them away in the hope of picking up two more diamonds and making a flush, or perhaps even a straight flush?

The old man continued. 'Not more than a few minutes after landing, I heard a sound, and spied a group of bandits holding a girl as their prisoner,' he said. 'I couldn't very well leave her to their devious intentions, so I crept back into the TARDIS for a very quick jump, over to their clearing.'

'I have trouble with the short trips, actually,' said the hobo.

'So do I, typically. But somehow I knew exactly what coordinates to set.' The old man rubbed his head. 'They just seemed to come to me.'

'I prefer to be surprised wherever I arrive,' said the jester. He arranged the cards in his hand and slipped one out, laying it face down by the old man. He raised an eyebrow and glanced around the table, nodding to himself confidently. Bluffing, the Doctor supposed.

The old man raised an eyebrow as he handed a new card to the jester. 'This trip had to be precise. Watching the bandits on the scanner, I materialised the TARDIS right next to the girl.'

'On top of the bandits?' asked the aristocrat.

'I counted on them scattering when they heard the TARDIS arriving,' said the old man. 'And they did, leaving the poor girl alone. So I opened the doors and pulled her in.'

'That was dangerous. You kidnapped her?' said the Doctor.

'I rescued her. She was frightened and confused by the interior of the TARDIS, but at least she was safe from the bandits. I watched them run away in fright, then opened the doors to let the girl go. But no sooner had

I stepped out to ensure that the clearing was empty, than a group of men in armour surrounded me. I only just had time to close the doors to keep them from the girl.'

'You might have just let her out,' said the jester, stealing a quick look at his hand and letting a tiny show of disappointment cross his lips.

'And into the hands of these knights? Who might have been as dangerous as the bandits?' said the aristocrat. 'Seems a rather irresponsible thing to do.' He took two cards from his hand and received two new ones from the old man, meeting the Doctor's gaze steadily, giving no clues.

'I suppose things are different in your day,' the old man said, glaring at the jester as he handed new cards to the hobo, still favouring one arm. What was wrong with his arm? the Doctor wondered. 'Wandering off without ensuring that everything's in good order. Leaving people behind to face who knows what?'

'Not deliberately,' said the jester.

'So who were these men?' asked the Doctor. He'd forgotten how his other personalities could clash. 'More bandits?'

'No, these knights had pursued the bandits. Now they were angry that I had interfered. "Return Lady Mary to us at once!" they demanded.'

'There's no pleasing some people,' said the jester.

'They should have been grateful that you rescued her from the bandits.' The hobo looked down at his cards, a grand smile spreading over his face before he caught the Doctor's eye, and forced his mouth into a straight line. He exchanged two cards for new ones from the old man.

The old man squinted at the Doctor. 'Did you want to exchange any cards?' he said.

'I'm thinking,' the Doctor said. 'Please, go on.' It was probable that the aristocrat and the hobo had somewhat worthwhile hands, and he was certain that the jester was bluffing.

'I went to open the TARDIS, of course,' said the old man. 'But then a rogue among them claimed he'd seen the TARDIS appear from thin air, and that I must be a sorcerer.' The Doctor had wondered if that ploy would get the old man into trouble. Always better to land off to one side, in the shadows.

'Primitive humans,' the aristocrat said. 'It reminds me of the time Sarah and I –'

'Can that wait until I've finished?' The old man poked the Doctor's arm. 'Are you ready yet?'

'Nearly,' the Doctor said. He shifted the twos and the diamonds back and forth, frowning at either choice.

'Are you delaying the inevitable?' The jester folded his arms across the table. The Doctor found it hard to believe that at some point he'd become this loud giant. Though he was as much of a contrast to his immediate predecessor, who'd faced the universe with a smile and a bite of candy.

'Someone suggested that my magic powers lay within the TARDIS,' the old man said. 'Another claimed that if they let me into the TARDIS, I'd make it disappear again and take the girl away for ever. They accompanied each new idea by hitting my arm or pulling on the bow case. The strap cut into me, and I started to wonder if they would tear me to pieces before deciding.' The old man rubbed his upper arm thoughtfully. 'And all the while two others pounded the doors of the TARDIS and chopped at it with their swords. Even if I got away I'd never get past them and inside. Finally one of them suggested that my will kept the TARDIS locked, so all they had to do was kill me.'

'And the doors would magically open,' the Doctor said. Taking a final look at his cards, he lay three cards face down and handed the pair of twos over to the old man, mentally crossing his fingers for the flush.

'Unfortunately, that plan sounded good to them,' the old man said, handing the Doctor two new cards. The Doctor turned up the first - the five of diamonds - and the second - the two of hearts. His hand was worthless. He should have kept the twos.

'You explained, of course,' said the hobo.

'I tried, but they would have none of it. Once they saw that I was frightened of their swords, one held me firm while the others debated which of them would have the honour of cutting off my head.'

'Barbaric,' said the aristocrat.

'Indeed,' said the old man. 'But the notion so appealed to them that they were momentarily distracted with thoughts of bloodlust. I seized the opportunity, kicking at one and breaking free. They grabbed at me from behind, catching the strap of the bow case, pulling my shoulder nearly out of joint. I struggled free and ran through the trees, feeling their feet pounding behind me and their collective breath on my neck. Somehow I managed to stay ahead.'

The Doctor shivered, remembering the rush of pursuit he'd felt in the console room, and the warm air on his own neck. The same as the old man had felt. A coincidence?

'I reached the edge of the forest and ducked through a narrow gap in the trees. The knights were slowed as they slipped through and I increased the distance between us. Just as I felt sure I couldn't run another minute, I reached the entrance to this castle and pulled up the drawbridge, keeping them outside.'

'Lucky no one was about,' the hobo said.

'Luckier still that this castle's still standing,' said the aristocrat. 'And that the drawbridge worked!'

'How did you manage to pull it up after running so hard?' asked the Doctor. 'And with your arm hurt?'

'The counterweights were still attached,' said the old man. 'I watched through the windows as the knights searched for another entrance. Finding none, they conferred among themselves, then all but two departed. I thought perhaps I might slip away but they camped by the entrance until their fellows returned, ready for battle. They brought extra men, with supplies and tools for crossing the moat and breaking in. I searched the castle for help, but found it empty. I was trapped, away from my TARDIS.'

'You did still have the bow,' the jester said.

'I'd never used it as a weapon,' said the old man. 'The emperor indicated that its power lay elsewhere. Besides, with this arm I doubt I could even pull back the string. I didn't expect to last long trying to fire arrows at more than a dozen running men in armour. I didn't know what to do.'

Listening, the Doctor imagined the fear the old man must have felt, the same fear he'd felt inside the TARDIS. And the old man had come here on his own... 'So you called us for help,' the Doctor said. Suddenly it made sense. Who else could he call?

'I did,' said the old man. 'Concentrating, I could feel the presence of my own mind - of my future selves - across time and space.'

'There are more than just us,' said the jester. 'Where are the others?'

The old man sniffed. 'That taller chap with the teeth and the scarf refused to come. There's a younger, handsome one, with hair dangling to his shoulders. He seemed quite confused and didn't respond. And of course I didn't bother with the short Scottish fellow. He'd try to turn things to his own ends. I can't abide that.'

So now it would fall to the four of them, the Doctor thought. They would have to face the knights and get the old man's TARDIS back. They had no choice. If the knights killed the old man the others would no longer exist.

'Thank you for coming,' the old man said. 'I'm far too old for such a battle. I feel my cells longing to rest, rejuvenate. Regenerate.' He patted the hobo's arm. 'But I do prefer that to happen in its natural course.'

'And it sounded as though their plan might have precluded a regeneration, in any case,' said the aristocrat. He frowned for a moment. 'I'm not sure really, would having our heads chopped off prevent a regeneration?'

The old man and the hobo exchanged shocked glances, but the jester nodded slowly. 'I'd expect so.'

'I always heard, double knife blow, one to each heart,' the Doctor said.

'As did I,' said the aristocrat.

'Anything short of that is repairable, given time,' the Doctor said.

'But still,' the jester said. 'Beheading. The brain's no longer connected to the body to start the regenerative process.' The Doctor and the aristocrat nodded their agreement.

The old man pounded the table twice with his good arm. 'Really now, this is all academic. No one's cutting off my head.' He watched them quietly for a moment. 'I propose that the lowest hand here might face these knights in my place. Any of you are far stronger than me and might have a greater chance of success.'

'Why don't we go together?' said the jester. 'The four of us –'

'Is that such a good idea?' asked the hobo. 'They already sound quite jumpy as it is.'

'And they might think we were more sorcerers,' the Doctor said.

'And you'd still be outnumbered,' the old man said. 'There were at least a dozen of them.' And just as likely to attack as listen to reason.

'Then perhaps it would be best if just one of us went to explain,' said the Doctor. 'At worst, it would let the rest of us know what to expect.' He couldn't say the word 'die' out loud. He met the glances of the others around the table, each nodding his assent. He looked at his worthless hand again, resigned to the probability that he'd be facing the knights. Unless the jester had bluffed quite badly, or his assumptions were incorrect about the others. Although... this might be the end of his time. It would be one of his stranger regenerations.

'Thank you,' the old man said. 'Now come, show your cards.' He turned to the jester.

'Two pair,' the jester announced, showing them. The Doctor noted tiny sighs of relief escaping from the other two. This didn't bode well at all.

'Three fives, I'm afraid,' said the hobo with a smile. That was fair; of them all, the hobo was probably least equipped for the battle ahead. In that previous existence, the Doctor recalled happily exploring the universe, enjoying the relative youth of his new body after hundreds of years in the first one.

'Full house,' the aristocrat said, laying them down with a slap on the table and smiling across to the Doctor. 'Did you pick up what you were hoping for, old chap?' His eyes remained kind, sympathetic. Beyond him the Doctor watched the jester smile nervously.

'No,' he said at last, folding his hand. 'I have nothing.'

Around the table, each man leaned back in his chair, letting out their breath as one. The old man smiled across to the Doctor. 'I know you'll do well, young man.' He pushed the bow in its case across the table to him. 'Perhaps this will help.'

The Doctor accepted it slowly. 'I'm not sure how.'

'You'd best go now,' said the aristocrat. 'Those knights are probably relaxing and deciding how to storm the castle. You'll have the advantage of surprise.'

'However that might help.' The Doctor looked out of the window, seeing the knights' camp-site across the moat, and the old man's TARDIS behind them where they'd dragged it from the forest. A few men lounged by the fire, the others probably in the tents they had raised. 'Brave heart,' he said to himself, nodding quickly to each of the others.

'Good luck!' said the hobo.

'I have every confidence,' said the jester.

The Doctor returned to his TARDIS, hoping that he could make this trip quickly and Peri would remain in the library as he'd told her. But he'd only just started working out the coordinates for the trip across to the knights' camp when she peered through the interior door.

'So why are we here, Doctor?' she asked. He looked up at her for a moment. There was no time to explain, even if he thought she'd understand the notion of him meeting his previous selves.

'Not quite finished,' he said. 'I might be a while, you should stay back in the library.'

She pouted. 'Can't I come out for just a moment?'

'It might be dangerous. I'm only going a short distance then coming straight back. I promise I'll explain later.' The TARDIS dematerialised and he hoped he'd set the right coordinates.

'You're not going to say that all the time, are you?' she asked.

'Only when there's no time to explain.' The Doctor tried to smile as he felt the gentle thud of the TARDIS landing. 'Don't touch anything. The TARDIS autopilot is set to leave as soon as I leave.' He opened the doors.

'What? Why is it leaving when -'

The Doctor didn't hear the rest. He pushed through the doors, closing them behind him and watching the TARDIS disappear again, returning to the castle passage. Hopefully Peri would stay inside - better that he explain the notion of regeneration than have her meet four examples of it. If this went well he'd have plenty of time later.

'What magic is this?' The knights stood just behind him, swords drawn. The Doctor turned, hands in the air.

'I come in peace,' he said, feeling foolish as their suspicious eyes worked him over. Had that line ever worked?

'Who the devil are you?' said the nearest knight.

'He stepped out of a box like the other one, and it disappeared, Henry,' said a second knight. 'He's another sorcerer.' The first knight looked back at him and squeezed the Doctor's arm.

'Feels real enough,' he said. 'Are you a sorcerer like the old man?'

'I'm an emissary,' the Doctor said. 'I want to apologise and settle this situation amicably.'

'Amicably, eh?' said Henry. 'Shall we be friends as we cut you to bits?'

They gripped their swords eagerly. The Doctor felt Henry's hand tighten on his arm. 'I promise I mean you no harm. Let me speak to your leader.'

'Or how about I take your message to him,' said Henry, 'along with your tongue.' He held his sword against the Doctor's cheek, the smells of blood and oil rising from it.

'If you kill me - if you kill the old man - you'll never get Lady Mary out of the box,' the Doctor said. 'It only opens for one of us.' Henry considered, allowing his sword to shift the tiniest bit away from the Doctor's face. 'If you find I'm lying, you can kill me later.'

Finally Henry nodded. 'George - tell Sir Edward this fool wishes to make a petition.' He breathed his night's fill of ale into the Doctor's face. 'I hope you are lying, emissary. Sir Edward takes great pleasure in silencing liars. With a sword through the guts.'

'I'll bear that in mind.' The Doctor turned towards the camp-site, but Henry shoved him to his knees just as a taller knight emerged from one of the tents.

The Doctor looked up, struggling to his feet. The tall knight met his gaze levelly. There was no trace of the lusty violence clear in the faces of the other men, but also no patience.

'Proceed with your petition, knave,' said Edward. 'I have many preparations to make for the battle tomorrow to rescue my sister from the magic that has captured her.'

'There need be no battle,' the Doctor said. 'I promise you, I can open the old man's box and bring her to you this very minute. This has been a misunderstanding. The old man never intended to keep her from you.'

'We heard this tale earlier today,' said Edward. 'Why should I believe you when I didn't believe him?'

'Send your strongest knight to escort me, to ensure that I don't try to escape. Or come with me yourself.' Though it would be best to avoid taking them inside the space-age interior of the TARDIS, he hoped that one man would be stunned to stillness while he found the girl. But there was a murmur among the men, and the Doctor realised his mistake.

'Take Sir Edward into the box, and that's the last we'll see of him!' said Henry. 'Was that your plan, sorcerer?'

'I'm not a sorcerer.' The Doctor watched Edward coolly consider Henry's suggestion. He may not be a patient man, the Doctor thought, but one doesn't lead men by making rashly formed decisions. Otherwise they would have stormed the castle already. 'I don't know what else to tell you to prove my honesty.'

'You'd best come up with something,' said Edward. 'Perhaps when he sees your body, the old man will surrender quickly to his fate.'

The Doctor struggled but Henry pushed him back to his knees, laughing. The Doctor wondered if his other selves were watching from the castle window. Would another of them attempt to startle the knights and give him a chance to escape? He listened for the cycling roar of another TARDIS about to materialise. But if they were watching, they'd have seen how quickly this went bad and would be trying to form a better plan. Or be leaving in their TARDISes, laws of time be damned.

He felt Henry's boot in his back and fell forward, the case hitting his side. Even if he'd been willing to use it, what good was a gold bow when a dozen men surrounded him? He felt the case bang into him again, as though attempting to answer the question. He felt its weight, thought of how the gold had gleamed at the card table. The jewels sparkling with life even in the dim light. Would the knights perceive its value as well?

'Henry, fetch my sword and we'll have done with this one,' Edward said.

'Wait!' With renewed strength the Doctor pushed himself up, toppling Henry to one side. 'I promise my story is true. I offer you this gift as proof of my good will.' Surprised at the strength of his voice, he handed the case to Edward, feeling utterly confident that he would accept it.

'More trickery?' Edward opened the case, his eyes glowing with the firelight reflected by the gold of the bow.

'It's solid gold, with priceless stones,' said the Doctor. 'Yours to keep for sparing my life and the old man's and allowing me to return the girl to you.' They were getting all the benefits - he'd be happy just to escape with his head on his shoulders.

'Your words do not persuade me,' said Edward, snapping the case closed. 'But your gold makes friends of us, for a moment.' He took the Doctor's arm and lifted him to his feet. 'Henry, take him to the box and keep him in your sight.'

'Thank you.' The Doctor pulled the key from the chain around his neck, feeling Henry's breath and sword at his back. He twisted the key in the lock and pushed the door open, feeling Henry follow him inside.

He squinted at the glare of the interior after the flickering darkness of the campfire. For a moment he took in the differences - he had changed this interior many times throughout his lives, as the mood took him, but this was the original, the console simpler, the roundels on the walls deeper. The room itself seemed somewhat larger, with an area off to one side containing a settee, on which a girl now lay.

Her eyes were closed tightly, as though if she didn't see the strange interior of the TARDIS it might not be there. The Doctor turned from the girl to Henry, who pressed his sword into the Doctor's back.

'What magic is this, sorcerer?' Henry asked, looking up at the unimaginably high ceiling, at the enormous space, trying to reconcile both with the box he'd helped drag from the forest. 'Your box is too small to contain all this.' As he spoke the girl opened her eyes, and at the sight of Henry she leapt to her feet.

'Sir Henry!' she said, grabbing his arm and distracting him from the Doctor. 'What is this terrible place?' Henry sheathed his sword and took her by the arm.

'Milady, your brother waits outside. Soon this will be over,' he said. His demeanour changed almost instantly upon speaking to her. These knights weren't unreasonable, they had only responded to their fear and confusion. Henry turned back to the Doctor with a quick nod. 'Lucky for you, Lady Mary appears to be unharmed. You've kept your word; Sir Edward will be as good as his.'

'Thank you,' said the Doctor. As they exited he heard a chorus of cheers outside. He watched the others surround Henry and Mary, clapping Henry on the back as though he'd rescued her with far more bravery than in reality.

The Doctor realised that no one was looking at him or the TARDIS. Fair enough, he'd kept his end of the bargain. Time to get this TARDIS back to the old man, and for them to leave before the crossed time-streams caused any damage to the continuum. He closed the doors and stared at the console. Where were the dematerialisation controls, again? He tried several buttons before the TARDIS vibrated into motion. On the scanner, the knights huddled around Henry and Mary, listening so intently to their tales that they didn't look up as the TARDIS faded from sight.

In the castle, the four other Doctors turned from the window and watched the TARDIS reappear. The old man was the first to reach the Doctor as he exited. 'Marvellous work, young man.'

'I'm sorry I had to give them your...' The Doctor trailed off. That was odd. Despite his sudden clarity when dealing with the knights, his memory was already hazy. 'What was it, again? A golden...?'

The old man frowned. 'A golden what?'

The Doctor's mind was blank. 'Whatever I gave them.'

'Well, no bother, the important thing is that you've brought back my TARDIS,' said the old man. Strange that he'd forgotten nearly as soon as he'd given it...

'Doctor, there you are!' The Doctor turned at Peri's voice, ready to give her a stern lecture on following orders. His mouth stopped halfway open... He'd seen her only half an hour earlier, but somehow she looked different.

'Peri, I thought I told you to stay in the TARDIS!' The jester had turned from the group and now had Peri by the arms, trying to lead her back into the hall.

'But Doctor...' Peri took them all in, her eyes lingering on the Doctor longer than the others. 'You? But you... changed.' She looked from the Doctor to the jester. 'To him.'

'Did I?' he said.

'It was right after –'

'Quiet, Peri,' the jester said. 'Don't say another word.' He pulled her out of the room, waving to the others with his free hand.

Change. While the Doctor knew he'd someday regenerate again, and that it had happened at least twice more already, he hadn't thought it would be so soon that Peri would be there to see it. Then again, did he ever know in advance?

'All good things...' the Doctor said, glancing at his former selves. Nothing to fear from a little change now and then.

With a history as vast and convoluted as that of astrology, it is no small wonder that some of the subtleties and primary attributes of this ancient science have been distorted or simply forgotten. The strangest of these is the legend of Capricorn, which stems from the myths of Babylon. The Capricorn was a deity called Ea who was half goat, half fish, a versatile and adaptable being, happy on land or in water. In the adjustment of the legend for Greek audiences, this beast became a fawn – half man, half goat – as represented by the god Pan. The Greek version seems to have been heavily inspired by the histories of Demnos, whose people, at least physically, matched this description. Whether or not the Greeks were in fact returning to the roots of the legend or simply welding on a different explanation remains to be seen, but certainly in neo-astrology it is the Greek iconography that has remained – the sea-goat being discarded as a less credible freak of nature.

Serious, sensible and effortlessly dull – these are some of the words that Capricorns might hear used to describe themselves, usually from those who have little or no understanding of the workings of the Capricorn mind. As hard-working as the Virgoan but without making so much of a dramatic production of it, the Capricorn is career-focused and often very single-minded. They are capable of blocking distractions from their minds while they deal with the task in hand. Yet they are also witty, mischievous, dare I say it – 'capricious' – while all the time having their feet firmly on the ground. As a counterbalance to this industrious, boring reputation, some Capricorns may feel the urge to play down the fact that they are, at heart, both sensitive and very wise. This is a temptation that must be resisted at all costs.

Kasterborus, *Our Destiny is in the Stars*

Kasterborus says...

If today is your birthday: *It's essential that you keep a clear head and avoid the usual excesses that social gatherings tend to put before you.*

'I Was A Monster!!!'

Joseph Lidster

And hence one master-passion in the breast,
Like Aaron's serpent, swallows up the rest.

Alexander Pope, *An Essay on Man* (1733)

Day One

Saturday morning. Pain and panic. So no change there.

Thoughts and memories all jumbled but starting to file themselves into...

Left the office and went to Maguires. Then on pub crawl around Dublin with workmates. Got very drunk and didn't know where I was. Went to one pub. Like Pizza Hut with a bar. Stood there. Took the mick out of the place with Billy. Thought that Gloria a 40-something colleague looked great. Oh God, did I say anything to her? Got chips. Went to a club. Danced. Drank. Danced. Drank. Danced. Blank.

Just woke up on the sofa fully dressed and still with my bag on my back. So confused. Hung-over. Grey. Did I say or do anything stupid or offensive last night? Remember me and Billy were loud but can't remember if I did anything bad myself. Could have offended half the people I work with. Was I just wrecked or did I make a real tit of myself? Darren lost his ticket and couldn't get his coat. Helped calm him down so can't have been that bad. But did get so lost and nearly die which is bad. But didn't fall asleep in a shop doorway which is good. Anyway, I digress. So woke up. Feeling bad. Had tea and toast. Had more tea and toast. Got quilt cos so cold. Have spent the last couple of hours watching *Student Bodies*, *USA High*, *Sabrina* and other teen-American crap. Now know the true meaning of friendship. 'I remember when you guys were all there for me when I was doing too much and was trying to organise my life with pills.' Flashback. So confused. Feel like the world has subtly changed. Things look the same but everything feels just that little bit out of phase. So I'm watching city guys from usa high student bodies being saved by the bell while having california dreams about sabrina the teenage witch, you know, learning about the true meaning of friendship and how you should follow your dreams – no wonder there are so many shootings in America – and Cody is in the comedy guidance counsellor's office. They're babbling on and I just don't give a toss. Cody comes through the door when suddenly – I'm there behind him. I'm on the TV. I'm just a character. God, I'm fu...

And then I remember. In. Glorious. Technicolor. Detail:

* * *

The music is hypnotic and euphoric with the lights swallowing all natural tones as everyone is bathed in a mysterious green and I'm dancing, I'm dancing because for that moment it is all I know. The vodka coursing through my body, its energy flowing through me like blood and I'm looking for my for my workmates, for my bestest friends in the whole world, but they're not here. Panic! Stumbling through the endless stream of office workers seeking respite from typing and emailing and spreadsheets and buses and bosses and colleagues – all looking good, all locked in their own paradises. A writhing mass of angels in suits.

Outside. The cold night air hitting me and my mind beginning to clear. Thoughts of angels and music and love and magic leaving my mind as the mundane realities of life beginning to slowly return to me. Still off my face but here outside it feels wrong not right. Starting to think about that thing I've got to do. That going home thing. Where am I though? Walking and becoming fascinated by the cool blue moonlight. Can still hear the music inside the club but now the tune of my feet crunching into the gravel beginning to take over. Looking up at the moonlit sky, clear and full of stars. Watching the tall trees sway gently in the breeze – the wind passing through their leaves like a thousand whispering souls. Unnerving. Must be outside of city. No walls. And now the staccato screech of the music is gone. I had been safe in my electric, false paradise and I'm not sure how to react in this new natural world. Decide to stop and have a smoke. Gliding over to a small stream and sitting down. Could have been there minutes, hours or years before remembering why I stopped.

Reaching into my pocket, taking the last cigarette from the packet and lighting it. The flame bursting into life, its warmth flashing across my face. Looking into the stream, my eyes staring into my reflection's. Inhaling, I see a whole other world reflected in the flowing water. This is the most peaceful, the most real moment in my life. Me, my reflection, the whispering trees, the bright silver moon and the glowing end of my cigarette. This is how I feel –

And I jump (fall?) off the sofa as I remember what happens next.

'Got a spare cig?'

My solitude being interrupted by a voice. Despite my state of mind, or, perhaps, because of it, I'm immediately noticing what's wrong. Can feel the presence of another person standing behind me. Wisps of red fabric darting in front of my eyes. There is someone standing behind me. Yet I know from the reflection in the water that there is no one standing behind me. Whoever this girl is, she isn't real.

And my head pounds as, collapsing on to the floor, I switch off the telly. Switch off the fake kids. Switch off the stars.

'It's my last one but you're welcome to share it.'

Am speaking which is good. She is sitting down beside me. Pale white skin, red hair, the same colour as her dress. A devil, tempting me. Beyond beautiful, she is breath-taking.

'What are you?' I'm asking as I pass her my half-smoked cigarette.

Taking the cigarette, placing it between her lips and smiling as she inhales. 'Why are you here?' she is asking.

A thousand answers rushing through my mind. Thoughts of offices and clubs and music and workmates.

'I'm lost!'

'We're all lost.' She is smiling as she leans towards me. Whispering into my ear: 'It's a defining characteristic of our generation.'

And I fall against the telly, my hand tingling against the static of the screen as I remember –

I'm not struggling while she is smiling. I'm not struggling as two of her teeth are growing smoothly down. I'm not struggling as she is placing one cool hand on the side of my neck and I'm not struggling as the teeth are piercing the skin of my neck and puncturing into my veins. Feeling the blood streaming out of my body and the natural paradise around me spinning out of all control. Pulling away from me and staring into my unfocused eyes she is telling me she can taste my ecstasy. She's going in for the kill but, now, hearing someone approaching, she is pulling back. She is running and I am falling. Falling backwards, a fall that is seeming to take for ever and ever. And my head is falling into the soft wet grass.

And my head rests against the hard, solid glass.

And I'm feeling the blood flowing from my neck.

And I feel hope, any hope that nothing happened, pour out of me.

And I'm lying on the grass and the world stops spinning and I feel myself changing. And I'm crying as I'm looking up at the stars.

And I turn to look at the screen but the stars are gone.

And I'm crawling to the flowing stream and I'm looking down. Drunk, tired and without hope, I don't make a sound at the fact that my reflection is gone. I am no longer part of the natural world.

And on the screen, the stars are gone. And there is just me. And I crave.

Day 12

> Murder always takes the victim by surprise. They waste precious moments of their final day applying lipstick or hair gel. They look at themselves in the mirror, not realising that they will never do this again. They grab their keys from their bedside tables and leave their homes just… just not knowing that they'll never see their bedside tables, bottles of cosmetics or their own reflections again. Sometimes, though, the murderer is as surprised as their victim. They don't realise, as they pick up their keys, that they're about to step on to an entirely new path.
>
> *The Capricorn Killer (*from the novel *I Was A Monster!* based on the 2003 film *I Was A Monster!* based on the posthumously-published diaries of the Capricorn Killer*)*

It's been some time since my rebirth. I have disappeared from society. I spend my days asleep and my nights in bars and clubs. Safe and anonymous. But still I crave. I desperately try to block out my hunger with alcohol and various drugs but, like my shadow, it's always there. And then…

The crushing reality of what I have become hits me as I leave the club. I run down a side-street, hardly noticing the lashing rain. I need peace away from the endless beat of the music but I cannot escape. In the distance, I hear a group of drunken tourists leaving an 'Oirish' bar and their laughter fuels my despair. I turn down a black, silent street and the darkness engulfs me. I lean against the soaking brick wall and the tears begin. The hunger inside of me is devastating and unending. I know what I must do. I've no choice. My body shakes with despair and fear. Can I? Is it possible for me…? But it's what I am. What I am become. My body shakes more violently now as the bloodlust consumes my entire body and I look to the stars and scream. An unending scream of rage and anger and hunger and… and someone is walking past me and –

he's wearing a Roy Keane football shirt and tracksuit bottoms. He's slightly taller than me and skinny. He's feverishly smoking a cigarette as he strides through the rain. He's looking at me through tiny black eyes. He's looking at me as I scream to the stars. He's looking at me –

'Freak,' he mutters as he sloshes through the rising puddles.

FREAK? My limbs are shaking uncontrollably as I launch myself at him. I jump on his back and we fall to the ground. FREAK? He's taller than me and been getting into fights since he was three but I am hungry. He's winded but rolls over to look at me. And I grab his ears and I pull his face towards me and I slam it into the –

his head… the rain pours… and his head jerks… and pours… and his head jerks back… and pours… and his head jerks back… and pours… and his head jerks backs and explodes into a red mist and the blood gushes out and there's a torrent of red flowing. So much red! And my face is streaming with red rain and I panic. Rising panic – I can't see! I hear a sound like crunching gravel and I wipe my eyes dry on the sleeve of my jacket and look down at my…

and his cigarette is extinguished in the puddle. The crimson puddle. The puddle that's becoming more blood than rain. FREAK? And I bring his head up once more and smash it down once more. More blood. I do this again and again and again and the back of his head just disappears. His left ear comes away from his face with a terrifying tearing sound and I'm left holding it. The fear in me is overtaken by something else as I, laughing hysterically, hold the ripped-off ear to my lips and whisper into it:

'Who's the FREAK now?'

Then the hunger takes over and I scramble over him and begin to drink. I crawl through the puddles drinking the diluted blood. And as I gorge, the rain and blood soak through my T-shirt and designer jeans but I just don't care. The blood fuels my body and soul and I feel alive. I have never felt so EUPHORIC as I do now – slurping the blood of my kill from the back of what used to be its head.

And now I am full. I reach into his pocket and pull out a soggy packet of Silk Cut. With difficulty I light one, inhale and then fall, that unending fall to the pavement, content.

Day 13

The following morning my heart hurts but I suspect it's more the cigarettes than guilt.

Day 19

I am not me. I stare into the mirror but there's no reflection. I no longer exist except on the TV. Watching the news.

'…has not been available for comment since escaping the *Big Brother* compound. In other news, police say that the murders of Lorcan Murphy, Sonia Fusciardi and Shane Fisher are, indeed, related. The three victims, all aged in their early twenties, were attacked and viciously murdered as they travelled home from the city centre at different times during the last week. The murderer, whom the press have dubbed the "Capricorn Killer" struck…'

The Capricorn Killer. That's who I am now.

I am not me. I am whatever you say I am and –

and his eyes stare at me dispassionately as I nail them into the wall – next to the photos of me in pubs and a joint-rolling mat. 'Why are you called the Capricorn Killer?' asks Kirsty from the photo in Mullingar. 'Yes, tell us!' asks the bar owner in San Antonio. 'Tell us!' ask my unblinking audience. 'Why shertainly!' I reply, putting on my best Sean Connery impression.

'The reason I am known as the Capricorn Killer is because of my goatee! I know – a crappy link, isn't it? But that's all you need these days. Any kind of connection and the public love it.'

And I explain to the wall of seeking eyes why I am now known as the Capricorn Killer instead of… well, you don't care who I was before, do you? Before, I was merely an office worker who did what all the other drones did. I was merely a non-speaking extra, a member of the public. Now, though… I am the Capricorn Killer because, although I can't see my own reflection in mirrors or windows or handrails on buses, for some reason I can be caught on camera. I suppose it's necessary otherwise I couldn't have the notoriety. I couldn't have the fame.

And the cameras show that I have a goatee.

Yep, it's as tenuous as that! Mad, isn't it? I have a goatee and that makes them connect me with goats and the devil and Capricorn and all that. Every killer needs an identity. According to the websites, the goat is an 'unclean beast, obsessed by the sex drive'. Apparently in tarot cards the goat appears on the Death card. And, supposedly, it represents a 'return to nature'. I suppose that bit could be true. 'Suppose there is something to it?' I ask Freda who stares at me from the office party photo. I have returned to nature. And yet, I yearn. I yearn more for the fame than I do for the blood. My hunger won't be sated merely by superficial earthly offerings such as blood – I crave the stars. I crave to be a star. And my new life, the life my red-haired devil gave me, gives me that chance!

Day 24

The WARMTH is leaving the publicist's body as I hug her tightly and I whisper into her ear:

'Did you know that when the police issue photo-fits, they give them mad staring eyes on purpose? Look at this terrifying inhuman monster! He could be coming for you next! So if you recognise him then you should shop him now! My picture didn't need touching up. My eyes really do stare like that! Look at them! LOOK AT THEM!'

But she ignores me because she's dead.

Day 27

You'd have thought the endless exposure to the results of my crimes would have depressed me. You'd have thought. Instead, it's had the opposite effect. Indeed, I now realise how it's all drama. The woman crying on TV pleading for her daughter's killer - her tear-stained face plastered over the front pages of every tabloid newspaper - could well have been an actress. If she was real, then surely she is enjoying this fame that I have given her! She will never be forgotten. My craving for fame and recognition is superseding my baser cravings. Frantically I type 'Capricorn Killer' into Google - twenty-three websites now mention me! Twenty-three - one for every year of my life! My face stares out from TV appeals and newspapers screaming out for the return of hanging. I decide to visit a chatroom but cannot use the nickname 'Capricorn Killer' as someone else has taken it. Nor can I use 'Capricorn2002', 'ZodiacKiller' or even 'DublinPsycho2002'. I have fans! But... but it's not enough. There are still people not talking about me. The stars on *Big Brother* have now gone but have been replaced by others. And the people I really want to notice me, the people who really matter, my peers, the drinking, working, Generation X, Y or Z or whatever we are... they still haven't noticed me. Have my murders stopped them going out? Do they huddle under electric lasers muttering my name? Do they heck as like. The rest of society has stopped but my peers are too drunk on spreadsheets, Guinness, Aftershock and the lap-dancers on Leeson Street to even notice me.

To reach them I need to be postmodern. I need to be ironic. For my fame to be complete I need to be more than a killer - I need to be a phenomenon. I need to be worthy of -

Day 32

'I WAS A MONSTER!' A TV MOVIE STARRING LEONARDO DI CAPRIO

Scene Eleven: A montage of newspaper clippings trailing the rise of the Capricorn Killer set to dance music which merges into...

Scene Twelve: Int. A trendy bar in the Temple Bar area of Dublin. The bar is crowded with beautiful people. The Capricorn Killer is standing at the bar, morosely sipping from a glass of whiskey (no ice!) and watching a group of twenty-somethings. Lots of 'NYPD Blue' camerawork and quick editing to appeal to the MTV generation

SARAH, 27, IS CHATTING TO HER FRIENDS. AS WE WATCH HER TALK, A MEMBER OF THE PUBLIC COMES OVER TO HER TABLE AND ASKS HER TO SIGN A BEER-MAT. SHE DOES THIS WITH A GRACIOUS SMILE AND THEN TURNS BACK TO HER FRIENDS. SHE'S TELLING THEM ABOUT HER NEW STORYLINE IN 'GIRLS ABOUT TOWN'. HER FRIENDS ARE NEVER MENTIONED BY NAME BUT GIRL#1 IS ASIAN AND GIRL#2 IS IN A WHEELCHAIR.

SARAH: So he's going to be my long-lost brother!

GIRL #1: No way!

SARAH: Yes way! How mad is that! It'll make a change. All I've been doing so far this series is Bridget Jones scenes in bars. They're finally giving me something I can get my teeth into.

GIRL #2: (GUSHES) Well done, Sarah!

(THE OTHERS ALL WISH SARAH WELL)

GIRL #2: So you'll be a genuine celebrity now!

GAY GUY: You could be on that programme!

GIRL #1: (LAUGHING) Everyone's talking about it!

GIRL #2: Isn't that *EastEnders*?

SARAH LOOKS DISHEARTENED THAT THE CONVERSATION HAS ALREADY MOVED AWAY FROM HER AS THE OTHERS LAUGH. SHE TAKES A SIP FROM HER VODKA. THIS IS THEN INTERCUT WITH A SHOT OF THE CAPRICORN KILLER SIPPING HIS WHISKEY TO EMPHASISE THEIR FUTURE CONNECTION. AT THIS POINT WE NOTICE THAT SARAH IS WEARING A RED TOP – SHE IS TO BE A VICTIM!!! VERY THOMAS HARDY!

GAY GUY: Isn't that *Big Brother* contestant going to be on *EastEnders*?

SARAH: Which one? The gay one?

GIRL #2: No. He's on that thing that Ant and Dec used to do.

GIRL #1: What? *Pop Idol*?

GAY GUY: I thought they presented *I'm a Celebrity... Get Me Out of Here!*

GIRL #1: Yeah, but before that.

SARAH: Oh, *Popstars*? So they gave us Hear'Say then?

THEY ALL LAUGH. A BITTER, CONTEMPTUOUS LAUGH! THEY KNOW THEY ARE BETTER THAN A MANUFACTURED BAND!

GIRL #2: One of them's just married that kid from *EastEnders*!

GIRL #1: What? The one from *Big Brother*?

GIRL #2: No. Wotsisface!

SARAH: So is it Hear'Say that have that 'sexy' song they were singing in *Big Brother*?

THEY ALL START THRUSTING THEIR HIPS AND GROANING 'SEXY!' A LA LIBERTY X.

SARAH: You know who I think is sexy?

GIRL #1: Ant? Brian? Nick? Tony Blackburn? Dec? Mel from *Big Brother*? Mel from *EastEnders*?

THEY ALL LAUGH.

SARAH: No! (SHE LEANS FORWARD, HER HAIR NEARLY CATCHING IN THE CANDLE FLAME – REMEMBER THIS IS ALL FROM THE CAPRICORN KILLER'S POV!) The Capricorn Killer!

GIRL #1, GIRL #2, GAY GUY: What???

CAPRICORN KILLER V/O (THINK EDWARD NORTON IN *FIGHT CLUB*): My heart is pounding! I've made it! Finally, someone – someone worthy – is talking about me!

SARAH: It's his eyes!

CAPRICORN KILLER V/O: And I'm starting to realise what I am and what I must do! These people talking have just summed up all there was to Summer 2002. But… but who's going to remember any of this in a few years' time? I can't even remember who won last year's *Big Brother*. The fame that they're talking about is fleeting which means the reality that they've gained is - pure and simple - temporary! And I'm just a footnote at the end of their conversation! I don't want that! If my fame is immortal then my reality will also be immortal. If anyone ever makes a movie of my life then this whole conversation will be incomprehensible because, in a few years time, no one will know who these people were. I don't want that! I can't be that!

SARAH LEAVES THE BAR AND THE CAPRICORN KILLER FOLLOWS.

CAPRICORN KILLER V/O: And as I watch her enter the nightclub, I realise the two things that I must do. I need to move from B-list to A-list celebrity-ville. To do this I'll have to remove one of the stars and take their place. The second thing I must do is to stop feeling the emotions, to stop seeing this as life and to start seeing it as it is - to start seeing it as everything is - a beautifully directed drama!

Scene Thirteen: Int. A trendy nightclub. The music and lights surround The Capricorn Killer as he enters – emphasising his role as our 'hero'. Just outside the club we hear a church bell chime midnight and so we move on to:

Day 33

As I step into the club I feel like I'm entering a film.

The beat of Amber's *Sexual* vibrates across the crowd - each individual lost in their own Ecstasy-fuelled paradise. As sweat pours down their faces, I long to be part of them. My body knows what to do as I unconsciously move my arms into the air. My legs are fluid, moving up and down and back and forth to the beat of the tune. We all brush against each other, aware of the presence of these beautiful others but not recognising them as people. As a silent group, we move as one. And there she is. Sarah, a celebrity. Someone else important. Her long blonde hair drenched with sweat, she appears as if she'll never leave her world. The smile on her face is the most beautiful thing I've ever seen. Suddenly, the tune changes, an energetic, screaming, staccato tune, electronic and yet pure, flies over our heads in perfect harmony with pulsing green lasers. As one, we explode. Every individual screams into action, our arms punching out and high - our fingers slicing through the lasers. Our smiles grow wider as we understand.

I move through these others and towards the blonde girl with the beautiful smile. She stares into my eyes and invites me to share in her world. Rhythmically, she creates a space for me and our actions become one. Our euphoric ecstasy flows like waves across those nearest to us as they understand that two kindred souls have, at last, found each other.

Although we don't touch each other, mentally we are as one. The screaming, staccato tune sounds once more and we fly. Her black, flowing top flaps at an impossible speed as she violently shakes her body from side to side. She looks into my eyes, begging me, pleading with me to join her physically as well as mentally. I move towards her, her face now lit purely by the pulsing green lasers. I reach out and my hand holds the back of her neck - electric. She begs me once more with her eyes and my lips move towards hers. Flash of green.

'Now,' she whispers.

My mouth moves from hers and towards her neck. Flash of green. She makes no sound as my teeth pierce her porcelain white - flash of green - neck. Her warm blood - red, black under the green - flows into my greedy mouth and I feed. Her life becomes mine as I drink and drink. Flash of green. She stops moving and I finish. I lay her beautiful, life-giving body down next to a discarded water bottle and, with one last glance at her unending eternal smile, I begin to slide rhythmically once more through the beautiful people.

As I leave the dance floor, someone violently interrupts our paradise with a scream. The atmosphere disappears as the individuals return from their heavens. Their beauty disappears, their clothes become cheap and the music stops. I ignore them all and push through the main doors into the biting cold wind as the screams intensify.

Day 35

And the papers have a field day. 'TV DRAMA STAR LATEST VICTIM OF SERIAL KILLER!'

It's happened! I'M THERE!

Day 36 in the Big Brother House

And I'm in a pub that looks like Pizza Hut with a bar... I WEAR MY SUNGLASSES AT NIGHT!

Day 38 (SCENE 433: A NIGHTCLUB)

SMILING. CAN'T STOP SMILING. LIFE SO HAPPY. LOVE. LOVE LIFE. BEAT GETTING FASTER. CAN'T STOP MOVING. NOW JUST HARMONY. NO BEAT. MELODY. STOP MOVING. SMILE TO THE SKY. ALL STAND STILL. BEAUTIFUL. NEVER BEEN SUCH HARMONY IN ALL HISTORY. WANT TO KISS EVERYONE. THEY WANT TO KISS ME. BREATHE IN. BREATHE OUT.

AND THE VOICE STARTS. TELLING US HE IS GOD. HE SPEAKS OVER THE MUSIC AND WE LISTEN. AND HE STOPS. AND THE DRUMS START. POUNDING DRUMS. BEATING DRUMS. AND WE DANCE!

And that night I have a dream but it ain't no John Lennon fluffy-bunny, cotton-wool dream:

And I'm flying. Flying high above all their little soap-opera stories of unplanned pregnancies and long-lost brothers. And there's a girl and she's pointing at me. 'What's that?' she asks the angel. 'Can't you see it? Coming towards us!' She doesn't know what I am. She doesn't know where she is but I do. A place where God and music and reality and dreams are swirling around in a maelstrom of confusion and unreality. I let myself fall away from them and suddenly - suddenly I hear the audience clapping and laughing. And I can see them! Amongst the thousands of grinning faces with staring eyes, I can see Mummy and Daddy. Their faces are distorted as they eat buttered crumpets and applaud the events they're watching. I try to fly towards them. Try to be with them once more but there's something between us. I'm trapped in a glass cage! And as the laughter - the unstopping, mocking laughter - continues I hammer on the glass. Won't Mummy and Daddy rescue me? Can't anyone save me? And in my panic I turn the world into what I want it to be. The towers are crashing down over and over again - the images that will be forever real and never forgotten. And I'm trapped here in the glass cage and I'm hammering on the glass but Mummy reaches towards me and switches over and I

wake up.

Day 44

and my skin smells like freshly baked bread. Homely. As I sit there, wrapped tightly in the dressing-gown Mummy got me last Christmas, I realise something. Sitting here in the semi-DARKness, I realise I am me. There will never be another me. I will never have another chance at LIFE. Every breath

I take, every thought I make - each one is unique to me. There are millions and millions of individuals in this world. I always used to hate it when someone DIED and someone else would say 'Makes you think, doesn't it? Could have been you or me!' Yeah, but what about the poor sod who's died? Their memories and thoughts are all gone for ever. Their consciousness has been switched off, SHUTDOWN. They can leave their belongings, their photos, toiletries and clothes but who really knows what was happening in their mind? Who really knows who they were? And now, they're gone. That person, that individual is gone. Only to be remembered in photos, fading memories and on websites. But what were they thinking as they last ran that hair gel through their hair? Were they thinking about shopping, dinner, sex, a film, *Big Brother*, their career, killing, life, death, babies...? We'll never know.

I need the FAME. I know I'll be gone soon. My Saviour will arrive and take me from this path. Well, I say bring on the Ferryman. COME AND GET ME! Just let me leave my mark on the world first. The dream showed me my innermost desire. I want - no, I need - to be 9/11 not *Big Brother*. I want to... I don't know what I want but I want something!

What do I want? I ask the eyes.

Day 46

And on the bus, a group of noisy clubbers LAUGH. Their shrill giggling piercing my mind, I turn with a friendly grin and the blood flows.

Day 49

iS ThiS reAl??

Day 50

i take the eyes off the wall cos i is sick of em staring at me everyone is staring at me

i don't understand what everyone wants none of it is real any more

they are all fake

Day 52

Sober again. But was it ever real? Was any of it? Even when I used to work in the office - it's like I was pretending. I didn't really have the high-powered job in THE CITY – I was acting. The office workers – the suited angels in the clubs of Dublin – weren't really office workers – they'd just seen all the TV dramas telling them how office workers were supposed to act. We're part of the 'work hard, play hard' generation so that's how we must act. And 'act' is the right word. Because it's all an act. And we all try to make it real! I'm starting to understand now. We praise a TV drama if it's gritty and realistic and rappers are singing about life on the streets and keeping it real and we all have endless phone numbers and email addresses as if we are trying to emphasise that we are real and that we are here and we all want to be famous because none of it's real any more.

TO MAKE OURSELVES FEEL REAL WE HAVE TO ACT LIKE THEY TELL US! BUT IT'S NOT ENOUGH! WELL, I WON'T DO IT ANY MORE! I'M GOING TO... I'M GOING TO... I'M...

drunk. I am lost. I am in the club. I am lost *(...defining characteristic...)*. Mummy and Daddy didn't come looking for me on the other side of the screen. I think they were real.

BANG a drum sounds. The light flashes. They all smiling false smiles. They not real as they not on TV. I will make them real. I will give them fame. I will bring them to my side of the glass. And then –

THE MUSIC... THE MUSIC GETS HIGHER AND HIGHER. THE STACCATO, PULSING RHYTHM NOW A HIGH-PITCHED SCREECH. THE EXTRAS ARE GRINNING MANICALLY AND DANCING FRANTICALLY.

But still they talk. Endless talk of cappuccinos and Beckham and *Big Brother* and manufactured bands but THEY are all manufactured. I'm on the right side of the screen and I will bring them to reality. I will –

BANG – A DRUM SOUNDS. THE CRIMSON LIGHT FLASHES. SMILING FALSE SMILES.

They're yearning to be with me, to be part of it. I will make them real! Together we'll all be immortal!

BANG – A DRUM SOUNDS. THE CRIMSON LIGHT FLASHES. SMILING FALSE SMILES.

But before I can, everything goes

DARK

BANG
RED LIGHT
I SEE DEAD PEOPLE
DARK
BANG
LIGHT
THE HUNDREDS OF FACES OF MY VICTIMS-TO-BE STARING OUT OF THE FRONT PAGES
DARK
BANG
LIGHT
WE'LL ALL BE REAL!
DARK
BANG
LIGHT
NOT *BIG BROTHER* REAL! NOT FAKE CELEBRITY REAL! WE'RE TALKING WASHINGTON SNIPER REAL! IT'S ALL THERE - IN THE GLASS CAGE!

DARK BANG LIGHT GRINS FASTER FASTER IMPOSSIBLE PANIC PANIC PANIC PANIC ABOUT TO EXPLODE DARKBANGLIGHT TEETH DARKBANGLIGHT CAMERAS DARKBANGLIGHT ACTION DARKBANGLIGHT HUNGER DARKBANGLIGHT STROBE FASTER FASTER HEART POUNDS MUST DARKBANGLIGHT DARKBANGLIGHT DANCE MUST DARKBANGLIGHT FEED.

MUST FEED! AND MY ARMS ARE RAISING ABOVE MY HEAD AND THE SHRIEK IS STARTING TO BUILD UP INSIDE OF ME AND THE MUSIC AND THE LIGHTS AND I'M ABOUT TO STRIKE WHEN

she appears

In an electric-blue halo, she stands. My angel!

'Come with me!' she mouths silently as the music returns and the crowds go wild. My breathing returns to normal and the sweat begins to cool.

I feel calm as I approach her. She is beautiful. Really beautiful. Small, she should be helpless but it's as if she is controlling the crowd with her smile as they part like the Red Sea and they let me through. The violins start to play as I reach her and I look down at my Saviour.

And she speaks. 'Come with me?' she asks - no commands! - with a cultured, unraised voice. I feel all my fame, my reality evaporate away as I follow her through a door I never knew existed.

As we walk down a grey, featureless corridor I ask her her name.

'Romana,' she replies.

Romana. Not Mel or Tracey or Kylie or any of those other real media names – it's different. Unique. Unreal. But is she real?

She doesn't ask me my name but tells me she will help me. I follow her as she glides down the bland corridor and then she stops and turns to me. She looks up at me and says:

'I know what you are.'

SHE KNOWS WHAT I AM! I don't know what I am but she does!

'Am I real?' I ask her.

'Are any of us?'

I look at her. She doesn't look real. Her clothes, her hair, her features... they don't... they don't... there's something... she isn't behaving like anyone else! She doesn't look the same! She isn't a reflection of what's on the telly.

She isn't trying to be real.

And then HE appears. A real devil. Tall, dressed entirely in red and carrying a long walking-stick. He smiles, revealing thousands of teeth.

'Hello,' he says calmly.

'What am I?'

'Ah, well, this could be rather awkward,' he says, acting shy. 'You see –'

I interrupt him. 'This isn't real!'

He smiles at me. 'Well of course it isn't. You think we don't know what we are? We know what we are, don't we Romana?'

'Yes, Doctor' she replies.

'Yes Doctor!' he shouts back before looking at me. 'Why are you doing it?'

I reply. 'They're all trying to act real! Trying to act like they're on the other side of the screen! But they're not and I am! I'm trapped here and I want to give them all what they want! I am real now. I am famous! I want them to be with me!'

My voice is rising as I start to panic once more. I don't understand what these two are. They're not trying to be real. They're not old or young or cool or uncool. They're not lawyers or the police or hospital workers. They're unique and original and I don't understand what they are!

The panic in me intensifies and I run at the man. He trips me easily, too easily and I fall the unending fall to the concrete.

He stands over me, tall and blocking the light. He looks down at me and smiles a toothy grin that screams out confidence, arrogance and self-belief. The jealousy bites into me as I yearn for that belief in myself.

I can still hear the music but the beat has stopped. Mourning violins wail a sad tune.

He raises the walking stick above my chest.

'You said you could help me?' I plead.

'I'm afraid someone brought you into our world. This is the only help we can give you,' he replies. 'Now hold still. This won't hurt a bit.'

('The Capricorn Killer, please leave the Big Brother House')

He plunges the stick through my chest and with the sound of smashing glass my ribs implode. He lied about it not hurting. But I suppose he had to, for the cameras. A tear rolls down my cheek. By the time it reaches my chin, my body has dissolved into ash. I am no longer real or unreal. I just am. And as the man starts to walk away, I feel myself rising into the air and then through into the wall. As he strides away, he shouts at Romana without looking back.

'I'm hungry, Romana. Are you hungry?'

She calls back, 'Famished, Doctor.'

'Fancy a steak? I know this wonderful little restaurant...'

And his voice trails off as he strides down the corridor, his work done. Romana starts to chase after him but then stops and turns to the pile of dust. The expression on her face changes and her widening eyes suddenly express raw emotion.

'Sorry,' she whispers before chasing after my killer.

And as I stare through the grey, glass wall I think of my Mummy. The mad music begins to play and the credits begin to roll and I, I am listed as 'Monster'. No name. No recognition. Was I ever real? Will I be remembered? A tear would fall if

The Aquarian legend is arguably the most difficult to pin down. For the Babylonians, the 'water bearer' was the bringer of life and so was the most revered of all the gods. Greek mythology is less straightforward. Was he Zeus himself, the god of water and of storms? Or was he Deucelion – with his wife Pyrrha the only survivors of the flood sent by Zeus to wipe evil and corruption from the planet? Once the waters had subsided, they were given the job of bringing life back to the world; Deucelion was, therefore, the 'water *bearer*' as both a survivor and a life-giver (this legend reappears in Judaeo-Christian mythology in the form of Noah and his ark). Or maybe Aquarius was Ganymede, the son of Troy, who Zeus appeared to in the form of an eagle and took to Olympus to be his wine-pourer and lover? Certainly, many zodiacs from the first millennium depict Aquarius as an eagle.

Aquarians are enigmatic, independent and eccentric. They are intellectual, forever thinking out every possibility in search of a better life, and are deeply sensitive and caring for those around them. Like the Gemini though, they hide their feelings behind a mask – in Aquarius's case, a mask that often makes them appear cold or distant. They possess a near-infallible judgement and an ability to juggle many tasks at once. This can, however, make them stubborn as they are loathe to admit the possibility that they might be wrong. Idealists at heart, they are willing to participate in – even lead – any revolution... just so long as it runs their way.

With all these complex and seemingly conflicting qualities it is no wonder the Aquarian is so misunderstood. Even their sign, the water-bearer – often depicted as a jug of flowing water – is frequently mistaken for a water sign when in fact it is a sign of air. But then, Aquarians are used to being seen as something they are not, content to allow others to grab the glory so long as their own uniqueness is recognised...

Kasterborus, *Our Destiny is in the Stars*

Kasterborus says...

If today is your birthday: *You have been in ultra-idealistic mode for some time now. But an intense period is fast approaching. Be prepared!*

The Invertebrates of Doom

Andrew Collins

The noises coming from up ahead were not encouraging. Laura Ainsell spat out a mouthful of brackish water and cursed under her breath as she wearily pulled herself through another tight, sightless corridor of rock. Corners and elbows of spiteful stone bit into her hands and snagged her overalls, while fingers of freezing water insinuated themselves down her neck and into her boots. She was cold, damp, and thoroughly pissed off. Flat on her back, three-quarters submerged, and blindly glaring in increasing frustration at the unseeable rocky ceiling just inches from her nose, Laura tried very hard to remember that she was meant to be enjoying herself. The joyful whoops of her companions were really not helping her mood.

Having a properly functioning torch might have helped. Was that so much to ask? She was going to kill Brian when they got back home. Although, come to think of it, why wait until they got back to the halls of residence when she could easily murder the sod down here and just dump his body in some dank and dripping cave? Grunting crossly, she forced herself forward another couple of inches and slowly began to sense a change in her environment.

The air - for so long icy but stale - seemed to prickle more on her exposed skin. Around her, the muffled cries of her friends filled out and became more resonant. The iron smell of the water lessened in its intensity, and comets of light darted around a chamber of rough, glistening rock. Blinking hard to regain her vision, Laura scrabbled at the lip of the tunnel from which she had emerged legs first, and shakily pulled herself to her feet, breathing in shallow gulps of relief.

'Yes! Oh, look at this place. Oh, yes!' Brian's excited baritone echoed round the jagged walls. Laura's eyes were slowly adjusting, and she fixed on one of the torch beams as it danced over stalactites, ledges and clefts. The ceaseless swirl of lights after such complete darkness was dizzying. Her tone was withering when she spoke.

'Congratulations. You've found a cave.'

'A cavern.'

'Right. Please yourself,' she said. Her disorientation was fading as she clicked into familiar patterns. 'Pedantic git.'

The space really was quite impressive. A huge natural auditorium with uneven sloping floor and the persistent sound of water droplets, the place seemed alive with the flickering shadows cast by the narrow torchlight. As she squished forward, Laura craned her neck to peer at the distant ceiling.

'What's that?' The awe in the voice made her turn. The speaker was Jason, a stocky shaven-headed daredevil from the Sports Science department. He was outlined against a ragged arch, and his torch beam was playing on a lumpy shape apparently jammed in a crevice. Seven pairs of booted feet made their way unevenly towards him across the treacherous floor.

'What is it?' There were mystified murmurs of confusion and surprise. The object was about the size of a lectern. Apparently made of stone, it was a dark grey in colour, and obviously carved or manufactured by precise tools because - on closer inspection - its swollen contours were smooth and delicate in detail. The solid, rounded trunk sprouted at the top like a mushroom. The head was panelled and five-sided, studded with whorls and fine ridges. As their torches explored the object's surface, intricate patterns were revealed.

Intrigued, Laura approached the object. Her fingertips brushed over its surface and she felt her fine wrist hairs prickle.

It began to glow.

The light was a dull orange, outlining the carvings on the surface as if a fire smouldered within. Laura found herself unwilling to take her hand away. The surface was warm. She felt her companions joining her around the object in fascination, their belt tools clinking. The glow cast eerie shadows over their faces in the gloom of the cave. Water dripped in the background.

It was only when she found herself unable to remove her hand that she realised how suddenly tired she was. And only when the monstrous shape began to appear in the air above the pedestal that she started to scream.

Clamping his straw hat to his head with one hand, the Doctor held his furled brolly straight out in front of him and squinted. 'Hmm, yes... Somewhere in this direction, I should think.'

Mel trotted gamely after him as he strode purposefully along the cracked flagstones. 'Exactly what are we looking for, Doctor?'

'We'll know when we find it, Mel.'

'Very helpful.'

'Think of it as a game,' he suggested, lifting his hat and turning in a slow circle. 'What could possibly cut across the vortex and knock us so far off course?' His paisley scarf flapped in the breeze.

Melanie eyed the heavy clouds with hostility. 'I'm just not really fond of drizzle. It makes my hair frizz.'

'Don't let it dampen your spirits,' he said innocently, replacing his hat.

She looked hard at him for a moment. 'Are you making fun of me?'

'Wouldn't dream of it, Mel.' The Doctor flashed her that irresistibly mischievous, snaggle-toothed smile. 'This way, I think.'

The TARDIS had materialised in a concrete wasteland of low post-war buildings and occasional scrubby trees. Apparently it was England, 1978. Clearly this was a secure site of some sort, as Mel had spotted barbed-wire fences and heard the distant bark of what could only be a guard dog. She also had an uneasy feeling they were being watched, or if not, that it was only a matter of time before they were noticed and chaos ensued. Drab birds flapped listlessly in the dull grey sky.

'Ah-ha! I knew it.' The Doctor spun round. Now he was clutching a small bleeping device studded with flickering red lights on extendable arms, and little spinning dials. The brolly was hooked over his arm. 'Something's up,' he pronounced solemnly. 'I can feel it in my water.'

'Really.' Mel pouted, raised an eyebrow, then tossed her red curls. She hated it when he looked at her this expectantly. With a small sigh, she caved in. 'All right Doctor, I'll bite. What's the problem?'

The Doctor knitted his brows and peered owlishly at the gadget. 'There's an anomalous concentration of artron energy from somewhere in this vicinity.'

'An anomalous...' Mel broke off and gave her companion a suspicious look. 'You're making that up, aren't you?!' She couldn't keep the laugh out of her voice.

'Anomalous concentrations of artron energy are nothing to joke about, Mel,' the Doctor scolded, rolling his r's. He turned ninety degrees and waggled the little device, which burped. He curiously eyed a flat-roofed, single-storey building up ahead. 'It can mean only one thing.'

Oh dear. She didn't like where this was heading. 'And what's that, Doctor?'

'Trouble.'

Dr Leech stooped over the artefact and peered at its etched and luminous surface in befuddlement. His assistant, a small pretty Asian girl in a lab coat, watched him. Her face was carefully neutral.

Some people possess a natural composure, an in-built unflappability. Dr Leech was not among their number. He had the harassed look of an underdog, and his failure to make any progress with this strange discovery was weighing heavily upon his narrow shoulders. He ran bony fingers through his thinning white hair. Tests had proved that the thing was many thousands of years old, but as to precisely what it was, its function, or the meaning of the delicate inscriptions, Leech was stumped. It was also very unsettling; the way it glowed. And the occasional low creaking noises it emitted - yes, he was sure it made noises.

'Shall we take a break, Dr Leech? You're looking tired.' Ly's face above the pristine white coat wore an expression of concern. Leech shook himself. He'd forgotten the girl was there.

'Um, yes,' he floundered. 'Well, perhaps a glass of water.'

'Good idea. I'm getting some coffee.' Ly turned on her heel and headed for the tiny kitchen.

Rubbing his face, Leech tried to focus again. The creeping tiredness was really not helping. It seemed he was permanently tired recently. Of course, he also had a sneaking suspicion what was causing the weariness, particularly since he had visited the medical wing and seen the state of the poor devils who'd brought the artefact to the surface. It was clear they were suffering more than just exhaustion from a strenuous caving experience. And it was obvious that others thought the same thing, otherwise they would be in a regular hospital.

Something bumped into his elbow and he turned blearily. 'Here's your water,' Ly said, handing him a tumbler.

A light rain rattled on the window. The lamps in the room flickered.

Huddled beneath the pattering brolly, arm in arm with her companion, Mel suddenly stiffened. 'Doctor, I hate to say this, but I think we've been spotted.'

'Keep walking, Mel.'

'They don't look too pleased to see us.' Off to the left, one of the uniformed men had started walking towards them. The other was speaking rapidly into his walkie-talkie.

'Not far now,' the Doctor said breezily.

'They're coming after us, Doctor!'

'Keep walking, Mel. Just keep walking.' The machine in his hand squeaked.

The water was clear and cold. Leech hadn't realised how thirsty he was.

'What the hell?' he yelled as the small energetic figure burst into the room, shaking off his umbrella. The odd-looking device in the newcomer's hands began to squawk raucously. 'This is a secure installation! What are you doing here?'

'Ah, here we are, Mel. The source of the problem.' This was directed to a second stranger in a pink trouser suit who had bounced into the lab. The young lady seemed the plucky and enthusiastic type, though right now she was soggily subdued. 'Hello, I'm the Doctor. This is Mel.' The man's smile flicked on and off like a light bulb as his attention shifted to the mysterious object in the centre of the room.

'What is the meaning of this intrusion?' Leech faltered as the glow from the stonelike artefact intensified, a sudden organic clicking noise emanating from it. 'It's never done that before.'

The small man approached it. He gazed in fascination at the carvings, and ran his fingers delicately over them. Then he started checking details and comparing them to the burbling readouts on his handheld device. His forehead crinkled. 'Aquatic?' he mumbled. The artefact made a further noise. It sounded like whale song and bubbles, the deep surge of currents below the waves. The lights dimmed.

'Yes,' he crooned, 'yes, this is the source, but the signal... the intensity. It's so powerful.' His face cleared with wonder and admiration. 'Of course! It's two-way. And it's drawing energy from its environment to boost the carrier wave!'

'I do apologise for my friend,' said the red-haired stranger, 'he gets like this sometimes.'

To Leech's embarrassment, it was his assistant who responded first. She turned to Melanie. 'I'm Ly. This is Dr Leech, the project's chief scientist.'

'Ah. Dr Leech, so nice to meet you. We're - um - from the Ministry.' The Doctor turned and grinned at Ly. 'Where did you acquire this object?'

Clearing his throat and striding forward, Leech tried to assert his authority. 'It was retrieved by potholers, a party of eight from the local university with which we are associated.' He glanced over at Ly who inclined her head in acknowledgement. 'It must have lain in those caves for thousands of years.' Hang on, he'd just given this stranger classified information. Damn.

'Fascinating,' said the Doctor, 'quite fascinating. Carried there no doubt by the flow of an underground river. It's alien, of course.' The air pressure in the room seemed to be changing, as if they were in a dipping aircraft or a diving submarine.

At that moment, the security guards burst through the door. Lumbering across the room, they grabbed the diminutive Doctor beneath the armpits and started to manhandle him away. 'Tell me,' he said, tripping a guard with his brolly and scampering back to the artefact, 'have you translated any of these inscriptions yet?'

There was the smell of ozone in the room. Mel hadn't noticed it before, but now it was difficult to ignore. Her hair was getting frizzy too as if there was a build-up of static.

'Well no, but we're working on it,' Leech replied, 'and some of the drawings are anatomically exact...'

'Show me.' The Doctor pulled him over. A guard made a grab for the Doctor and Leech waved the man away.

'Images and sounds from another world...' His wistful expression abruptly crumpled in worry. 'Oh no...' The whistling in Mel's ears increased. She swallowed, trying to release the pressure. There was a background noise... a whooshing sound like an untuned radio. It was getting louder. A chill snaked down her spine.

The light was changing as if a cloud was smothering the sun. Shadows were being cast at strange, unnatural angles.

'Transference beam...' said the Doctor, 'a homing signal and transference beam.' He became suddenly animated. 'Mel, Ly, what do these pictures remind you of?' The two women slid over to the artefact and looked where he was pointing. They saw a meticulously rendered image, a line drawing of a domed creature.

The security guards, relieved of their purpose, were standing at the door, shuffling their feet. The background whine was becoming unbearable. As she identified the itching familiarity of the carved picture, Melanie Bush looked slowly up at the Doctor, her mouth open in astonishment. The Doctor was nodding darkly.

'Medusoid coelenterates,' he breathed.

Mel's ears popped.

There was a sudden impact on the flat roof. She gasped. Then something else thudded into the ground outside, followed by another thud, and another.

Everyone in the room jumped as an object hit the windowpane hard and slid down it. There was a fleeting impression of something soft, damp, and very squishy. It left greasy smears down the outside of the glass. The noise on the roof became a steady drumming.

Moving to the window, they looked out on to the chaotic scene.

'Doctor, I never thought I'd say this, but... it's raining jellyfish!' Mel's eyes were wide.

Jellyfish. There were thousands of them, falling from the sky and slamming down to earth. The floor outside already looked like a beach after a stormy high tide. Glistening invertebrate bodies were everywhere, some twitching. Many had disintegrated from the devastating force of hitting the ground, and the concrete was slick with guts, tentacles, and sticky fluids. More of the creatures rained down.

'I've heard of it raining fishes or frogs,' began Mel.

'Or cats and dogs,' offered Leech, immediately wishing he hadn't. The Doctor's scowl did not make him feel big or clever.

'Everyone, wait here,' the Doctor snapped, and stormed towards the door.

'But Doctor...' Ly began.

'And don't touch the artefact!' The door slammed behind him.

The Doctor slipped and skidded on the uneven, treacherous surface. The air was heavy with a thunderstorm smell, and soft things squelched beneath his feet. The noise was incredible. He leant heavily on his umbrella for balance as he stumbled a few more feet into the open, slimy wet bodies slamming down all around him. He looked up, and almost fell over.

Filling the sky above him was an immense spaceship.

The craft was huge. Viewed through the soaking rain of jellyfish, the metallic grey underside steamed with water vapour. He could make out ducts and hatches and the glow of five engines, dotted equidistantly around its disc-shaped rim. The jellyfish were raining down from the ship.

The Doctor steadied himself, then bellowed into the storm. 'What do you want from us? Who are you and what do you want?'

A falling jellyfish hit him square in the face. It stung.

Gagging and spitting, the Doctor paused for a moment in thought. He wiped his face absently with his scarf, then turned and made his way gingerly back to the lab.

'Slight change of approach,' the Doctor said, re-entering the room and leaving puddles in his wake. He had to raise his voice to be heard over the persistent hammering on the roof.

Leech and Ly were warily backing away from the artefact. It was making rasping noises and the air above it was rippling. 'It went crazy just after you left,' Ly told him, 'and it's hot to the touch.'

Mel was still at the window. Her voice was small and incredulous: 'Is that a spaceship?'

'Yes, yes.' The Doctor took a deep breath. 'In 1977, the National Aeronautic and Space Administration launched its two Voyager probes. They were designed not only to gather information on the universe and beam it back to Earth, but also to send a message to the universe. They included images and recordings from this world, giving a flavour of life on Earth.'

'We remember, Doctor,' said Leech, 'they were launched just last year. What's your point?'

'I believe this device is a similar construction. It's a hello to the universe, a cry for recognition from a curious and optimistic race of beings, launched many thousands of years ago.' He beamed enthusiastically, then his face became sad. 'Of course, they never expected it to come crashing to earth. They probably never knew why it stopped sending signals back home. But its discovery caused it to be reactivated, sending the energy wave that knocked the TARDIS off course. A homing beacon across time and space. And now I think they've come to retrieve it...' He froze when he saw where everyone's attention was fixed.

Floating in the air above the artefact was a huge rippling jellyfish. Its bell was transparent and blobs of green throbbed within. White radial canals and pulsing muscle could plainly be seen as the creature expanded and contracted majestically. Below, long wormlike tentacles waved and curled, strands trailing and wafting like paper streamers. It was both magnificent and terrifying.

'I am Commander Hydra Sowerbii of the Imperial Cnidarian starship the *Water Carrier*.' The gurgling voice echoed around the room. 'Your world belongs to us now.'

Nearby, a very surprised angler in a boat watched as a shower of gelatinous shapes splashed into the lake. The downpour seemed to be localised over the scientific facility, but its edge reached as far as the lake's east bank. Ripples radiated from the points of impact like rings around a bullseye.

Things started to swirl beneath the surface, swelling and uncoiling.

The angler reeled in his line, picked up his oars and started rowing. Shapes seemed to follow him beneath the surface.

The hovering holographic jellyfish was chuckling malevolently. 'Resistance is futile. Our time-space technology is far superior to anything you creatures possess. When our ancient probe was reactivated, it took mere days to track it down. Viewing your planet from space, we realised how much of its surface was covered in water. It is perfect for our needs. When we sent out the probe we were a naïve idealistic race in its infancy. Now we are conquerors. You will fall to the might of the Cnidarians. Even now, my troops rain down upon you!'

Everyone in the room looked out of the window at the pathetically twitching blobs on the ground.

'I don't think your invasion force is being terribly effective, Commander,' the Doctor observed. 'You're over dry land right now.'

The hologram froze for a moment. 'I knew that.'

'Your troops are being decimated. Stop this foolishness and let's talk reasonably.'

With a graceful undulation, the Cnidarian leader jet-propelled himself out of the picture, presumably to cease the ill-conceived attack. The Doctor turned to the others and rubbed his hands.

'Right. We may not have much time. We can't rely on these creatures responding to reason. We need to gather all our information.'

'What do you suggest, Doctor?' Melanie asked as Leech and the guards crowded round. Ly looked on curiously. One of the guards - Baines - unhooked his radio as it crackled, and retreated to a corner to talk.

'Earth jellyfish don't possess a brain or a heart. These Cnidarians are obviously highly evolved, extremely intelligent. We know this artefact can function by absorbing energy from its surroundings... Dr Leech, you said it was discovered by potholers: what happened to them?'

'They're in the hospital wing, suffering from some form of extreme fatigue.'

The Doctor peered at Leech. 'You're looking a little green around the gills yourself. Are you all right?'

'Been around the artefact too long, I think. I'm a little drained.' He sat.

Baines returned. 'They've got into the lake,' he reported. 'I just got word that an angler's been attacked by monsters.'

The hammering on the roof slowed then stopped.

'Doctor...' Mel nudged him. The Commander was back.

'A slight miscalculation, that's all,' the creature gurgled sheepishly. 'But soon you will tremble at our might.' Something snaked past the window.

'Tremble,' intoned Leech putting his head in his hands. 'Wibble wobble. Jelly on a plate.'

Ly looked uncomfortable. 'He's not well,' she said.

'Commander Hydra,' the Doctor began, 'you must listen to me...'

Suddenly the glass exploded inwards, sending stinging shards flying, as a powerful metal tentacle whipped into the room. It slithered around the Doctor's waist and he was pulled off his feet. It happened incredibly quickly. He was dragged protesting through the shattered window and up. Mel screamed.

'Oh, you want to talk, little creature?' Hydra taunted. 'Let's talk.' The hologram faded along with the gleeful tittering.

Suspended upside down, the Doctor struggled uselessly against his constraints. He was lifted higher and higher towards the underside of the spaceship. The ship now resembled a giant jellyfish itself: a ring of metal tentacles hung down from the craft, flexing sinuously. The Doctor was hoisted uncomfortably to a hatch which looked disturbingly like an oral cavity. Metal arms around the gap grabbed him and guided him inside the ship.

In the shocked moment which followed the Doctor's disappearance, Leech let out a groan and folded to the floor. Mel turned to Ly in anguished determination. 'We need to get to the hospital wing.'

Baines said briskly, 'I have to go to the lake - contain whatever's happening there.' He gathered his men and left.

The water was churning with bloated life. The creatures that had landed in the lake had rapidly mutated into terrifying battle-jellies. Stinging tendrils whipped through the air, grasping at the men who had already arrived. Guns were proving ineffective against the monstrous foe.

There was a terrified shout as one man was plucked from the bank and into the depths, his rifle falling uselessly away.

The Doctor found himself floating. Hordes of differently coloured jellyfish swam by, tendrils trailing in the murky water. Some were huge, some tiny, some had transparent bells and short tentacles, while others displayed exotic colours and their tentacles seemed endlessly long and graceful. Strings of bubbles rose slowly through the water. There was a pressure in his ears as he held his breath and all he could hear was a muffled glugging. Stacked white polyps clung to stalks of drifting weed.

He became aware of five fluorescent purple jellyfish hovering menacingly in a semicircle around him. Apparently he had an escort. He opened and closed his umbrella experimentally, trying to emulate their movements and propel himself forward. After a couple of failed attempts he gave up and swam. Bubbles escaped from his mouth and nostrils.

'This inefficient specimen cannot absorb oxygen from the water,' observed one of the creatures in a slurping voice.

An air bubble appeared around the Doctor and he was gratefully led onward.

Mel and Ly dragged Leech in a stumble-run across the paved area to the medical wing. It was a difficult journey, picking their way through the carpet of slippery remains, and all the while the spaceship hung over them like some oppressive omen, metal tentacles waving. As they arrived a man was being brought in, dripping wet, on a stretcher. His skin was a tender mass of puffy welts.

'The angler,' said Mel. 'The poor man.'

A couple of nurses came and fussed over Leech. As they guided him to a bed and fitted him with a drip, one of the nurses yelped. 'I think he stung me!' Everyone crowded round and looked in astonishment as the nurse delicately rolled up Leech's sleeve. Ridges of stinging cells were raising themselves on his pale flesh. The nurses rushed the bed into the isolation ward, Mel and Ly trotting along behind.

As they passed a darkened room, Mel halted curiously and pulled Ly aside. Quietly, they entered the room. A number of beds lined the walls and Mel stepped towards the closest. She looked at the patient's chart. Her name was Laura Ainsell. The woman looked dreadful: dark circles round her eyes contrasted with the pasty whiteness of her skin, and her long mousy hair was plastered in sweaty strands to her forehead.

'The potholers,' Mel breathed. 'Wait, something's wrong...' The sheets over Laura's prone form were rippling. Trembling, Mel pulled them back. Extending from the woman's fingers were thin transparent threads, writhing like a nest of snakes. Suddenly her eyes snapped open.

'Water,' she gasped, 'put me in water!'

This seemed to provoke a response in the other patients who started pulling themselves upright, sheets slipping to reveal that they too had developed wriggling tentacles.

Ly stepped up behind Mel.

Mel looked on in horror, then blinked. 'Wait a minute. I thought there were eight people in those caves. There's only seven in here. What happened to the eighth?'

'Oh,' Ly's face was unreadable, 'that was me. I led the expedition.'

Out on the lake, the detachment of security guards had rapidly been augmented by the military. It had been quickly established that the threat must be contained: several rivers fed into this lake, and the last thing anyone wanted was for the aggressors to spread upstream. A manned powerboat churned through the water, dropping depth charges. A thick rubbery tentacle snaked over the side as the boat banked and Corporal Flavell was yanked overboard. The last thing he saw as he thrashed underwater was a gaping black maw coming closer and closer.

As he entered the *Water Carrier*'s control grotto, the Doctor looked about in curiosity. It was full of flowery coral and glowing stone panels covered in levers and flashing lights. Weeds wafted in the gaps between the panels. Huge screens were embedded in the rock, one showing a view of the battle at the lake. He watched it for a moment in concern before his attention turned to the imposing figure at the centre of the chamber.

Close up, Commander Hydra Sowerbii was even more arresting than the hologram had suggested. He was huge, like an immense elephantine polythene bag full of phosphorescent green gunk. The edges of his bell rippled and his surface was mottled and swollen.

'What do you call this world, little creature?' Hydra gurgled, his tendrils curling in fiendish pleasure.

'Earth.'

'A foolish name for such a watery world. We will rename it New Aqua.'

'It's not your world, Commander...'

In a rage, Hydra grabbed the Doctor in his stinging tentacles and slammed him against the nearest wall. The Doctor bit his tongue, the salt taste of blood flooding his mouth. And it was then that he identified what had been troubling him.

'You... you're one of them?' Mel backed away from Ly in horror.

Ly stepped towards her, smiling beatifically. 'Commander Hydra appeared to us in the cave even as our life force was being absorbed. He made us see that we couldn't fight the Cnidarians: our only hope was to be absorbed.' Slowly, slick cords of rippling grey tentacles slipped from her white sleeves and flexed in the air. She shuddered and gasped in apparent ecstasy. The patients were getting shakily to their feet; all the while their new tentacles waved sickeningly. Laura's face was slick with perspiration, her expression one of torment.

'Then you're responsible for Leech's condition too?' Mel asked.

Ly tilted her head and chuckled. 'Microscopic zooplankton in his drinking water. It was thriving in the waters of the cave, carried there on the artefact from the Cnidarian home world. You see, we were infected as soon as we entered the cavern.'

'You should have fought it,' Mel said.

'Look at me!' Ly spat. 'Look at these poor wretches. How am I supposed to fight?' She advanced on Mel.

Mel backed away, sweating, and bumped into something which clattered. In a reflex, she reached behind her, grabbed for the object, and hurled it towards Ly. The small woman began screaming as the saline drip stand slammed into her, the bag bursting, and salty water spilling over her face and body. The other patients hissed and cowered.

Mel stood for a moment, dumbstruck, then a light went on in her eyes.

Baines watched as the plane flew over, dropping its payload. He doubted he'd forget today in a hurry - it wasn't every day you saw tactical air strikes on aggressive giant mutated jellyfish.

There was a muffled crump and a huge spray of water. A ragged cheer went up as a clump of disembodied tentacles crested the surface, twitching forlornly, then sank out of view. Suddenly his radio hissed into life. 'Baines... Baines, are you there? This is important.' It was the voice of the red-headed stranger. He lifted the radio to talk.

'You're freshwater jellyfish, aren't you?!'

Inasmuch as a jellyfish can look disdainful, Hydra looked disdainful. 'What are you talking about?'

'The water in this ship - it's fresh.'

'Well we'd hardly live in dirty water...'

The Doctor shook his head in frustration. 'No no no, you don't understand. The seas of this world are salt water. They'd be poison to you.'

Hydra seemed to deflate slowly. 'You've got to be kidding me.'

'I'm afraid not.' The Doctor looked suddenly sympathetic.

The Commander seemed to gather himself. 'Well, we'll just de-salinate the oceans. Yes, that's it...' His tentacles waved vaguely.

'Oh give up, Commander,' the Doctor snapped. 'You're unprepared for conquest. You're out of your depth.'

One of the screens suddenly filled with static and, to the Doctor's surprise and delight, resolved into an anxious-looking Mel. 'I think this is the way to do it,' she was saying, 'I'm used to Earth computers, not bits of aquatic alien rock... Er, calling occupants of interstellar craft...'

'What do you want, Earthling?' Hydra rumbled.

'Oh! Hello.' Mel looked startled. 'I hacked into your probe to let you know your human agent wishes to come aboard.' Behind her, the Doctor saw Ly step into view. She seemed to have developed extra appendages.

Hydra sniggered in glee. 'Come aboard, my pet.'

In a few short moments, Ly had been lifted up to the ship and was floating into the control grotto, escorted by a cluster of purple jellyfish. She didn't need an air bubble, and swam with graceful ease, tentacles wafting. As she approached, the Doctor saw she was clutching a large container tight in her hands. His eyes widened. Ly swam serenely up to the Commander, smiled coyly, and opened the catering pack of table salt. The white substance swirled and dissolved in the water around her, and Hydra began to choke.

The artefact had been loaded aboard the ship for its journey home.

'How are our patients doing?'

'Getting much better. The saline drips are doing the trick. The alien infection should be out of their systems in a matter of hours.'

'So that's all they needed - a dose of the salts!'

The Doctor smiled. 'Yes. And the battle jellies at the lake were beaten by a salt assault! I hope the Cnidarians have learned their lesson. Ly was very brave.'

'I never liked jellyfish.' Mel wrinkled her nose. 'I was stung once on the beach at Bournemouth.'

'Hmm. They're ninety-five per cent water themselves, you know,' said the Doctor, taking her arm. 'As with many things, it's the five per cent you have to watch.'

'I can't believe they thought they could take over the world and they couldn't even live in salt water.'

The Doctor looked reflective. 'I don't think they're natural conquerors, just opportunistic, drifting on the tides of circumstance. With Hydra gone, they may think twice in the future. They did rather over-face themselves with this plan - they were like fish out of water.'

Mel winced. 'Oh dear.'

Wiggling his eyebrows, the Doctor grinned. 'Time we were leaving, I think. I've worked up quite an appetite. How about jelly and ice-cream?'

She slapped his chest in fond exasperation. 'Doctor...'

Overhead, the *Water Carrier* was a receding dot in the hazy grey sky. Birds chirped experimentally as the sun struggled through the clouds, and the damp world glistened. The friends strolled off arm in arm to fresh adventures.

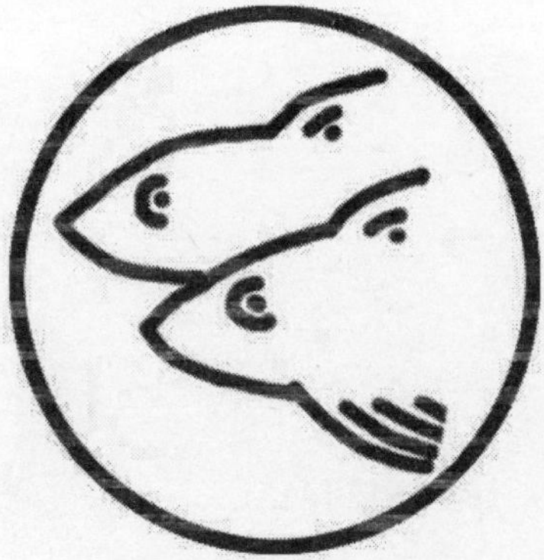

The final house of the zodiac is that of the fish – Pisces. The typically romantic legend with this one concerns Aphrodite, goddess of beauty, and her son, Eros, the god of love. When they were confronted by the giant beast Typhon, they leapt into the ocean depths to evade him and were dragged to safety by two fish. The fish were, like all of the animals in the zodiac, rewarded with a place in the heavens to mark the moment in time when love and beauty were saved from destruction.

As any astrologer will tell you, nobody is 'typical' of their sun sign. That is because all of the signs work together to different degrees to make us who we are. The sign of Pisces is an example of how all the signs of the zodiac can work in harmony as, being the last sign of the zodiac, Pisces has the good fortune to have the benefit of experience from and empathy with all the other signs. It is also easily influenced by *the other signs and the Piscean's well-being is closely in tune with its environment. When others are happy, you will often find a Piscean at the centre of the party; when there is discord, though, they retreat, for Pisceans dislike conflict as it upsets their desire to view the universe through rose-tinted spectacles.*

Kasterborus, *Our Destiny is in the Stars*

The next morning, Tom felt fantastic. He hadn't felt so good in a long time. For the first time in what seemed like months, he had smiled at his wife before leaving the house and had walked to work with a spring in his step. It seemed quite clear to him that this sudden surge of healthy feeling must have been caused by the boost his system had been given by the fish serum.

After a couple of hours out on the pontoon on his own again – Trevor the netsman was off sick with flu – Tom stopped for a break. This work was only done once a year and had to be done between October and January. It was cold and wearing work, numbing the mind as well as the body. Tom poured some tea from his flask into the flask lid. He sipped at the brew, staring at the injecting pistol, doing that dangerous thing: thinking.

It did me no harm yesterday. In fact, I feel great. What harm can another dose do? I may feel even better still. I don't really want to have to inject myself with the gun, though.

Tom picked up the pistol and fired three shots into his tea. Then, not pausing to think, just in case he changed his mind, he drank the tea down in one. Gone. Didn't even taste funny. That morning he got through 5465 smolts – a personal record.

By lunchtime Tom had a bit of a headache – right in the back of his skull. It wasn't like any headache he'd had before, but it wasn't too bad – certainly not worth tramping all the way home for painkillers. He was probably just cold or tired. Or both. As he removed the first vaccinated fish of the afternoon from the pistol's loops, Tom had a very odd feeling that the fish was looking at him. Silly really.

'What you looking at, mate?' he said playfully.

You.

Tom stood open-mouthed, looking blankly at the fish. He could have sworn he had heard someone speak, yet there was no one in sight. He must have imagined it.

'So you're looking at me, are you?' Tom teased the dumb fish.

Yes.

His head pounding from the strange headache and his hands shaking, Tom threw the smolt hurriedly down the chute into the second holding tank. He was scared.

'What's happening? That fish spoke to me! Fish can't speak – this is ridiculous.'

We can speak, Tom.

This time it was more than one voice – thin and faint and high pitched and a little difficult to make out, but definitely more than one voice. Tom realised that the voices weren't audible, but that they seemed to be

The final house of the zodiac is that of the fish - Pisces. The typically romantic legend with this one concerns Aphrodite, goddess of beauty, and her son, Eros, the god of love. When they were confronted by the giant beast Typhon, they leapt into the ocean depths to evade him and were dragged to safety by two fish. The fish were, like all of the animals in the zodiac, rewarded with a place in the heavens to mark the moment in time when love and beauty were saved from destruction.

As any astrologer will tell you, nobody is 'typical' of their sun sign. That is because all of the signs work together to different degrees to make us who we are. The sign of Pisces is an example of how all the signs of the zodiac can work in harmony as, being the last sign of the zodiac, Pisces has the good fortune to have the benefit of experience from and empathy with all the other signs. It is also easily influenced by *the other signs and the Piscean's well-being is closely in tune with its environment. When others are happy, you will often find a Piscean at the centre of the party; when there is discord, though, they retreat, for Pisceans dislike conflict as it upsets their desire to view the universe through rose-tinted spectacles.*

Kasterborus, *Our Destiny is in the Stars*

Kasterborus says...

If today is your birthday: *You find yourself in a perfect position to change your situation, but you must restrain your sense of independence – few goals can be reached without the help of others…*

The Stabber

Alison Lawson

Tom Watson adjusted his scarf so that no flesh bared itself to the October wind. Inside the waterproofs, woolly hat and wellies, there was very little of Tom that was visible. He stood on his own at the end of the pontoon, trying not to think of anything in particular.

Using a net on a long pole, he lifted a smolt from the holding tank to his left. He took the young salmon in his left hand, on which he wore an old cycling glove, and slipped it into the copper wire loops at the end of the gun. The fish in place, he pulled the gun's trigger with his right hand, then removed the fish and tossed it down a chute into the holding tank on his right. This was the 2347th time he had 'stabbed' a fish today. On a good day, with the help of a netsman, he could get through as many as ten thousand. The smolts were counted automatically by a sensor as they entered the new holding tank. He didn't even have to do his own counting. It wasn't the most edifying of jobs, but work was scarce and it paid the bills.

His hands numb with cold, Tom paused for a while to warm them under his armpits. Tom was soon back at his task, however, netting fish number 2348. He didn't want his mind to wander. He had to do the job without thinking, automatically. This was the only way he could function – if he started to think about the fish it made him feel queasy. It was only Monday and he had a whole week of 'stabbing' to do. Just get on with it. Forget those inconvenient vegetarian principles.

Suddenly Tom yelped as his numbed hands fumbled. He dropped the young fish and the gun stabbed straight into the ball of his left thumb. He sucked on the injured thumb and started, for the first time that day, to think about something properly. Just as the gun had injected antibiotic serum intended for smolts into his thumb, so fear now injected adrenalin into his system.

Think, think! Should I tell anyone? Should I see a doctor? Is it dangerous? Should I be sucking it like this or is it already in my bloodstream anyway? Will I lose my job? Is it dangerous?

Then:

Well, it does the fish no harm. It's good for them. And people will eat the fish eventually, so it must be safe. Better not tell anyone. Just get on with the job.

Fish number 2348 of the day lay at his feet. Tom picked it up, positioned it in the copper loops of the pistol and gave it its shot of antibiotics, carrying on as usual.

* * *

The next morning, Tom felt fantastic. He hadn't felt so good in a long time. For the first time in what seemed like months, he had smiled at his wife before leaving the house and had walked to work with a spring in his step. It seemed quite clear to him that this sudden surge of healthy feeling must have been caused by the boost his system had been given by the fish serum.

After a couple of hours out on the pontoon on his own again – Trevor the netsman was off sick with flu – Tom stopped for a break. This work was only done once a year and had to be done between October and January. It was cold and wearing work, numbing the mind as well as the body. Tom poured some tea from his flask into the flask lid. He sipped at the brew, staring at the injecting pistol, doing that dangerous thing: thinking.

It did me no harm yesterday. In fact, I feel great. What harm can another dose do? I may feel even better still. I don't really want to have to inject myself with the gun, though.

Tom picked up the pistol and fired three shots into his tea. Then, not pausing to think, just in case he changed his mind, he drank the tea down in one. Gone. Didn't even taste funny. That morning he got through 5465 smolts – a personal record.

By lunchtime Tom had a bit of a headache – right in the back of his skull. It wasn't like any headache he'd had before, but it wasn't too bad – certainly not worth tramping all the way home for painkillers. He was probably just cold or tired. Or both. As he removed the first vaccinated fish of the afternoon from the pistol's loops, Tom had a very odd feeling that the fish was looking at him. Silly really.

'What you looking at, mate?' he said playfully.

You.

Tom stood open-mouthed, looking blankly at the fish. He could have sworn he had heard someone speak, yet there was no one in sight. He must have imagined it.

'So you're looking at me, are you?' Tom teased the dumb fish.

Yes.

His head pounding from the strange headache and his hands shaking, Tom threw the smolt hurriedly down the chute into the second holding tank. He was scared.

'What's happening? That fish spoke to me! Fish can't speak – this is ridiculous.'

We can speak, Tom.

This time it was more than one voice – thin and faint and high pitched and a little difficult to make out, but definitely more than one voice. Tom realised that the voices weren't audible, but that they seemed to be actually inside his head.

We did not intend to alarm you, continued the voices. *It is true that we cannot speak in the manner you are used to, but we can communicate directly by the power of thought.*

Out loud and feeling just as foolish as he was scared, Tom asked, 'Who are you?'

We have no names, came the voices.

Tom looked into the holding tank of vaccinated fish. 'I've gone mad. I think the fish are talking to me.'

No, you are not mad. Your mind is receptive, that is all. Before, it was not receptive, although we tried hard to reach you. Now we can talk.

Despite himself, Tom felt his fears subside as he was drawn into the conversation as if in a dream.

'What do you want to talk about?' he asked.

We want to know why you hurt us so badly. Why do you force us to grow unnaturally? Why do you hate our kind so much?

'I don't hate you,' said Tom. 'The vaccine is for your own good.'

But it hurts.

'Only for a second,' replied Tom, feeling less sure of himself as the conversation continued.

No. It hurts our minds.

Tom didn't know what to say to that. He was still coming to terms with the fact that he could communicate with smolts.

We can see into your mind, Tom. We know you do not believe in your work. We know you would rather we were free. Set us free, Tom.

'Look, just leave me alone.' Tom was annoyed now. 'It's not my fault. I can't help you. I'm sorry. I must get on with my work.'

Tom netted a fish and prepared to inject it. He wavered, his finger on the gun's trigger, as the smolt looked him in the eye. Had all the smolts looked so pleading? So sad?

You can help us, Tom. You can help us without anyone knowing. You can send a distress call for us. Someone will come. Someone will help.

'Okay,' said Tom finally. 'What do you want me to do?'

Sit down and close your eyes.

Tom sat on the wet wood of the pontoon and closed his eyes.

Now concentrate.

Tom heard the voices becoming increasingly distant, telling him to concentrate, concentrate, concentrate. He felt warm and sleepy and the dark behind his eyelids seemed strangely all-enveloping. And then it took him completely.

Tom felt a tap on his shoulder and woke with a start. Two people – a man and a woman – stood in front of him. The man was tall and broad with blond curly hair and looked as if he'd got dressed at a colourful jumble sale. The woman was shorter, with shoulder-length brown hair. She wore warm trousers and a fleece jacket.

'Hello!' said the man brightly.

'Hi!' said the woman. Her accent was American.

'Did you answer the distress call?' asked Tom, getting to his feet.

The newcomers exchanged a quick glance and then the man replied, 'Yes, probably. I'm the Doctor and this is Peri. What seems to be the problem?'

'We must save the fish!' said Tom.

Peri looked at the Doctor and raised an eyebrow. The Doctor ignored her and replied to Tom. 'Save the fish, must we? Very laudable.'

Peri looked at the waterproof-clad man. 'Who are we saving the fish from?' she asked in a voice full of sarcasm.

Tom didn't reply. He lifted his hands to his head as if he were in pain, and appeared to be confused.

[*Explain to them why we need their help.*]

'But I'm not sure why. I'm not sure how they'll help. Can we trust them?'

[*Yes, you can trust them. We see no malice in their minds. They will help.*]

'How do you know?'

[*We just know.*]

The Doctor and Peri watched and listened while Tom appeared to talk to himself. Peri raised her hand and tapped the side of her head with one finger. The Doctor scowled at her.

'He's a loony,' Peri mouthed at the Doctor, nodding over to Tom.

The Doctor approached Tom again. 'Perhaps we should start with your name and why you sent the distress call?'

'I'm Tom Watson. I work here, fish stabber.' Tom indicated the bench with its vaccinating gun and the net propped up by the side.

'Fish stabber?' Peri was appalled.

'He means he vaccinates the fish against disease, don't you Tom?' said the Doctor helpfully.

'I shouldn't call it "stabbing",' Tom went on, 'that's just a joke between me and Trevor. The fish are farm bred - they have no natural immunity - so we have to vaccinate them against ISA.'

'That's ischaemic salmon anaemia,' put in the Doctor.

'Yeah, because if one of them gets it, they'll all get it,' finished Tom.

Peri looked down into the holding tank. 'It looks like they've already had it, to me,' she said. The smolts lay unmoving in the water.

'They're anaesthetised,' explained Tom. 'Benzocaine in the water. We'd never catch them otherwise.' Tom paused and seemed to be staring into space.

Peri and the Doctor again exchanged a glance. This time they both raised an eyebrow.

[*Explain why we must be released.*]

'I was coming to that,' said Tom.

'Coming to what?' asked the Doctor. 'Who are you talking to?'

'Well, I know it sounds a bit, you know, mad, but, well...' He trailed off.

'Well, what?' The Doctor was losing his patience and had an idea he knew what was coming anyway.

'Well, it's the fish.'

'You're talking to the fish!' Peri said with a snort that turned into a laugh. 'Oh come on!'

Tom and the Doctor looked at Peri, one with a mixture of embarrassment and hurt and the other with mild disdain. She stopped laughing as best she could.

'I thought as much,' said the Doctor.

'And we have to save them,' continued Tom, pressing home now it was clear that at least one of the strangers believed him. 'We have to release them because the injection hurts them and it's wrong to keep them in tanks like this.' He gestured at the tanks. 'I couldn't do anything myself, so they said I should send a distress call and that someone would come to help.'

The Doctor patted Tom on the shoulder, comfortingly. 'That's right. We're here to help, aren't we Peri?'

'Oh yes, Doctor,' she replied, thinking that the Doctor had clearly decided the best course of action was to humour the man.

'Why don't you just sit down and relax,' the Doctor said to Tom, 'while my assistant and I work out the best way that we can help?'

Tom sat down heavily. He looked tired out. The Doctor and Peri walked back down the pontoon so they were out of earshot.

'There's something fishy going on here,' began the Doctor.

Peri groaned and rolled her eyes. 'The man is obviously unhinged, Doctor. He thinks he can talk to the fish.'

'Maybe he can,' said the Doctor.

'Doctor, we're on Earth. This guy is from Earth. People from Earth can't communicate with fish!'

'Maybe he's not an ordinary human. Did you see his eyes? He can't focus on us properly and the pupils are oddly dilated. Maybe the effects of a drug.'

'Well that clinches it,' said Peri. 'The guy is tripping.'

'Or the side effects of a drug,' continued the Doctor. He suddenly turned and strode back towards Tom. Peri had to run to keep up.

* * *

Tom looked up as they approached. He felt he could trust these people, even though they were a bit strange.

'How are you?' asked the Doctor.

Tom looked blankly at the Doctor. This seemed an odd question at this juncture. Before he could get a word out, the Doctor went on. 'How have you been, recently? You know, since the fish started to talk to you. Has anything unusual happened?'

'Well, I've had a bit of a headache today,' said Tom.

'Go on,' said the Doctor encouragingly.

'I felt pretty good this morning.' Tom didn't elaborate further and began to rub the ball of his left thumb with his other hand.

'Hurt your thumb?' asked the Doctor. He took hold of Tom's left wrist and turned it so the ball of the thumb was visible. A small puncture mark with a purple bruise was revealed.

'It was just an accident,' said Tom. 'It did no harm. I felt fine afterwards.'

The Doctor seemed to be waiting for more information. How could he know?

Just tell him. He will help you and us!

'I had a few shots of it in my tea, too,' he admitted.

'I see,' said the Doctor, casting his gaze around and seeing the flask on the bench.

With his wrist clasped in the Doctor's hand, Tom could see the face of his watch. How had it got so late? 'I'd better get going,' he said. 'I'll never hear the end of it if I'm late for dinner.'

The Doctor and Peri seemed taken aback by the way the conversation had suddenly changed direction.

Peri watched as the Doctor moved round the bench so he had his back to it. 'Dinner, eh? That sounds like a good idea! I expect Peri's hungry.'

'Well, no, I –'

'Good, good,' continued the Doctor, strangely enthusiastically.

'You can come back with me,' offered Tom, looking over at Peri.

'Thanks,' she said, grinning through gritted teeth. How had the Doctor got her into this? What was he up to? She managed a quick glance in his direction to see that behind his back he was pouring some of Tom's tea into a glass test tube. Where had he got that?

'Coming Doctor?' she added icily.

'I'm not all that hungry. And I've got some things to do,' he replied irritatingly. 'You go on with Tom and I'll meet you back at the, er, guest house later.'

Resigned, Peri watched while Tom packed up his things ready to go home.

* * *

'It's probably best not to mention, you know, the fish,' said Tom as he and Peri approached his house. 'I don't want to worry Mary.'

'Okay,' replied Peri, who had been planning on steering clear of the subject anyway.

'Hello, love,' said Tom as he went in. 'I hope you don't mind - I've brought a visitor. She and a colleague are here on, er, business.' He winked at Peri conspiratorially and, playing along, she winked back.

The front door opened straight into the lounge, which was a welcome oasis of warmth from the bitter cold outside. An open fire burned, keeping the room warm and gently toasting a nearby armchair and sofa. At the far side of the room was an old kitchen table with four chairs. Tom took Peri's fleece and his own waterproofs and hung them on hooks inside the front door.

'That's no problem,' replied Mary as she came out of the kitchen and headed into the front room. She was about the same age as Tom, mid thirties, Peri guessed, and although she smiled, Peri could see she was exhausted. Her long dark hair was scrunched up in an untidy ponytail and her face was pale with dark eyes. She carried a toddler on her hip. The girl hung on to her mother and looked over at Peri briefly before turning her face to Mary's shoulder.

'Hello, I'm Mary,' she said, holding out her free hand to shake Peri's.

'Hi, nice to meet you,' returned Peri. 'I hope I'm not going to be in the way, dropping in like this.'

'No, not at all. It makes a change to have company, doesn't it, Tom?'

Tom had disappeared upstairs and didn't reply.

'So you're visiting the plant on business, are you?' asked Mary.

Peri thought quickly. 'My boss is here on business - I'm just his PA.' This seemed to satisfy Mary.

'And who's this?' asked Peri, tickling the child's midriff. The child shifted position, but didn't smile or laugh or make any other reaction.

'This is our little Linda,' said Mary. 'And you're a sweetheart, aren't you?' She directed this at the child, who, again, made little response. 'She's very sleepy,' explained Mary, 'but she likes to stay up until daddy gets home, don't you Lin?'

Peri didn't mind children, but she wasn't all that keen on the way that doting parents talked half to the adult with whom they were conversing and half with the child, who clearly couldn't reply.

Changing the subject, Peri asked if she could help out in the kitchen, as the smells of something cooking were wafting into the lounge.

'No, no,' Mary said, 'I'll manage, but you can come and keep me company while Tom gets changed.'

Peri followed Mary into the kitchen. 'So how old is Linda?'

'She's just two years old last month,' replied Mary, stirring a pot of something unidentifiable with a wooden spoon. Peri detected a slight tension in her voice, so decided not to pursue the subject.

'You really are in the middle of nowhere here, aren't you?' she said. 'The village seems to be very small. The peace and quiet must be great.'

'It's okay,' said Mary, turning her attention to the oven while not moving the child - clearly a practised manoeuvre. 'I'd have preferred to stay in London but my parents are nearby.'

This answer raised more questions than it answered. 'So you moved up from London?'

'Yes, about eighteen months ago. Linda has a kidney problem. It took ages to diagnose and when they told me what it was, the name of it meant nothing to me. In the end I had to see it in practical terms of how Linda's life and our lives would be affected.'

Peri hadn't been expecting this. 'So you moved up here to be near your parents?'

There was a pause before Mary answered. 'Yes. I couldn't really cope on my own. I was so exhausted. And it's good to be close to home - I can help mum and dad out and they can help me.'

'And Tom?' Peri regretted the question as soon as she'd asked it. It sounded accusatory. Mary didn't interpret it like that, however. Perhaps she was used to explaining the situation to others.

'Tom, bless him, is the most wonderful man in the world.' Mary popped her head out through the kitchen door and shouted upstairs that dinner was ready. 'He dotes on Linda and me. When things got really tough and we talked about moving up to the borders, he wanted to do what was best for us all. Give me a hand with these plates, would you?'

'Sure,' said Peri, helping to carry plates full of food into the lounge. She and Mary set the plates down on the table.

Mary glanced up the stairs then turned back to Peri. 'I know he doesn't really like his job. He puts a brave face on it, thinks I don't know how much he hates it. I'm hoping we can move back south in the new year. Linda's much better now than she was. Ah, there you are Tom.'

Tom appeared down the stairs and gave Mary a big hug, encompassing Linda too. 'Hello my little angel,' he said. 'Are you going to sit on daddy's knee for dinner?'

Cutting short the baby talk, Peri said, 'It smells fantastic. What is it?'

'Leek and aduki bean stew with herb dumplings and veggie gravy,' replied Tom, who clearly recognised the dish. 'My favourite!' And he seemed to mean it.

The Doctor stood in the doorway to the TARDIS lab and thought it looked a trifle messy. He shrugged and pushed Bunsen burners, retort stands, old petri dishes and other long-untouched items to one side so he had some space to work.

He took the test tube containing some of Tom's tea out of his pocket and held it up to the light. It looked like tea. He sniffed the liquid. It smelled like tea. Stopping short of tasting the liquid, the Doctor instead prepared a slide and slotted it into a microscope. He hoped that answers would come quickly.

'So you don't eat fish?' asked Peri.

'Certainly not salmon, anyway,' replied Tom. 'You wouldn't want to either if you saw what I do on a daily basis.'

'What do you mean?' persisted Peri.

'Oh don't get him started,' said Mary. 'He can talk for Britain about the evils of GM foods.'

'Well, it's almost everywhere in the food chain now, isn't it?' Tom started, clearly about to make oft-repeated points. 'The salmon aren't big enough or don't grow quickly enough for people, fruit isn't sweet enough or goes off too quickly or is too inconvenient to peel. How long before we see oranges with a ring pull?'

'Tom, calm down,' interjected Mary. 'You're exaggerating.'

'Yes, okay, but when we breed animals that have no natural immunity to disease, I think we're just asking for trouble.' It was clear that Tom felt strongly about the subject. It occurred to Peri just how much he must hate his job if he felt this way.

'Well, this seems wholesome enough,' said Peri, trying to lift the mood. 'It's delicious.'

'Yeah - there's no preservatives or colouring in this,' said Tom.

The meal over, Peri offered to help with the dishes, but again Mary said she could manage. Tom took Linda upstairs to put her to bed - the little girl had fallen asleep on her father's knee during the meal.

Mary made some coffee and returned to the lounge. The mood was more relaxed over the coffee, and the conversation turned away from genetically modified foods to more amusing topics. Peri talked about her home and her family - the first time she had talked about them to anyone for ages. In their turn, Tom and Mary talked about London and how much they missed the hustle and bustle of the city. Peri didn't mention her own experience of London as theirs seemed so much more enjoyable to imagine.

'Well,' said Peri, downing the last of her coffee, 'I really had better be going. Thanks so much for dinner and for a lovely evening.'

'It was our pleasure,' said Mary. She didn't rise from her armchair - she looked even more exhausted now than she had before dinner. Instead, Tom got up and passed Peri her coat. He looked strangely preoccupied. He put his hand to his head and frowned slightly.

She cannot fail to help us now. You have shown her such excellent hospitality.

The Doctor came out of the lab and closed the door on the additional mess he had made. In his hand he carried a small flask of colourless liquid. He looked very pleased with himself. 'That should do the trick,' he said, smiling broadly.

Peri's voice floated in from the console room. 'What have you been up to?'

'Ah, Peri,' said the Doctor. 'Have you had a good evening?'

'Not bad, we talked about –'

'Yes, yes, tell me tomorrow,' cut in the Doctor. 'We've got a busy day ahead and need a good night's sleep first.'

The next morning, the Doctor and Peri set out in different directions.

'See you in an hour,' said the Doctor.

'I've heard that before!' called Peri over her shoulder as she headed out to the pontoon.

The Doctor walked confidently into a very neat, sanitised, orderly laboratory and looked around appreciatively.

'How did you get in here?' asked a man's voice behind him.

He didn't turn round, but leafed through some papers on the bench in front of him. 'Why do people always ask me such dull questions about what I've done instead of interesting questions about me?'

'This is a restricted area,' continued the voice.

Now the Doctor turned round. 'It's always the way, isn't it?' He looked at the voice's owner – a young man in a white chemist's coat. He looked nervous, biting his lip.

'What do you want?' the man asked.

'I want to talk to you about this,' said the Doctor, waving the man's own sheaf of papers at him. 'And, more importantly, I want to talk about the consequences of your work.'

The man looked even more nervous and, perhaps, a little panicky, but said nothing.

'I'm the Doctor,' continued the Doctor, unperturbed. 'And you are?'

'Dr Harden. Dr Grahame Harden.'

'Well, Dr Harden, I think we need a little chat. What do you know about the hallucinogenic properties of the formula that you're injecting into all the fish here?'

'Hallucinogenic?' said Harden lamely.

'You haven't actually tested this formula thoroughly, have you?' accused the Doctor.

Harden's face reddened, not with embarrassment but with anger. The Doctor had struck a raw nerve. 'I told them repeatedly that I needed more time to test it properly, but I was shouted down. Testing isn't as important as money, apparently. Now they've got me working on the next loony project and I still don't have time to analyse the results of the first formula.'

The Doctor sighed heavily, as if to express extreme disappointment in a student. He threw down the sheaf of papers, picked up a pen from the bench and ringed one of the formulae on the top sheet. 'I think you'll find that's the main problem,' he said.

Harden examined the formula in question and frowned. 'Oh,' he said.

'Yes, "oh" indeed,' said the Doctor. 'You've been mixing impure steroids with the standard anti-ISA formula and haven't considered the potential side effects.'

Again Harden looked angry, but he spoke calmly enough. 'The managers know nothing about science. All they know about steroids is what they read in the press about athletes testing positive, bodybuilding and so on. They thought it would improve the yield.'

'Improve? That's a funny way of putting it,' said the Doctor hotly.

'But this can't affect humans,' Harden protested.

'Do you know that for sure?'

There was a pause.

'I thought not,' continued the Doctor. 'You do realise that this is already being injected into the fish?' he asked. 'And that the men doing the job of vaccinating might occasionally come into contact with the formula?'

'I should have insisted on more time to test this,' said Harden with a tone of anguish, looking again through his papers.

'Yes, you should have done,' confirmed the Doctor. 'Now, what are you going to do about it?'

Harden's shoulders slumped as he realised the extent of the work that lay ahead of him. 'I'll have to develop some kind of blocking agent to eliminate the side effects of the drug.'

The Doctor produced the flask of clear liquid that he had carried with him from the TARDIS lab. 'Don't worry. Here's one I made earlier.'

Harden gaped. 'What?'

'Well, you can take it or leave it,' said the Doctor.

'Okay. Thanks,' said Harden awkwardly, taking the flask. He bent straight to the task of analysing and identifying the components of the liquid. After a few minutes, he spoke over his shoulder. 'This is really helpful. Who did you say you were, again?' He turned round, but the Doctor had gone.

Peri waved to Tom as she approached. 'Hi,' she said cheerily. 'How's it going today?'

'Oh, you know, same as ever,' replied Tom.

'Fancy a quick tea break?' asked Peri. 'I've even brought my own cup.' She produced a plastic mug from her fleece pocket and smiled.

'Good idea,' said Tom. He propped his net against the bench and opened his flask, pouring a little tea into Peri's cup and his own.

'Thanks again for dinner last night,' said Peri.

'That's okay.'

They sipped their drinks. Peri needed to distract Tom's attention somehow. 'So, how are you feeling?'

[*She is being kind. She wants to help.*]

'I'm fine,' he said. 'I've still got a bit of a headache, but it's not as bad as yesterday.'

[*Give her the drug. She will understand. She will help. Inject her with it, Tom.*]

Tom picked up the primed gun and aimed it at Peri. 'Are you sure?' he said.

'Hey! Watch where you're pointing that thing!' exclaimed Peri.

[*Go on. Do it now.*]

Tom swayed and raised one hand to his head. He frowned, closing his eyes. 'No, it doesn't feel right.'

'Tom!' shouted Peri. She knocked the gun out of his hands.

Tom looked at her in confusion. 'What am I doing?' he asked.

'Tom, it's okay.' Peri was shaken. 'It's okay.'

Tom stood hunched with his eyes closed, breathing heavily.

Peri quickly poured the clear contents of a small test tube into his tea, then returned the tube to where it had been hidden in her glove. 'Here,' she said, 'you haven't drunk your tea.'

Tom straightened up and took the cup of tea from Peri, downing it in one. He blinked and his frown flattened out. 'Will you be staying long?' he asked, as if nothing untoward had happened.

'No,' replied Peri. The relief on her face was plain. The antidote was working. 'The Doctor and I will be leaving pretty soon. He's meeting me here.'

Just as Peri said this, the Doctor appeared at the other end of the pontoon, striding towards them. 'You're looking well, Tom,' he said, with a glance in Peri's direction. Peri winked. 'Well,' he continued, grasping Tom's hand suddenly and shaking it, 'we must be going. Mind yourself with that needle, now!' With that he turned and strode off back down the pontoon.

'Bye Tom,' said Peri, smiling. She followed the Doctor, jogging to catch up. Falling into step with him, Peri asked, 'Mission accomplished?'

The Doctor nodded vigorously. 'And you?'

'Yeah, there was a minor hiccough, but in the end he drank it all down and didn't even notice. Back to the "guest house" then?'

'I think so,' said the Doctor.

Tom watched the Doctor and Peri walk back towards the offices beyond the pontoon. A bit odd, but they seemed nice enough. He netted another fish, vaccinated it and dropped it down the chute. His headache seemed to be clearing.

No! What is happening?

Yes, his head was feeling much clearer. He thought he could hear something and looked up. Perhaps Trevor had finally showed up for work for once. But there was no one there. So what was that noise?

No! You betrayed us! You betrayed us!

He must have imagined it. Tom shook his head to clear it, thankful that his headache seemed to have gone completely. It was a beautiful, clear, silent October morning. He netted the next fish and got on with his job.